D0170151

# THE HUMPTY DUMPTYS

a novel by

*Reba,*
*Thanks for the support. I hope you enjoy the read.*
*Best,*
*Greta*

GRETA SHERMAN

The Humpty Dumptys. Copyright 2014 by Greta Sherman. All rights reserved. Printed in the United States of America.

www.gretasherman.com

Cover Design by Gordon Linderman

ISBN: 0990808807
ISBN 13: 9780990808800
Library of Congress Control Number: 2014913025
CreateSpace Independent Publishing Platform
North Charleston, South Carolina

Humpty Dumpty sat on a wall
Humpty Dumpty had a great fall
All the king's horses and all the king's men
Couldn't put Humpty Dumpty back together again

*An early English nursery rhyme dating to 1797, author unknown*

to Rick Purvis,
who saved my life

# PRELUDE

Just about everyone comes from a dysfunctional family. Most people just grow up and become dysfunctional adults and can't figure out what happened to their lives. It's partly the genetic roll of the dice and partly the exposure one receives during those formative years when brains are being developed and self-value decided. Each generation hopes to make fewer mistakes and develop children who are more whole, but in reality, families tend to simply rearrange the deck chairs. Different generations, different problems. Few have the courage to look at their own realities and attempt to cut out the rotted spots. Their lives are happy enough.

Most families are just garden variety dysfunctional, but not the Andersons. They were Olympic gold medal level dysfunctional. Five daughters, a mentally ill mother, and a highly functional alcoholic father. At one point, the family also had a dog named Henry, but the mother chained the dog to a horseshoe spike, piled the girls into the car, and drove around in circles until she hit and killed the dog. Thump. The girls all got out of the car and waited for their father to come home from work and remove the body. There was no reason to cry.

Each Anderson girl had her role in the family, and they grew into adults made of steel. Nothing could compare to their childhood; no one could compete with the betrayals. They shared a background that made them strangely loyal to one another, almost a single unit, but unemotional. When each graduated from high school, she left for college, unaware of how broken she was. They were determined to never inflict the kind of physical pain they had endured on their own children, but they were so accustomed to a world of hate and harsh judgment they did not recognize their sharp differences. They didn't realize they also needed to abandon the skills that had helped them survive the emotional abuse.

They had hidden so much for so long, they appeared perfectly normal and believed themselves to be free once they left their childhood home. But they would never be free.

# ONE

October 2012

Hedy punched her iPhone as discreetly as she could, given she was in a boardroom filled with seventeen executives from the Johns Hopkins Health System. She was supposed to be focused solely on them, not whether she was going to make her flight out of DC. Her time was their time because they were paying a high price for what she was advising.

The conference room was tight and hot, the water bottles mostly depleted. People had the bound books her colleagues had silently laid out in front of the attendees after Hedy's initial presentation. Passing out the books earlier would have guaranteed distraction, and they needed to focus on what she was saying. Some were now taking notes, flipping through the pages, which were alive with colorful graphs and charts; others were poised to ask questions.

Hedy had finished outlining the complex proposal almost three hours ago, but the discussion about the system's 2013 recruitment advertising strategic plan was still going strong. Two hundred and forty-three pages and a sixty-slide PowerPoint presentation were a lot to digest. It represented weeks of her strongest team's research. It was her job to sell it.

"Search engine optimization" was all one gentleman in the room stated. "Search engine optimization."

"When individuals are looking for very specialized positions, you must appear on the first page after they have asked the search engine a question," Hedy responded, indicating with her hand the higher the better. This was old news, and she couldn't believe she was explaining it one more time. "We can't expect them to go through six pages from Google to find you. People won't do it. You want to appear among the top three on page one. It's more than a key component. The whole plan will not work if you don't have appropriate search engine optimization and marketing. It is essential to what makes the plan work."

"It's a lot of money," he continued while tapping his expensive-looking pen on his book. "A lot of money." Hedy nodded in agreement, but she wasn't going to discuss the budget with him. He was not the decision maker, and she wasn't going to let things get derailed.

The plan was more out of the box than the executives were comfortable with, but they needed to embrace the changing world of advertising. Digital. Mobile. Forget printed materials—no one read on paper anymore—at least not the individuals they needed to recruit to work at one of the best hospital systems in the world. They needed young generation Ys who were brilliant, well educated, and steeped in entitlement.

The room's occupants looked a lot like Hedy herself—highly accomplished, well-dressed, and solid baby boomers. They were not the target audience, and she tried to help them understand the need to think like professionals thirty years younger. What would attract that generation to accept a new position at Hopkins? The last slide projected on the wall was nothing more than a big blue-and-white Q&A. Hedy didn't think she could provide another A to another Q.

Four forty-seven appeared on the iPhone's screen. The meeting was to have lasted two hours, and they were now almost into the fourth. Didn't these people have somewhere else they needed to be? Time was slipping away. The last thing Hedy wanted to do was spend one more night at the Marriott, as nice as the new one was on Aliceanna Street in Baltimore. The black car was waiting outside to whisk her to the airport—had been for hours now—but it didn't look as though she was going anywhere soon. She was booked on the last flight from Dulles. Maybe Reagan had a later flight. She didn't think so. She'd need to get to Atlanta in time to connect to the Louisville flight. It would be tough to get to BWI at this hour even though they did have a direct to Louisville on Southwest. She'd have to start making calls as soon as she got into the car.

Questions were still coming at her rapid fire. Focus. Quit thinking about getting home.

"The Cerebrovascular Center is going to continue to burn through their neuro nurses unless the culture is changed," Hedy said, less careful than she had been earlier in the presentation. The administrator was an old-school hard-ass who ran off highly trained professionals as fast as the advertising that Hedy and her team developed could attract them. "It's a small medical world, and there isn't an experienced neuro RN at Mayo, the Cleveland Clinic, or Mass General who doesn't know the culture. It doesn't matter if you're the best neurological hospital in America. The RNs in Jakarta at RSPAD don't want to work for her. You can't pay them enough."

Silence. Hedy had been doing this for so long she knew exactly when to be diplomatic and when to bluntly state the obvious. Many times it took someone outside the system to put it on the table. She loved the challenge of getting it just right. Most people didn't have the skill.

"I know she's been there for thirty-four years," Hedy said pointedly, "but the world has changed. We must have leaders who understand the not-so-subtle differences of the generations. The center will not fold in on itself if she decides to retire or go into a research position."

"What are we doing about the needs of our Middle Eastern clients?" a slight woman in a Prada suit proffered. Hedy hadn't worked with her directly, but she knew she was the Senior Vice President of International Medicine for the entire system. She also knew her small, demure behavior belied her aggressiveness.

"It's laid out in detail in the plan," Hedy said pleasantly. She got the message that while everything was in the plan, the woman expected to be treated with extra care and that her needs would require personalized attention.

"We've targeted King Faisal in Saudi, Tel Aviv Sourasky, and Alsalam in Kuwait based on your individual needs. There are other great facilities, but these three match you most closely. We have a blanketed approach to Turkey because they have so many outstanding facilities, but Turkish medical professionals are not always totally welcomed by the individuals coming to Baltimore. They want what they consider 'true' Middle Easterners."

The woman smiled, pleased that Hedy knew her audience. "What about the concierge team?" she continued. Hopkins had just purchased much of the newly built Ritz Carlton Residences to accommodate the entourage that accompanied a Middle Easterner seeking medical treatment. If the private jet was coming to the States, why not tag along?

The "tag along" women would arrive in full burkas, but underneath, their clothes were exquisite. No budgetary constraints. The international Hopkins team regularly worked with Nordstrom's to open after hours to accommodate female family members who spent more on shoes in one day than much of the world's population earned in a lifetime.

"We are working with the military for individuals who served in the Middle East but who don't have health care transferable skills. You simply need to speak the language to work with these families and then be trained to accommodate their needs while in the States. We are also sensitive to how a candidate must present. I feel very good about filling those roles," Hedy responded. She started straightening up the papers in front of her, indicating the meeting needed to end. You had to know when to draw the line.

"So the total budget for 2013 is about $4.6 million," the Executive Vice President for Human Resources said to the group. "It's a lot of money, but I have reviewed the plan carefully and think this is where we should go." Hedy had spent hours explaining every penny to the ultimate boss, a woman who was minutia oriented.

Hedy gave herself a silent high five after the endorsement. This was what she needed to hear. Support from the top. The system's many hospitals would fall into line, and she'd work hard to make them happy.

"I'm not sure the smaller facilities can afford a plan like this," came a male voice from the back of the room. The man represented a community hospital that had been absorbed when health care in America had changed and hospitals had merged into systems. "Taking our medical records digital is costing us every penny we have. We have to have that completed by 2014."

"The budget will be based on size—you'll just be charged a small percentage," the Hopkins executive countered. "We're not asking you to pay $4.6 million."

Hedy knew this was the time to step in. "John, we ran the numbers on your open jobs report, and if you just reduced your vacancy rate by 1.8 percent, you would save about $600,000 in the first quarter. Agency RNs are killing you since you end up paying them about three times the cost of salary and benefits of a regular employee. And then there is the consideration of how much you want regular Hopkins-trained personnel delivering Hopkins-quality care." A one-two punch delivered. Cost and quality.

"As a system, we spent $22 million in overtime last quarter," the top executive continued. Hedy had fed her the information. "We need this plan. I am challenging each of you to reduce your open jobs rate by two percent in 2013, and then we will truly celebrate—not to mention regain our designation as the best hospital in the United States."

The issue of not being number one was raw at Hopkins. The annual rankings from *U.S. News & World Report* had named Massachusetts General in 2012 as the number-one hospital system in the country, a designation Hopkins had held for over twenty consecutive years. Times were changing, and without extraordinary employees, a health-care system could not deliver extraordinary health care.

The room became quiet. The budget had become a nonissue. Two percent reduction in vacancy and regaining the number-one designation was what they had heard, and if this plan was going to help accomplish that, it looked just fine. There was nothing else to say. Hedy felt relief. The meeting was ending. Hedy wanted to run.

"The staff servicing each of your facilities will be calling next week to set up appointments for us to start the implementation,"

Hedy said with a broad smile to the executives who were packing up and leaving. She had brought six staffers to the meeting, and they had been sitting quietly behind her waiting for this very moment. They were from both the Philadelphia and Boston offices, based solely on agency politics. It should have been handled by one office, but Hedy had learned long ago what battles to fight in order to survive corporate America.

It was a little after five o'clock, and the sun had started to wan. After warm and perfunctory good-byes, the Philadelphia crew went one way and the Boston group the other. They got along, but they disliked having the account in two offices. It wasn't ideal. Sole ownership was important.

"I'll call you tomorrow," Hedy said quietly to the advertising agency's VP overseeing the operational aspect of the account. They were quickly walking out into the parking lot. "I'm worried about their Applicant Tracking System," she continued while waving to the black car. "It's not compatible with our proprietary products. It's not going to work, and it is a big part of that budget."

"What do you want me to do, Hedy?" Jim Simmons asked with a note of despair, "You know we have to sell our products. I have to sell our products," he emphasized. Jim had two children, one with special needs, and he needed to keep his well-paying job. He'd been "eliminated" once before and knew how it felt not sleeping, worrying about money. When asked to return to the agency, he had jumped at the chance and did what he was told.

"In about six months, it's going to be a disaster, and it's my face on this account," Hedy responded, knowing there wasn't anything she could do. She might be the Senior Vice President of Health Care Strategy, but her hands were tied when it came to doing what was best for the client as opposed to what the CEO wanted. What Rachel Weiss said was law, and it always involved her need to look good in front of the investors.

Rachel had no life other than the advertising agency she headed. No family, no hobbies, no friends. She was socially inept and was driven only by the bottom line. If it wasn't good for the client but was profitable for the agency, sell it and move on once everything fell apart. Rachel was a survivor. She had worked her way up and in the beginning was as good as anyone servicing the clients, but she had grown cold, bitter, and petty. She had become worse than a bully, she was a bully with power. The salaries were impressive, and they became the chains that bound the top-tier employees. Everyone knew he or she could be dismissed with a wave of her hand, and they groveled anytime it might be necessary. She was especially cruel to the men.

If an employee was diagnosed with any kind of illness that might slow him or her down or raise insurance premiums, she found a way to get that person out the door. Once, when her second-in-command had taken two weeks off to go to China to adopt a baby girl, she threw a fit and forced him to come back early. "Isn't that why you have a wife?" she had asked him on the phone. Calls on Christmas morning to discuss numbers was the rule, because she didn't really celebrate any of the holidays. Certainly not a Christian holiday, and certainly not because of any consideration of what her staff might celebrate. Who would she celebrate with?

Hedy got into the car quickly and started calculating. She wasn't going to make Dulles; Reagan was her best bet. She let the driver know that she was trying to make a change but to start driving in the direction of DC as opposed to Baltimore and the direct flight on Southwest. She felt sure it would be overbooked and she wouldn't stand a chance.

"Reagan," she called out to the driver. "There's a 6:50 flight, and I can make that easy if the traffic isn't too bad." She sat back in the plush seat and crossed her legs, looking out the window. She had status with Delta Airlines and could change her itinerary if any type of seat was still open. It made traveling much easier, but who wanted to be traveling four days a week? She'd get back to Louisville somewhere around eleven thirty in the evening if there weren't delays. Hedy was spent, but she still had hours to go before she pulled into her parking space at her condominium.

The ill-advised Hopkins product interface with the new Applicant Tracking System gnawed at the back of the mind. She couldn't figure out a way to make it right. She should be happy with the big sale. She should be calling her boss, the CEO, but Rachel Weiss hadn't spoken to her in more than three years. It was a horrible working relationship and Hedy knew she had to do something, but she didn't want to if it meant sucking up to Rachel. She didn't like Rachel. She didn't agree with the path of the agency. In all of her professional years, she had never really been unhappy, but she was very unhappy now.

# Two

"Any interesting bodies today?" Hedy asked quietly as she slid her body close to the one already warming the king-size bed. It was past one in the morning, and she wasn't ready for sleep. Baggage had taken forever, and the plane had been late leaving Atlanta. That last flight to Louisville was almost always late. On occasion, they'd hold a plane for a passenger to make the connection, and while that sometimes worked to Hedy's benefit, it still got old when she was on the plane counting the fifty minutes it took from Atlanta to Louisville, wheels up to wheels down. Finally she was in bed, and she slid her hand along the well-toned thigh next to hers and felt the smile as opposed to actually seeing it in the dim light.

"Not unless you count a shooting in the West End," continued the conversation easily. "A guy named Ray found his wife, Fay—seriously, those are their names—in bed with another man. He pulled out his gun and shot her directly in Scarpa's triangle." Hedy had no idea what Scarpa's triangle actually was but could make a pretty good guess. After fifteen years, she had picked up a lot of medical jargon. The mental picture was complete.

"Evidently, the first guy grabbed his pants and ran. Ray, who told the police she'd never need that again, nicked the femoral artery, and she bled out in about fifteen minutes. Wasn't exactly a difficult ruling for cause of death."

Hedy rolled over on her side and smiled. Most people would find the conversation disturbing, but then, they didn't sleep with the Chief Medical Examiner for the Commonwealth of Kentucky. She'd heard much worse. Hedy was always amazed at how her lover could keep conversations with the dead so separate from conversations with the living. Clearly, Fay's body hadn't needed to say a lot other than she'd gotten caught having sex with a man who wasn't her husband. The husband had a hot temper and a gun, and that was enough to end a life with a well-placed bullet. Close her up and move on to the next case.

The breathing next to Hedy grew heavy, and she knew she was again alone with her thoughts. Tomorrow was going to be packed, mainly because she needed to make time to deal with her sisters. Why couldn't someone else take the lead? She thought wearily of her mother, a bitter, untreated mentally ill woman filled with hate. Because it was her job. It had always been Hedy's job to deal with Dorothy. It wasn't that she was more burdened with Dorothy than her sisters; she was just burdened differently.

Sleep crept silently into Hedy, and she let go for the first time in the last twenty hours. It wasn't exactly easy sleep, but fatigue took control. In what seemed liked minutes, she reached over to the other side of the bed, and it was empty. She jumped to punch her phone, and it read 8:10 a.m. She was normally up by 6:00 a.m. Her first conference call wasn't until 8:30. She'd be OK, but relief poured over her when she remembered they wouldn't be able to see what she looked like. If the staff ever started Skyping, she would be in trouble.

Teeth brushed, hair combed, blood pressure pills consumed, and a large glass of cranberry juice sitting by the computer. "It's Hedy," she said into the phone. "Who's on?"

"We've got the Chicago team in the conference room." She recognized Jill's voice.

"Dallas is on." Jennifer was in place as usual. She knew these employees had come in early since they were in the central time zone; it was only 7:30 a.m., and they were in an office. She thought about when their alarms might have gone off, since they had showered, dressed, and driven as much as forty minutes in Dallas traffic. No one complained.

"What's the weather like?" Hedy tried to sound friendly, interested. She couldn't care less about the weather; she just wanted to fill the dead air until everyone had checked in.

"It's October, Hedy," said Jill. "Chicago is getting crisp."

"For Dallas, we're going to hit a hundred today."

Hedy was grateful for the pleasant fall in Louisville. She looked out at the trees and their brilliant colors.

"What about Phoenix?" said Hedy, wanting to get started.

"We are here," came the response after a beep had indicated another caller had joined, "and the weather is going to be hotter than Dallas." Laughter was easy. The employees genuinely liked one another.

You would have had to put a gun to Hedy's head for her to admit she had scheduled the call so early because she had personal business in the afternoon. She felt bad enough but told herself it was Friday and everyone would feel fine taking off a couple of hours early if possible. "Possible" being the operative word. These employees worked grueling hours.

Hedy jumped in immediately. "Vanguard isn't going well." She wanted to get this call finished. "Chicago and Boston are especially unhappy, and I'm not sure why. We are on the verge of being fired," she said pointedly. She explained that she had gotten a call from the Human Resource vice president for the twenty-eight-hospital system, and complaints were coming in from the field. Most of the hospitals were unhappy. "Phoenix is the only one who is remotely happy."

"They hate us," said Jill. "They didn't want to leave their agency, and when they were forced to work with us, they were determined we'd fail. And, according to them, we are failing," she continued. "Our direct-mail campaign produced forty RN applicants, and it wasn't enough. Forty experienced RNs. If I lined up a perfect candidate for every opening, they wouldn't be perfect enough."

Hedy remembered when they had won the Vanguard account. It had been a big deal. The corporate office was located in Nashville, and it was pretty much a unilateral decision from the top, requiring all twenty-eight hospitals to use one agency in an effort to save money. Most of the hospitals had liked their current agencies—had personal relationships with their account teams—and the last thing they wanted was to hear one more order from Nashville that would change their personal working relationships. They had already changed insurance companies and medical equipment suppliers. Obamacare, or the Affordable Care Act, was changing the face of health care, and no one knew it better than Hedy.

"Have you been over there?" Hedy asked, knowing Jill hated making office calls when they were unpleasant.

"Did you hear me say they hated us?" she answered, avoiding the direct answer.

"I want you over there, as often as they will let you in the door. Make them at least see you as a person. Get to Boston as soon as they will schedule an appointment. Keep overproducing. Please." The pause before please was clear. Jill needed to step up. Hedy had respect for Jill, but she needed to make it plain what was needed.

"San Antonio isn't all that unhappy," Hedy told the Dallas group, but they weren't exactly happy either. "They account for seven hospitals, so I've scheduled a meeting to let them bitch. Jennifer, you and Tom will need to join. What does the first of November look like for you?"

"Filled," Jennifer stated bluntly. "But you know I'll clear it. Do we have to be there in the morning?"

"The meeting is at 9:00 a.m., so you may be able to get a flight from Dallas early enough. I am going to be coming from Houston, as I have MD Anderson the day prior. I'll be at the downtown Marriott. Don't forget there are two Marriotts, right there together, so book at the Riverwalk."

Hedy hated the details, but getting teams together from across the country took time and attention. "You'll have the account summary," she directed to Jennifer in a presumptive close, knowing the hours it would take to put everything together. "You'll need to lead the meeting with the account team, as Ronald wants to have a private meeting with me."

Silence. Hedy jumped in quickly. She didn't need drama this morning.

"I think I know what it's about," Hedy said, calming the troops and explaining why she was having a private meeting with the executive vice president. "My contact at Blackstone tells me Tenet is getting ready to acquire Vanguard. It's all hush-hush, but Blackstone owns about forty percent of Vanguard, so it's a pretty completed deal. They are talking about $1.8 billion, so it's robust. They don't want any moans from the field, so we need to just keep them happy for a couple more months, then we'll be the least of their worries. Tenet is happy for the moment, so we can make this very clean if we are just careful." It was good that Tenet was already their client.

"The middle managers of Vanguard have no idea, but when they start to hear rumblings from some of the other suppliers—and they will—we want to be their best friend."

Tenet had been a client for eight years, and while there had been some ups and downs, the main contact was fair and efficient. If the deal went through, Tenet would once again be a major player in the for-profit health system world. Years ago, they had been caught overcharging the government and insurance companies and had paid a high price, going from 120 hospitals to about 50. The financial penalties had been tremendous, and they had sold just about everything any other health system would purchase. Only recently were they climbing back into the game. The Vanguard purchase would change things considerably.

Few people understood health care like Hedy. Most assumed everyone was treated about the same, but Hedy knew that what kind of treatment you received was often based on how much your insurance would pay, whom you knew, or which hospital was providing your care. While institutions like the Cleveland Clinic touted an open-door policy, one didn't just walk in and get treated. You might get examined eventually, but people without money or insurance didn't receive the same treatment, and they died at different rates.

Hedy had worked her way up, so she normally consulted only with the most prestigious facilities. But she could not escape working with the for-profits because they translated into a fatter bottom line for the agency. For-profits were exactly what they sounded like: for profit. They were businesses and executed deals in a clean business manner. The not-for-profits oftentimes mixed messages of health care along with religion and politically charged decisions, which grated Hedy's last nerve. Hedy was a businessperson, and she operated on facts, not emotion.

For-profit facilities cut client care everywhere possible. Unless some test was oddly categorized and paid for by insurance or Medicare and Medicaid, it wasn't administered. Staffing ratios were, at times, so low that care was unsafe. There were always exceptions, but generally, nurses were underpaid and fatigued, and their skills had often grown old.

As the Phoenix office reported on how things were going with their Vanguard hospitals, Hedy recalled once having just finished dinner at a high-end restaurant with a client in Los Angeles when he got an emergency call in the car reporting an elderly man had just died.

"He wouldn't calm down," the nurse had told Hedy's client hysterically. "I couldn't get a doctor. We had one of those rent-a-docs for the evening, and he wasn't answering his page. We have sixteen patients tonight, so we decided to look into the box and see what we had," she continued, referring to the other RN on the shift and a box of leftover drugs they had saved to use when they couldn't find a doctor and secure an appropriate prescription. "He had an adverse reaction."

"That's putting it mildly," the client responded. "The man died. I'd call that adverse." The car was making a U-turn going back toward the hospital, and Hedy knew she'd be taking a cab. Time was of the essence, and if they hadn't been in a rough part of town, she'd have gotten out of the car at the next stop light. She didn't want to hear anything more.

"It happens more than you know," said the client. "I hate it. I've got to get back to a real hospital. Shit. It doesn't matter that he was going to die in a few days anyway. Those girls are about twenty-three years old, and their lives are ruined. The man is dead. The box. What do you think might have been in the box?" The question was rhetorical. Hedy said nothing.

Hedy brought herself back to the conference call and remembered what the Vanguard/Tenet merger would mean to the agency. Do what you need to do was the message. Do it now, and make the client happy.

"Will you be coming into the Dallas office," Jennifer asked Hedy, "since you'll be in Houston with MD Anderson?" In other words, Do we clean up, pick you up at the airport, make sure reports are up to date?

"No, no. It's an easy in and out," said Hedy. "Besides, it's Houston. No need for a Dallas stop." She could almost hear the sigh of relief. "MD Anderson is joining forces with Vanderbilt to study pharmacological inhibitors. They need some very specialized people who work in bromodomain proteins. I had to do the research myself," Hedy explained. She was a whiz at finding information and oftentimes did the work herself, as opposed to farming it out to some recent college graduate who sat in some cubicle in Chicago. It kept her skills sharp, and she enjoyed digging around the Internet. "I had no idea what they were talking about when they first called, much less where to find these scientists."

"They actually have an association of these geniuses," she continued, pleased with what she had found. "Can you imagine how exciting those annual conferences are?" Hedy laughed a little. "Boston

University isn't going to be happy when we start poaching their people, but best of all is the fact that the Olivia Newton-John Cancer & Wellness Center in Melbourne is really where we want to lure the researchers. They have the best. Somehow, I won't be able to get *Grease* out of my head when calling our Sydney office." Hedy laughed. "It's a small world."

Conference calls continued throughout the morning, but Hedy was able to organize her upcoming travel schedule. Cedar-Sinai that Tuesday in Los Angeles for a workshop with the recruitment team, Houston on Wednesday with MD Anderson, and then San Antonio on Thursday. She loved weeks when she was home on Monday and Friday. It would be a different Marriott every night and a lot of time in airports, but she generally loved her job.

She put the last file into her Tumi backpack, which worked as a portable office, and smiled. The clients that week would be getting more than what they were paying for. The advice would be sound and accurate. She wouldn't be selling something half baked that didn't really work, and she wouldn't be suggesting unsuitable products. Hopkins haunted her. She didn't know what to do. She had built her reputation on always doing what was right for the client, even if the answer wasn't the most profitable for the agency.

Things were different now. It wasn't as if she could call her boss and complain. She wasn't even sure who her boss was. She operated so independently that she felt like an island. What had become of her professional life? Over the last few years, her refusal to grovel to the CEO meant she had slowly been cut out of everything important. She maintained the health-care accounts and found appreciation from the clients and her coworkers. She made a New York salary while living in Kentucky. Things could be worse.

# THREE

While the morning had gone well, Hedy was dreading the afternoon. Lily would bitch, Eva would go along, and Sophie would basically present as forgotten and pitiful. Every spring, they went down to start the summer at their mother's home at least moderately clean and then go back in the fall to close everything up for the winter. The time for organizing had arrived. They'd all appear, the work would get done, and then they would go back to their independent lives.

"I'd like someone to rake my leaves and get everything ready for winter," Lily had shot back on the phone when Hedy asked if she and her husband would agree to meeting a week from Saturday. Their mother lived alone, and if they didn't do it, the yard would fall into even more disrepair. The call wasn't a surprise to Lily, they had been doing it for years.

"We'll all do it together, and it'll go fast," Hedy had reasoned while looking out of her home office window from the sixteenth floor. She could see the rides at Six Flags Kentucky Kingdom in the distance, along with planes easing down into Louisville International Airport.

She knew if Lily agreed on Saturday, the other sisters would be easier to convince. Lily was number three of the five Anderson girls, unemotional and tough as nails. "You can paint. Dorothy can't...won't," Hedy responded to Lily, using her mother's given name. She never referred to her as Mama, Mom, or Mother. Nothing endearing, ever.

She felt Lily coming around. "I can do a lot of things," Lily said. Her voice was brittle, edgy. "What about the young man who's been cutting the grass?"

"He went to college," Hedy replied. "He's in Arizona and won't be home very often. I haven't been able to find anyone else." It never mattered how much she overpaid; it was almost impossible to get anyone to work for her mother for very long. Plumbers. Cleaning women. Hairdressers. Auto mechanics. Hedy felt as if half her life was spent begging people to consider doing something her mother needed. She never quibbled about the money. They deserved every penny.

Lily laughed sharply into the phone. They all knew the only way they had gotten the young man to cut the grass for so long was because his father, the local Southern Baptist minister, had convinced him it was his spiritual duty to endure, forgive. Regardless of anything Dorothy had uttered unfairly to the young man, he had always met it with a smile and undeserved kindness. Guilt had been much more effective than money. Nonetheless, his graduation gift had been more than generous.

Lily agreed to come, and her husband would do whatever she asked. "Sure. Sure. It'll be great. A ball of fun," Lily said, closing the conversation with dripping sarcasm. "But only if everyone else is on-board." There was always a hook with Lily.

"I'll tell her she has to buy us chicken," said Hedy, determined to keep things light. "Can you believe they have a Kentucky Fried Chicken in Hardinsburg?"

The small town where the sisters had been reared, where their mother still lived, consisted of fewer than 2,500 people. Everyone knew everyone else. There were several hundred more families who lived out in the county and farmed, but it was an exceedingly small world. Hedy had wanted nothing more than to run as fast as she could from rural Kentucky, and she had done just that. She was a successful advertising executive, employed by a large international agency headquartered in New York, but she never forgot she came from Breckinridge County.

The exhaustive travel, the corporate politics—it was, in many ways, a hard way to make a living. Sometimes her sisters acted as though she had somehow just gotten in the good-salary line and been lucky. Hedy remembered the twenty-hour workdays and the emotional toll of meeting sales goals along with the clients' expectations. It hadn't all been expense-account dinners and trips to fun cities. One Marriott looked like all the others, and oftentimes she was so tired she couldn't keep the boardrooms separated.

After stints in Chicago, New York, and Los Angeles, she decided she wanted to move to Louisville. Kentucky was home, and Louisville wasn't Hardinsburg. She was happy, but dark clouds could creep into her mind, and she thought there must be something wrong for wanting to move back. It didn't matter how many accounts she won or how many promotions she attained; there were always doubts. She picked up the phone to call Eva, the oldest of the sisters.

"What about next Saturday?" she said as she walked to the window and looked down at the green trees outside her building. The changing colors were stunning. The sky was a beautiful blue with little puffs of white clouds. She would be going out to dinner later, and details about this "cleanup day" would be boxed and left on a shelf in her mind somewhere far away. She would be back to normal. It was Friday, and she was home.

Hedy crossed her legs as she leaned back into her office chair, having returned from the window while the conversation dragged on. Eva could talk forever. Hedy loved working at home and had a room in her condominium she used exclusively as her work space. She kept things separate and organized. She dropped a shoe onto the oriental rug.

"I've already called Tom Bennett, and he says he can be there at ten o'clock slow time." She cringed at the use of the term "slow time." They had grown up on the time zone line, with half of the county in the eastern time zone and the other half in the central time zone. Much of her childhood had been spent clarifying, is that slow time or fast time? Ridiculous wording. Time was time. Two of the sisters lived in the central time zone, and two lived in the eastern time zone along with Hedy. She had to revert to another language. Her head was beginning to ache.

"He'll put down a layer of gravel for $125. I told him to take it all the way around to the back door." Their mother didn't want people to see if she was home or away, so she had taken to hiding her car behind the house, driving over the grass and creating an ugly dirt path. Hiding the car was just a mutation of teaching the girls, when they were younger, to hide and not answer the door if someone, clearly not from Hardinsburg, knocked on the door.

Eva agreed to supply the hedge trimmers, and Hedy said she'd pick up the paint. It was coming together. Eva lived almost next door to their mother, and while she was universally accommodating, she chaffed at Dorothy. Too many tongue lashings. Too many cruel put-downs. Eva was over Dorothy and agreed to help only because everyone else was pitching in. Besides, if the leaves blew into everyone else's yards, local people would expect her to do something. She was grateful for the help.

There was always guilt associated with calling Sophie, Anderson sister number four by eight minutes. Hedy hated asking her to do anything since she took care of their sister, Sophie's twin, Patty, who suffered from tonic-clonic, or grand mal seizures. It was never totally clear what had happened, but Patty had gone from a happy, bright child to someone completely withdrawn and mostly non-communicative.

No one ever really explained Patty's condition, but Hedy remembered the day Dorothy swung a golf club, hitting Patty in the temple and driving her across the back room. She was out cold, so everyone gathered Patty up and got her into the car and ultimately to the back door of the doctor's office. Hedy wasn't old enough for a driver's license, but that was of little consequence. She sat up as tall as she could, looked through the extra circular bar around the steering wheel, and put the car in gear. She didn't have far to go. Eva held Patty.

"Miss Finney?" Hedy said quietly when the doctor's nurse came to the normally unused back door of the clinic. "It's Patty. She hit her head." It wasn't the first time the girls had appeared at the back door and it wasn't the first time the wound did not match the explanation. No one ever said anything, but the doctor was soon at the car, and he carried her into an examining room.

Patty came to, and the doctor sent her home with no questions asked. The girls stayed up with Patty all night, as the doctor had told them. Keeping her awake. Hedy had always thought that incident had led to the seizures, even though they started years later. It just wasn't talked about. Sophie and Patty were twins, and Sophie just assumed the responsibility. When Sophie went to college, Patty followed after a stay at a Louisville psychiatric hospital. They were a package deal.

As language problems and the loss of cognitive abilities became more pronounced, Patty did little more than rock in a chair in her bedroom and listen to police radio. Radio Shack had changed her life. One day she seized on the buzzing and crackling of the little handheld device, and for less than a hundred dollars, she had access to the communications of over five hundred police jurisdictions. It had been a godsend for Sophie, who worried that Patty would stop talking completely. With the police radio, she would occasionally share details and become animated. It also kept her occupied.

Patty liked Chicago police radio the best, with Cincinnati a close second. "I always know some people are worse off," Patty had told Sophie on one of her few speaking days. "I love it when the police come and help the children. A lot of children are hurt in Chicago."

In addition to the domestic abuse in Chicago, Patty was obsessed with germs. She washed her hands at least forty times a day, and she followed the washings by wearing little white gloves. She felt secure and soothed wearing the gloves, which were increasingly hard to find but still available at church supply stores. Louisville had more than its share of those, with all the Catholics, Baptists, and occasional Presbyterians. Sophie made sure Patty had boxes of the gloves and a ready supply of batteries for her radio.

Sophie's husband, Paul, fortunately loved them both, and the living arrangement seemed smooth. They would all join the cleanup effort. Paul would bring the lawn mower with the attached leaf catcher. It would be one more year down.

Hedy hadn't talked to this many sisters in months. She promised to bring cold drinks. She'd do just about anything to get the yard and house ready for the winter. She wanted off the phone and on to her real life. Dinner and a nice cold glass of sauvignon blanc couldn't come fast enough.

# FOUR

Lily couldn't believe she was the first to arrive, and she had to go to the bathroom. Dorothy certainly wouldn't be awake at midmorning. There didn't need to be any discussion between Lily and her husband, Howard. He knew to sit down by the picnic table and wait silently. He'd been doing that for over thirty years. Lily would sneak into the house and go to the bathroom without making a sound or waking Dorothy. She was a professional at not bothering Dorothy. All the girls were.

Howard watched as Lily opened the unlocked door and slipped smoothly into the enclosed back porch. He wondered if they could get everything done before Dorothy got up. He thought about his own mother, who would have been so excited about her children coming home that she would have cooked for three days, stood looking out the window until she saw them drive up, and then run out into the yard. You didn't have to worry about Dorothy doing too big a welcome—she wouldn't even wake up. Howard didn't want to have to deal with her today, so he was hoping things would move fast. It had already been a tense and silent ride to Hardinsburg. God, Lily could be so cold, and there was no negotiating with her. It was her way, no discussion, and then the icy stare. She was shut down and in control.

Howard looked around the property and surveyed what needed to be done. He didn't want to mow, trim the overgrowth, or paint. He wanted to run. There was never another woman he had wanted the way he had wanted Lily. Even now, he could grow hard just looking at her, long legs and tight little ass. He'd gotten through many a high school English class because she sat in front of him. He'd followed her to the University of Kentucky and majored in Lily. She had dated plenty of other men, but he had been patient. He was comfortable and always there. He loved her. He demanded little, and he understood her.

Lily always held a little something back. She had said she loved him, but not convincingly or very often. He had always tried not to notice. He loved her enough for both of them. At first they had been a good team. Raising the kids, moving from one house into another, snapping up the promotions, becoming financially secure.

Howard didn't notice Hedy walking up the driveway.

"Got to move that rattle trap," she said to Howard, smiling in the morning sun and pointing to the new Mercedes-Benz. "Tom Bennett is going to lay new gravel, so we have to park the cars out on the street," she continued. That was the way it was with the Anderson girls. No pleasant discussions. No warm greetings. They were all business with no time for emotions. He was sure Hedy didn't mean anything by her immediate orders; it was just what was needed. All the sisters would be wound tight today. This was an emotional land mine.

Howard stood up as Lily emerged. "I'm moving the car to the street," he said to no one in particular, saying just enough to keep Lily informed. This day would mean just taking orders. He slid behind the wheel wondering if anyone would notice if he just kept driving.

"She's asleep," Lily said to Hedy in a low voice, even though she was outside and well distanced from Dorothy. "Why again are we doing this?" The question was rhetorical.

Hedy held her hands out and pointed to the hedges, which were overgrown and dying, the leaves spilling over the gutters and the rusting swing set. "I can't get anyone to come here and do this work," Hedy said. "It's a mess."

Eva and Don were the next to arrive, toting clippers and a bag of tools. "The gutters are on their last leg," Don announced as he turned the corner, stepping from the driveway to the overgrown grass. "I've milked them as long as I can." He had become as good at non-greetings as his sisters-in-law. He'd been around the longest. Eva was the oldest, and they had married the summer after she turned seventeen. It wasn't legal in Kentucky, so they had slipped to Tennessee, where she didn't need a parental signature for being under eighteen years old. Dorothy had said it wouldn't last six weeks, but forty-six years later, he was still around.

Don was the most abused son-in-law simply because of proximity. They lived in Hardinsburg, and Dorothy did not hesitate to call and demand. He already knew everything that needed fixing because he'd been fixing things all summer. He was grateful for the other sons-in-law as well as the sisters, who would tackle a project as quickly as any man.

"There is a lot of rotting wood up there," Don continued.

Howard was back, considering what job he wanted to sign up for. Dress shoes had not been a good idea. He needed to carry his load, or it would be hell with Lily.

Sophie, Paul, and Patty arrived with a lawnmower and a box of black trash bags. "Does she have a ladder?" Paul queried after overhearing the discussion about the gutters.

"In the furnace room," said Hedy, thinking of the coal-burning furnace that had warmed the house in the winters of their childhood. She and Eva had always been in charge of making sure the fire didn't go out. Responsibilities for the two oldest. They weren't more than ten and eight when they assumed the furnace duties. Eva had once burned off her eyebrows and much of her hair by throwing kerosene into smoldering coals, desperate to bring the fire back to life. There was nothing like having to tell Dorothy you had let the fire go out, so Eva made the unfortunate decision, resulting in an explosion.

"I'll get it," responded Hedy, taking off for the house. Only the girls would go in, as they knew exactly how not to wake Dorothy.

Patty headed to the metal lawn chairs. She was groggy from a very rough night. It was rare that she suffered cluster seizures, but sometime around nine the night before, she had felt the aura and soon was shaking violently, eyes rolled back and her face and lips turning blue from lack of oxygen. She could hear Sophie in the distance urging her to breathe. Twelve seizures in an hour had brought the whole house to a stop. Sophie had helped her ride them out, but when Patty would come out of one, she was violent in her movements and disoriented. Patty was shaking still from the sheer number of seizures her body had endured the night before.

As Patty made her way into the yard, she clutched her police scanner and chose both a channel and a seat for the day. The chairs were ancient and needed painting. Dorothy liked green, so Hedy had bought hunter green paint for the seats and backs; white for the legs and arms. There was no rocker, but Patty could bounce in the lawn chairs, as the legs consisted of one continuous hollow pipe running from the front and looping under the seat. She was soon self-soothing by bouncing and rubbing her gloved hands on her lips. The police radio crackled lightly, enough for only Patty to hear clearly. This would be a very difficult day for her, but she was happy to be part of the action, the seizures at bay.

"I'll do the painting," said Lily, reaching down and taking the brushes and paint Hedy had deposited. "Didn't they have spray?" she asked, holding up the gallon bucket.

"This is what the Home Depot guy suggested. Adheres to metal," Hedy responded. If she had bought spray, Lily would have wondered about a can, she mused.

"I'll mow," said Hedy, ending the paint conversation, thinking about the immediate gratification of making those long rows of freshly mowed grass along with the full bags of leaves.

Paul pushed the mower toward Hedy and gave her his best "be my guest" smile. Eva said she'd pull the dead flowers and clean the flower beds in the front. Howard picked up Don's tools and went to the decrepit swing set. It had been rusting in place for fifty years. How was it still standing?

Eva picked up the box of tools and headed to the mailbox. "It's falling down. I'll even take some of your paint, Lily, and green and white it up."

"I've got my truck," said Don to Howard as the swing set easily disintegrated. "All this needs to go to the dump. You know, past St. Romuald." Don was pointing in the direction of the school where all the girls had attended at least elementary school. Eva was the only one who had graduated from high school there. Dorothy had had a blowup with a priest when Hedy was in ninth grade, and she suddenly found herself going to the public high school. Just one more change to endure, but the teachers were much better, and everyone was actually credentialed. Going to public school had been a blessing for Hedy, but she never let Dorothy know or she would have been back down at St. Romuald.

"How about all this grass and the leaves? Can you take that too?" Hedy was sweating in the midday sun, dragging a black plastic bag.

She hated this kind of work. Hated it. She had finished mowing the back portion of the yard and scooping the leaves. There was a lot more to be mowed, bagged, and hauled away. "I put the cooler on the front porch," she continued. "It's full of everything."

Sophie rounded the house with gardening gloves and a black bag full of clippings. "The front is weeded and raked," she announced, looking up at her husband perched on a ladder. Paul was nailing back the cleaned gutters and shaking his head. "It won't last another winter."

"Maybe if it falls down around her, we won't have to do this again next year," Lily announced. "If we didn't do it, maybe she'd be nicer to other people." Some ugly words were beyond sequester. No one answered Lily. That wasn't the way it worked. The girls had been programed from an early age to take responsibility, no matter how painful and undeserved. In turn, they had programmed the husbands.

"We need a new section of gutter," said Don. "That last three feet is gone. I wish I'd realized it before I put the old stuff back together. We could have replaced it all."

"I'll go to Glasscock Brothers," said Hedy. "What do I ask for?" she said to Don. "How big? Will they have gutters in stock?"

"Let me measure exactly what we need and have them cut it to order. They'll do it," Don said. "I'm going to need your help, Paul. If we can just get through another year."

Hedy pulled her keys out of her shorts pocket and took off down the freshly graveled driveway. How could Dorothy sleep through all this? Hedy wondered, knowing she had no idea how many pills her mother consumed each night. Pills to go to sleep and then enough caffeine to light a city. It was tough not being able to face the day.

When Hedy rolled back up the driveway, everyone was sitting around the picnic table drinking various containers of soda, water, and beer. It was a nice sight. They had all known one another for a lifetime. No one needed to explain anything, and everyone carried his or her weight in different ways. They all knew their places.

"Are we otherwise finished?" asked Hedy, holding out the new guttering. It was late afternoon, and they didn't need to be as quiet. She'd be getting up soon.

"Almost. Just that piece of gutter," said Don. "We need to get into the house to attach it appropriately. Who's going in and telling her we need to get in?" He smiled tauntingly as he laid it out.

"I'm not," Hedy responded resoundingly. There was only so much she'd do.

"Well if you think I am, you are dead wrong," responded Lily. "I'm here under duress already."

"You're always under duress," said Sophie. "I don't think it's that bad. Hell, everything is finished. We are ready to go home."

"Seriously?" Lily shot back. "Not that bad? Be my guest, then." She pointed to the back door.

Eva sat quietly. She lived close enough that she took the majority of the calls and problems. With everyone else in town, she could completely withdraw.

"Why don't we just go into the back room quietly? And then, if she gets up, we'll deal. Otherwise, nail up the stuff and move on," Hedy suggested.

"Sounds logical," Don said. "But Paul and I will be the ones on the ladder, and we'll be defenseless. One swift kick would be all it'd take."

"I'll stand in the hallway and protect you boys from a surprise attack," said Sophie, chuckling. "Geez. Grow some tits."

"Grow some tits," Paul said to the other men. "Come on, boys."

The gutter work went easily. Howard took the scraps and loaded everything into Don's truck. Dorothy did not rise, and even the girls were a little surprised. It was five o'clock, and everyone was starving.

"What about that chicken?" Lily said to Hedy as they reached the freshly mowed and raked back lawn and the afternoon sun. "Mmmm. Sure would be good about now."

"I'm thinking we all head out and stop by the KFC," said Hedy. "We can make a quick drop at the dump and be ready for some grease." Hedy didn't usually eat at Kentucky Fried Chicken, but she knew there wasn't much else between Hardinsburg and Louisville. She'd grown accustomed to eating in the finest restaurants because much of her job consisted of taking clients out to dinner, but KFC was looking great at the moment.

"I've been starving for hours," said Howard. It was amazing how the girls didn't stop for things like a meal. They just keep going when there was work to do. Who needed food? Lunch had consisted of PowerBars.

"Are we really just leaving without saying anything?" Sophie was motioning to Patty, who was rocking close to the picnic table, her eyes wide. "I expected Dorothy to come out at least by four, even if just to tell us how shitty a job we've done."

"I don't care what we do," said Lily. "But I'm leaving."

"I'm going in to at least tell her we've been here and we are leaving," Sophie announced. "Patty, get in the car, and we'll be leaving as soon as I tell Granny good-bye."

Sophie was always the one who would break down and act as though Dorothy was somehow normal. That she deserved a good-bye. Sleeping all day was normal. Kids came home and worked in the yard without food, drink, or greeting. All normal.

"Sure. Thanks, Sophie. We'll wait here," Hedy responded. "Tell her it's all taken care of." There was a weariness Hedy couldn't quite pinpoint. The work had been strenuous, but her fatigue wasn't just a result of the manual labor. She was tired of making sure everything was OK. She was just tired. She was tired of acting as if things in this part of her life were normal.

# FIVE

Sophie walked out the back door, not bothering to stop the slam of the screen door. It was a group stare that greeted her. "She's dead," was the simple announcement. "She's dead."

"What do you mean dead?" said Lily in a semi-disgusted tone. "Really? Like heart-attack dead?"

"It's her head, her neck. There is a lot of blood, but it looks as though she was hit with a rusty pipe from the swing set." Sophie brought her hand up and showed blood on the tips of her fingers. "There is no pulse. The pipe is still there, and it has blood on the end."

"Did it look like she's been dead for a long time?" Paul asked his wife. "I mean, she couldn't have just died. We were all right here. All day."

"It's fresh blood," said Sophie. "The pipe is from the swing set Howard just broke down. She hasn't been dead that long. I don't know. The blood is all over the couch and her head. The pipe is just laying on the floor. She's not that cold. She was asleep, I guess. She was still wearing those stupid underpants on her head." Every Anderson girl knew exactly what Sophie was saying. Dorothy kept from having to do her hair for a week by putting silk underwear on her head each night. Most people would have gotten something made for keeping helmet-head hair in place, but not Dorothy. She used underwear.

No one said anything for what seemed like minutes, but it was, in fact, only about twenty seconds. Everyone's mind was racing. Hedy broke the silence. "Are you sure? Dead? Really dead? Like someone murdered her?"

Finding their mother murdered did not rattle the sisters. They had learned to deal with anything. Nothing in their adult life could compare to their childhoods, and their tolerance for the outrageous was off the charts. No one blinked. The husbands, on the other hand, could deal with a lot, but a dead mother gave them pause.

"Who do we call? Shouldn't we call someone?" Eva said to the group. "The sheriff? The coroner? Hardinsburg Police? Who investigates?"

Considering next steps seemed unbelievable. Patty was the only one who screamed, a small, terrified cry that sounded like a wounded bird. Sophie went to comfort her.

"Well, I've seen enough *Law & Order* segments to know we shouldn't all go rushing in there, but you are sure, Sophie, that she is dead. Murdered?" Hedy continued in disbelief, projecting how important it was that Sophie was accurate. Hedy was tired and sweaty. It had been a long day.

"I'm telling you she has been hit in the head—well, the neck—and there is blood all over the couch. She has no pulse. I'm a damned RN. I know dead. No pulse."

Patty started to laugh and rock in place even though she was standing. Time seemed to stand still. Sophie wiped her bloody fingers on a tissue.

"Wonder if she knew who did it?" said Lily. "I'd like to know that she knew someone had finally had enough."

No one else said anything, and the men stared at Lily. The girls let the thought roll around in their heads, and some even smiled. Paul looked away, and Howard sat exhausted on the picnic table, where he had started.

Hedy slipped her iPhone from her pocket and punched in 911. "This is Hedy Anderson." She used her maiden name even though she had been Hedy Miller for almost thirty years, a small leftover from a brief marriage. "Oh, hi. It's my mother. Yes. We think she's been murdered." Hedy listened as the familiar voice on the other end became alarmed. Everyone knew everyone else, and Hedy could envision the overweight woman sitting in the basement of the courthouse taking 911 calls. She just couldn't remember her name. Mary Ann? Betty Lou? One of the Floods? How many calls a day would she answer? Hedy wondered, knowing this was going to be a big day for her. "Yes, Dorothy. Murdered." The line almost crackled with the news.

"Only Sophie has actually seen her," said Hedy. There was no need for an explanation of who Sophie was. "We don't think there is a need for an ambulance, but I'm sure we'll need one eventually. There isn't a pulse. OK. That's good." A non sequitur.

Hedy looked up and explained that an ambulance had been dispatched and that both the sheriff and Hardinsburg Police would be on their way. There was a collective gasp, and everyone started moving around, going nowhere and wanting to go anywhere but in the backyard of this home that now held a murdered woman. Dorothy had done a lot of things in her life that had resulted in confusion and chaos for her daughters, but this topped everything. "Could she have done this to herself?" Hedy said to no one in particular.

"I wouldn't put it past her," said Eva.

Don stood speechless by his wife. Some things even surprised him. "How could she stab herself in the neck? Wouldn't you stab your heart?" Don continued in the absurdity.

Everyone looked away.

Howard reached out for Lily, but she turned and walked to the car. "How did this happen? I didn't want to come in the first place," she mumbled. Sophie continued to comfort Patty, and Hedy leaned against the concrete block wall that comprised the coal room addition. The sirens began to wail almost immediately, rushing down Main Street. It was close to six o'clock, but they would still have at least another hour of light.

The county sheriff was the first to arrive, with the Hardinsburg Police right behind him. They roared up the freshly graveled driveway with an urgency that wasn't needed.

"I'm Bobby Clinton," said the sheriff to the group as he rolled one leg out of the cruiser. They knew he was the sheriff because it was written everywhere—on the car, his shirt, and his hat. His big badge gleamed in the late afternoon sun. His belt was heavy with attachments—a gun, a baton, keys. His uniform was a light khaki with brown trim. They knew he was Bobby Clinton because they had grown up with him in Breckinridge County.

"Hi Bobby," Paul responded, walking over and holding out his hand. He had been a year ahead of Bobby's class. Patty and Sophie had graduated with him.

"What do we have here?" Clinton said, pulling up his pants.

Hedy had a brief vision of Don Knotts and the one bullet in his pocket from *The Andy Griffith Show*, but she quickly put that out of her mind. She didn't want to grin when asked about her murdered mother lying in the house. She was so glad she had gotten out of Hardinsburg. Just being in the backyard brought pain.

Don stepped up behind Paul and explained, according to Sophie, that it appeared Dorothy had been hit with a rusty pipe and was dead. Don knew Bobby well; they had both lived in this small town their entire lives.

"You're telling me Dorothy is dead," he said flatly. "We haven't had a real murder in Breckinridge County since 1946, when the local English teacher shot her married lover. It was written up in the *New York Times*," he continued. Everyone knew the story.

The chief of Hardinsburg Police stepped up and stood beside the sheriff. "Should we take a look? Maybe she isn't dead."

"She's dead," Sophie said tiredly. "It looks like she bled out from a neck wound."

"Let's go in and take a look," said Hedy. "I'll show you." She motioned to the back door as both men started putting on latex gloves. Hardinsburg has gone high tech, thought Hedy as she opened the door and held it for the men who were now following her.

Everyone else filed in behind the initial trio and made an immediate right, which led into the kitchen. Hedy and the law enforcement officers went straight ahead and into the living room. The house was a circle, and the larger group went around the corner from the kitchen and into the dining room. It looked into the living room, where

Dorothy was prone on a hideous flowered couch. She never slept in her bed but maintained a bedroll on the living-room couch. A large mirror hung above the couch and provided a nice view of Hedy and the two men as they looked at Dorothy.

The sheriff reached down and felt for a pulse and shook his head. "She's starting to get cold."

"Well then, I guess she's dead," the Hardinsburg police chief said, stepping back and away from the body. He'd never actually seen an honest-to-god murder. Blood was everywhere.

Geniuses, Hedy thought. Cold wasn't the only thing that proved Dorothy was dead; she also wasn't up and cutting everyone to pieces with her tongue, which could substitute for a machete. She would have been furious that people were in her house—her space. She was definitely dead.

"We don't have many murders," the sheriff repeated while trying to make sense of the situation. This was going to be trouble. Everyone was pretty much the same in Breckinridge County, no one much more important than the next. But all things considered equal, the Andersons were a tough bunch. They had mostly all gone to college and done better than the average Breckinridge Countian. Dorothy was beyond difficult. And while he could see she was dead, he also knew he couldn't get this one wrong.

The local coroner had gotten the news and let himself in the back door, and now he appeared in the living room. "Do you want me to take a look?" he queried. Jim Bandy had served as the Breckinridge County coroner for twelve years and had been given the Advanced Coroner Award last year from the Department of Criminal Justice and Training. He took things seriously, but like most local coroners, being the coroner was a part-time gig that paid $900 a month, supplementing his farming income. He was not a medical doctor but had forty hours of training and then another eighteen hours each year covering topics such as crime-scene investigations, patterns in injuries, and evidence for death investigation. The problem wasn't so much not having enough training to do an adequate job, it was that he'd never gotten to use any of his knowledge. There simply weren't murders to be investigated in rural Kentucky. People kept their back doors unlocked and the keys in their cars.

"I see a blood pattern right here," he stated, motioning to a spray that went from the edge of the couch to the middle of the room. "That would indicate she had the pipe rammed into her neck from someone standing behind her. It would go pretty fast if the carotid artery was severed, which appears to have happened with this much blood." The coroner stood back and looked at Dorothy from another angle.

"People bleed out in a matter of minutes. You also have the jugular, and it looks like the pipe was pushed so hard that it could have severed that too. If the larynx was crushed, she wouldn't have been able to speak." The scenario he was painting was violent, and while everyone listened intently, they all appeared horrified. The sheriff was watching the reactions intently while listening to the coroner.

"But wouldn't she try to get up and call for help?" Hedy responded, surprised at the knowledge the coroner was displaying. "I'd think she'd thrash around, throwing a lot more blood in the room. You know, looking for help. Couldn't she have come out where we were working within fifteen or twenty minutes?"

"You lose consciousness pretty quickly," he continued. "If she were asleep or lying down, she should have been able to get up, at least for a few seconds. It takes a few minutes to die, but she'd be out pretty quickly. It is a little odd that she's right where she seems to have been sleeping. Normally she would have been able to move a little."

containers she saved, and paper bags. Their father would dutifully bring the box of food into the house and put it on the kitchen table. Dorothy would be waiting, and she would just as dutifully take it and put it all in the trash cans in the back. Maggots prevented the girls from trying to salvage the food, but they all walked out and watched it sit in the can. No one ever said anything, but the chicken looked so good.

"You are nothing but millstones around my neck," Dorothy would often say. "I could have been something." Sometimes Dorothy tried— on rare occasions, she would cook a pot of beans. Other times, a pot of macaroni and tomatoes. They would be sitting on the stove cold and tasteless, but at least she had tried. If Dorothy herself had eaten that day, which she normally did not until late evening, there might be a hard fried egg left in the grease of the frying pan. The days she tried were few. She simply couldn't hold it together.

When she found out she was pregnant the last time, it was decided that Eva and Hedy would be sent away to their paternal uncle's house for the summer. Lily was farmed out to another local aunt.

Uncle Otis was an accountant for the L&N railroad company, and Hedy and Eva were put on the train from Louisville to New Orleans. It was as far as they could go without switching trains, so Otis drove from Houston, where he and his wife lived, and picked up the girls. They were four and six years old, but they weren't afraid. Hedy knew Eva was in charge, and she did what she said even when it meant flushing the little mints a woman on the train had given them. She was coming home from her son's wedding and they had been the fa- vors, but Eva flushed them. You weren't supposed to take things from strangers. They had a little compartment, and the train porter brought them meals in little boxes. It was wonderful. Roast beef sandwiches, little bags of nuts, and an apple.

Dorothy didn't recover when the twins were born. Eva and Hedy were back because school had started, but people stepped in when

Dorothy remained hospitalized. She stayed in a Louisville hospital for six weeks, and all the Anderson girls were placed with relatives. No one talked much about which hospital, but Hedy later found out it was not where she had given birth; rather, she had been moved to a psychiatric hospital. Everyone said it was kidney stones. Everyone knew better. Dorothy talked a lot about kidney stones when she returned and about how painful they were. It was the 1960s, and people just didn't go for mental treatment. People didn't talk about it.

Hedy hated it when others witnessed her mother's "sermons." Dorothy could stand and yell for hours. You had to listen because sometimes she asked questions. Hedy was always embarrassed. She knew it was their fault. She just wasn't sure how to make it right. A mother always loves her children. No matter what. No matter how awful they were. The Anderson girls developed an ongoing, continuous feeling of dread and sadness. The moment one of them let down and did not watch to make sure things were as even as possible, something happened.

The girls quickly learned they needed to sleep under the bed. Dorothy roamed all night because she slept all day. The girls had places upstairs where they slept. Lily had an old army cot, and Eva had a room off the attic. Hedy's bed was more in the open, and Dorothy loved to sneak up on her and beat her in the night. Hedy learned to sleep under the bed to be more prepared. You couldn't be responsive if you were tangled up in sheets, so Hedy kept her ear to the wooden floor and was ready when Dorothy started mounting the steps. Hedy knew she had to take it, but she could get prepared. A shoe heel to the back was much less effective than a shoe heel to fingers. Fingers broke easily.

Hedy was mostly the target in the night, but once, Eva saw her coming with a butcher knife. That was unusual, and the girls never figured out what the plan really was because Eva came screaming and got between Hedy and Dorothy. Dorothy dropped the knife, turned, and went downstairs.

Dorothy liked driving into Louisville to shop, and she took the girls with her. Those days were both good and bad. On the way home, you got to have a cheeseburger at the McDonald's on Dixie Highway, but you could be publicly yelled at in a store if something went wrong. Something always went wrong. People would stop and stare for a moment, but they walked on. The Anderson girls just had to stand there with their heads down.

The girls were smart. Very smart. They loved school, even when they would come in late and the other children would make fun. No one could match them academically. Of course they were going to a small rural Catholic school that was not accredited by the State of Kentucky, but they were always the best in the class.

In first grade, Hedy already knew how to read. Some of the kids who lived out in the county were repeating first grade and still couldn't read. Most times, it was because they missed too much school. It was Sister Mary Joseph's first year, and she seemed to like Hedy. She allowed her to help some of the slower kids.

"We are going to break up into three groups," the nun had told the students. "We are going to have the turtles, the automobiles, and the jet planes." Hedy knew she didn't want to be a turtle, so when she was put in the jet plane group, she felt proud and was quick to tell Dorothy she was a "jet plane." Hedy knew it was a mistake the minute it came out of her mouth.

"Really?" said Dorothy. "You're a jet plane. I guess you don't get it, do you?" she told the six-year-old. "You might be in the jet plane group, but you know you have a green tint." Hedy looked at her hands and then turned them over for another look. "Everyone sees it but you, and they laugh behind your back because you can't see it. And you think you are smart, but you aren't really. You have a green tint, and you think Sister Mary Joseph likes you so much. Ha! She's making fun of you. You're not smart. They are laughing at you because of the green tint."

Hedy didn't understand exactly about the green tint, but she did know that she didn't want Sister Mary Joseph laughing behind her back. Later, when she was asked to help, she was slower to get up from her desk, slower to point out the correct pronunciations of the words, and she never again trusted what anyone said to her. They saw the green tint, and she did not. Hedy needed to take care of herself. Trust no one. They were all laughing behind her back.

Hedy looked at the sheriff and wondered if he saw the green tint. That he somehow knew something she didn't. Hedy was now sixty-one years old and a successful businessperson, but the green tint could come back in a second. On good, solid days, she knew there was no green tint, but on vulnerable adult days, the green tint could still crush her.

# Eleven

"I know you all want to go home, but you are walking evidence," said Bobby Clinton, the sheriff. "There is nothing to suggest that anyone else came or went from that house—with the exception of Tom Bennett, who laid the gravel. He's being questioned, but he was there early morning and barely got out of the truck, and the doc from Louisville says Dorothy was dead four to six hours when you found her. Tom was long gone.

"You are the suspects. Right here," he continued, pointing to the group. "We think one of you did it. No one else had access." The room fell quiet. "Or motive. I've never seen so much motive."

Clinton was over being nice. Acting like someone else had done this. As far as he was concerned, this was a bunch of lunatics. Killing her with a leg of lamb, crushing up pills. He had been so jealous of both Sophie and Patty in high school. Hanging tobacco had been a picnic. He just hadn't known.

Bobby knew he was totally outmanned, but it didn't mean he had to be outsmarted. He was going to get this right.

"Mary Theresa is going to take all of the women to the court-room, and you'll need to change your clothes and leave them behind." The girls looked at one another in disbelief. Were they driving home naked?

"I called the hospital, and they are bringing sterile scrubs. You'll have to use them for clothes to get home. They have two techs on to-night, it being Saturday. They are going to scrape your nails and other stuff." Clinton waved his hand, trying not to think about what "other stuff" might be. Was he leaving anything out? What else should he do?

Hedy looked down at her perfectly manicured nails. She cringed at the thought of them being cut. She'd need to get to the salon and have the lacquer evened out. Lily simply crossed her leg and sneered into the air.

"I will be with the men in this room," he continued. "You'll do the same. When we are finished bagging and taking physical evidence, you can leave. But we'll need to interview each one of you individually tomorrow, Monday, Tuesday, however long it takes."

"I can't do it," said Hedy immediately, very accustomed to giv-ing directions that were generally followed. "I'm in Seattle, Phoenix, and New York next week." She didn't realize just how outrageous she sounded.

"Well, la de da, Miss Hedy. Don't let the stabbing of your mother get in the way of your job," said Lily. All of a sudden Lily cared about Dorothy being dead? "Are you nuts? You'll need to cancel. We are go-ing to have to bury her, you know."

"And we need to find out who killed her," Clinton inserted quick-ly. Weren't they at least interested in who had killed her? How many cities did she reel off for next week? What kind of work did she do? Each year, he saved so he and his wife could drive to Atlanta to watch the University of Kentucky Wildcats play in the SEC basketball championship. It was more vacation than most people took around here.

Patty started to cry. Sophie looked up at Clinton, begging with her eyes. "Patty too?" The police radio static was in the background. She looked clean. They all looked clean.

"I'm sorry, but Patty too," said Bobby.

"I'll help," said Eva, always the peacekeeper. Patty was melting down fast. She suddenly became stiff and fell backward toward the floor. The seizure had come on without the usual warnings. Sophie knew the triggers, and she was surprised it had taken this long. They hadn't eaten appropriately, and the stress was off the scale. Sophie moved in quickly to let Patty fall backward into her body, and they went down together. Eva took Patty's arms and rolled her over on her left side. They all had been doing this for years. The shaking was violent, and Patty started hitting her head against the terrazzo flooring. Sophie slid under her and took the blows and waited. There was nothing more she could do. She was turning blue.

"Breathe, Patty," said Sophie. "Remember to breathe."

She took a breath and then clinched her teeth. Her eyes were closed, but Sophie knew they had rolled back into her head. Patty tried to come out of the seizure but couldn't. It lasted for a little more than sixty seconds, and she was still completely disoriented as her body eased and stopped jerking violently. Eva and Sophie held her tight, hoping to calm her and avoid violence.

"Patty too," Sophie said again to Clinton as Patty finally opened her eyes and Eva helped her into a sitting position.

"I'm sorry," Patty said to the group. She was embarrassed; she knew what had happened. She was disappointed because she had controlled her seizures fairly well with new medication. This one on top of last night's cluster was defeating.

Bobby Clinton lowered his eyes and shook his head no. He had never seen someone have a seizure, and he was humbled. Today had been too much for him. He had fought in Vietnam and had seen men punch their fists straight into a women's faces, but this had been too much.

The hospital staff had arrived, and the women agreed it would be better if they stayed in the conference room and the men went to the courtroom. Everyone moved quickly and companionably.

Hedy quickly started taking off her clothes, and Lily followed as Clinton walked out the door. Today had been too much. Too much for everyone. The scrubs were so big that Hedy rolled them up to her knee. She was the first to be cleared for evidence, and she walked to Sophie.

"I'll stay with her till you get changed," she told Sophie, taking Patty and moving her face to look toward the wall. They all knew what to do to calm her, and in her mind, she was somewhere else. She wasn't in this room. She hadn't just lost complete control of her body, she had also taken her mind somewhere else. She wasn't speaking.

Hedy looked down and realized Patty had soiled herself during the seizure. It happened when the seizures were especially violent. "What should we do?" Hedy looked at Sophie for guidance.

"Let it go. I'll get her home. She's just wet. Clean up the mess, will you, before he makes me strip her right here."

"She just hates it when it's so public," Sophie said quietly, although she knew Patty had quit listening. "I've got pills that will help her sleep. I think there should be paper towels in the bathroom."

Hedy started out of the room.

"How did this happen? How did we get here?" Tears were in Sophie's eyes. "Dorothy won't go away. She'll never go away. I'm standing naked in the courthouse. Naked—in so many ways."

The technicians were young and efficient. They worked quickly folding the clothes, marking them, and adding little ziplock pouches of dirt and other things that had been lodged under the girls' nails after a long day of yard work. They looked in ears and armpits, behind knees, and around heads. No one complained. They didn't know exactly what they were looking for because they weren't crime technicians. Just common-sense girls who knew they had been told to look for blood and rust and anything else that might seem out of the ordinary. What was ordinary?

"I'm serious about not knowing what to do about work," Hedy said slowly to Lily as they walked out in the hall looking for a trash can. She would understand the most. "It's not the biggest week, but things haven't been as good lately. I don't know what to expect with this investigation, but I'll cancel everything. I'll be totally available next week. But this can't go on too long."

Lily nodded in agreement. "Can you talk to Barbara?" she said, referring to both the chief medical examiner and Hedy's partner. "Will she tell you anything?"

It sort of surprised Hedy that Lily would bring Barbara up. No one talked about her much, even though they had been together fifteen years.

Hedy shook her head no. "There is business, and then there is us. Two different things. She's way too ethical. I know she's rushing things, but she'll go through the proper channels. She told Bobby she'd talk to him at eleven tomorrow, so it isn't that much longer anyway."

Hedy and Lily looked up as Frankie Jones, the state trooper, came up the steps. "We're finished with your house," he said straightforwardly. "There isn't much of a crime scene except for the living room. I've got men standing guard. They'll be there around the clock."

"Is it a circus?" Hedy said to Frankie, who smiled.

"What do you think? Seems everyone in town is up late tonight and walking on South Main Street." He really didn't need to answer. "I'm so sorry," added the trooper sincerely.

"It's OK, really," Hedy said. "I think we are all in shock. I think it is important to remember people respond to these situations in different ways. She wasn't kind to us as a mother. She was mentally ill, so please don't judge us. I know everyone thinks we should be sobbing and feeling a loss. We lost our childhood years ago. There isn't anything left for us to mourn, but I don't think any of us killed her."

"It sure points to one of you. No one else had access. The front door was barricaded. It hadn't been opened in years." They all knew that to be true. The front door simply was not used.

"Windows?" Lily said.

Frankie shook his head. "The assailant went through the back door. Your husbands said they really weren't allowed in the house. That leaves you five girls. Did you see anyone around? Anyone at all? We have almost nothing to go on. A partial print of a shoe with some blood on it in the hall. That's it. It's a woman's shoe; we just aren't sure what type or size yet. Unfortunately, it's not really clean, so it's not a lot to go on," Frankie paused. "Hedy, did you really have to tell Bobby you hatched a plot to kill her?"

Hedy went quiet. She had gone to the same therapist for eight years, and he had demanded that she roll back the layers of the onion that was her life. She had looked at what her life had been, learned what damage had been done. Some things she told him stopped him cold, and she was always surprised because they didn't seem so bad to her. Everything was relevant. Once, when Hedy asked Lily if she had read the book *Mommy Dearest*, about Joan Crawford and how she beat her children with wire hangers, Lily's only response was "amateur."

Over the years, she had worked at learning to tell the truth and not just stand and take the beatings. Physical beatings, verbal beatings, the beatings of being taken advantage of. She had learned to take that little six-year-old Hedy and love her. To hold her and teach her that being touched didn't always involve a blow. In all her years, Hedy could never remember a hug or even a gentle pat from her mother. You learned to stand back.

Hedy told that little girl she shouldn't have had to worry about finding food or sneaking into the back room at the doctor with a sister who was out cold. It had been some of the hardest things she had ever faced. She couldn't seem to find a center, but she knew now she shouldn't have told Bobby she wanted to beat Dorothy to death.

"I'd show you my shoes," she said, "but they have them in a black plastic bag. I've got little scuffs to go home in," Hedy said, trying to lighten the moment. "We really were all together."

Frankie nodded. "There isn't anything good about this situation." He had known the Anderson girls all his life. They were a little younger, and when he had just graduated and made state trooper, they started driving. When they got out, which wasn't often, the whole town knew it. They were hot looking and a lot of fun. They drew a crowd.

Frankie had been steadily promoted, and he rarely did these kinds of investigations anymore. This was a big one, and he had volunteered when he heard it was Breckinridge County. It made it harder, and it made it easier. He couldn't see any of them ramming a rusted pipe into Dorothy's neck, but everything pointed toward it. He had learned to consider only the facts.

"I know you did the whole yard, but where were you exactly?" Frankie added.

Hedy wondered if she should get a lawyer. She'd get one in Louisville, and Barbara would know whom to call.

Lily took the question and explained that Hedy had been mowing the grass. "The backyard is pretty large, so it was just up and down for like over an hour. Don or Paul would help empty the leaves when the bag was full. It all went into Don's truck. I painted the chairs, so we were both in the back. Eva and Sophie worked in the front with the flower beds, the leaves, and the mailbox. Howard disassembled the swing set, and Paul and Don worked on the guttering. We were all over. Well, Patty sat and rocked. That would be right next to me. I had to move her to the picnic table when I needed to paint her chair."

"How is she doing?" said Frankie. "I never understood what happened." Most people didn't have the nerve to actually ask the question.

"She just had a seizure," said Lily, skirting the actual answer. "Eva and Sophie are getting her ready for the ride home. Sophie has pills."

"Well, it's been a long day, and I have to drive back to E-Town," said Frankie as Bobby and the husbands emerged from the courtroom.

"Patty had a seizure," said Hedy to Paul, Don, and Howard.

"Bobby told us," Howard said.

"What is the plan for tomorrow?" Hedy asked. "What about if I'm here for questioning at 11:00 a.m. your time?" she asked Bobby. "Will that give you enough time? Too early, too late? I want to get my part over. I guess we'll need to make burial arrangements. I can sign for the body if the medical examiner is finished and then get it shipped back to Hardinsburg."

No family member wondered why Hedy was taking the lead on the body. There were few secrets in Breckinridge County, and Hedy had not hidden the fact she chose to live with a woman, but the locals didn't know which woman. Hedy was a Breckinridge County girl, and if she decided to sleep with a woman, she was still a Breckinridge County girl. If comments were made, they weren't made to her face. Just like the fact one of the Pile boys was born with only three fingers and Billy Moorman was rumored to liked sheep better than his wife.

# TWELVE

Hedy didn't ask if she could walk to her car. She simply left the courthouse in the scrubs, scruffy shoes, and star-bright sky. They had let her keep her purse, so she had her phone, her driver's license, and a little bit of money. She passed the Farmer's Bank and kept walking until she reached the post office at the end of the same block. She stopped and looked up at the flagpole. The moon was out just enough that you could easily see where you were going. It didn't matter too much anyway; Hedy knew every inch of this route. It appeared that finally, the curious had gone home for the night. Hedy was alone on the street.

Her father had served as postmaster for twenty-six years, until he was forced to retire because of high blood pressure. They had done everything they could for him in Louisville, and then he had been sent to Vanderbilt in Nashville. It couldn't be controlled. The physicians brought Dorothy in and told her she needed to make some changes. It was never clear what Owen had told them about Dorothy, but the medical team placed much of the problem squarely on her shoulders. She didn't change.

Owen didn't change either. He retired and then took the job as chief of police of Hardinsburg. He smoked four packs of Camel unfiltered cigarettes every day, and his fingers were brown from the tobacco stains. It was hard to smoke that many cigarettes; he often-times lit one off the end of another.

He also drank a case of beer every night. He had a special glass. The drinking began exactly at six o'clock every night and stopped when the last brown bottle was lined up on the kitchen table. It was the girls' job to take the bottles away and put them back into the little slots in the bigger box. When Eva and Hedy could walk well enough to balance the bottles, they started the transferring. As the other girls got older, the job was handed down. Lily, being Owen's favorite, got out of it most of the time, but it was just something that had to be done. It didn't take long.

Because Breckinridge County was a dry county, Owen drove to the next county each Saturday and bought seven cases of beer. Sometimes he would buy eight or nine if snow was in the forecast. There was al-ways a little extra. You didn't want to run out.

When the girls got old enough to drive, they took over the task of beer procurement, even though they were far from the age of being able to buy liquor. Sometimes they started making the run before they were old enough to legally drive, but no one said anything. They would pull up and place a check on the railing outside a tavern called Dead Horse Hollow. Two men would bring out the cases and fill the car, and then the girls would drive home.

Dorothy hated the case-a-night ritual, but what could she do? It was about the only time he ever stood up to her. She didn't let him come into the living room, where the television was located, to watch the evening news, so he would stand in the corner of the dining room, holding the glass of beer, and watch the news just out of her sight. She knew he was there and secretly congratulated herself for exerting such control.

Owen knew she beat the girls, but she beat them less in front of him. Screaming was more her style when he was home. Sometimes, if she was really going strong and it involved Lily, he'd pick her up and put her on his lap. Lily had a problem with her nose bleeding when she was being hit, so everyone was grateful when she was spared. There was no cleanup.

Owen slept upstairs, where the girls also found sleeping places. Dorothy slept on the couch downstairs. Oddly enough, the downstairs bedroom was not used. No one questioned why. With their father on the same floor, it seemed a bit safer even if you had to sleep with your ear on the floor.

Hedy thought about the day her father died. She had been on a business trip. He had been diagnosed with throat and esophageal cancer in August and died the next February. He had just turned sixty-five that January but said he was glad to "find some peace."

The people at the post office had liked him as a boss, and they flew the flag at half-mast when the procession turned the corner from the funeral home and headed down to St. Romuald. The remembrance of the small tribute caused Hedy to stop. It hadn't changed in twenty years.

Owen wasn't Catholic, but he was buried at St. Romuald anyway. Dorothy was Catholic, and that was all that mattered. She believed if you went to mass every Sunday and to confession, heaven was a guarantee. It didn't matter what you did the rest of the time; it could all be forgiven. Owen's mother was a strict Southern Baptist, and she prayed every day for Owen's soul. Hedy wondered who won in the end.

His government retirement benefits and the fact he was a decorated war veteran covered his medical care, but getting to Louisville for cancer care was always a problem. Dorothy had to drive him because by then, all the girls had escaped. Louisville was an hour ahead, which just made things worse. Getting to a 4:30 p.m. appointment was next to impossible. He missed a lot of cancer treatments.

Hedy resumed her walking, past the old Marathon station, Blancett Motors on the left. One more block, and she could see the yellow tape. She paused. She didn't want to just walk up the sidewalk to the house, so she made a quick left and went into the backyard of the house next door. It was well past midnight, and she made quick work of covering the small incline that put her right into the backyard. She slipped the car keys out of her purse and hit the button to unlock the BMW. The lights came on, the sound beeped, and out came three police officers.

"It's just me, Hedy," she said into the night, to the approaching officers.

"Did Bobby say you could leave?" one asked.

"They are finished with me until 11:00 tomorrow morning," she said pleasantly. "Frankie says you are guarding around the clock." She wanted to let them know she had spoken to everyone.

"Are you driving back to Louisville tonight?" the young man asked in a somewhat astonished tone. Most people from Breckinridge County didn't just drive to Louisville. It was normally a big occasion. Christmas shopping, doctor appointments.

"I want to sleep in my own bed," Hedy responded. "I'll be fine." In fact, she was looking forward to the ninety minutes. Her car, a five-series champagne-colored BMW, was fun to drive. It had been a splurge, but one she enjoyed every time she put her foot on the pedal.

Hedy eased down the driveway and left the men and yellow tape in her rearview mirror. As she passed the post office on US 60, she took one more look. Should he have stopped her? she thought. Should he have done something that would have made us more safe? Should I be angry with him? Her father was dead. She hoped he had found some peace.

She wasn't angry with her father. She had been grateful. He had let them get food at the grocery, and when Hedy applied to the University of Kentucky, he wrote the seven-dollar check. He was a man of integrity, and people respected him in the community. World War II had damaged his generation, and he lived with what he had signed up for. He had married Dorothy, and he had stayed.

Hedy hadn't felt anything when he died. She had thought he wanted to die and was oddly grateful for the cancer. No one questioned the exit, and he left Dorothy with a government pension and social security.

After eight years of intense therapy, Hedy didn't know how she should feel. The therapist thought she should be angry at not just her father, but at lots of people. The nuns who took Lily's frozen fingers and thawed them when she walked to school in zero degree temperatures. The doctor who sewed them up and sent them back. The family members who knew the beatings were daily. The ones who just stayed away. It was the 1950s and '60s, and people didn't say anything. People minded their own business, and if they could, they helped in small ways.

Hedy was always grateful for a ride to speech competitions and knew not to say anything if she won. She was grateful when the mother of a classmate would stop after dropping off her own children at school and turn around and take the three of them. It was what it was, and there wasn't any time for anger or expectations.

# Thirteen

"Where are you?" she asked into the phone, which was part of the car. You just told the car whom to call, and it did. No hands involved.

"I'm still at the morgue," said Barbara. "What about you?"

"I'm just leaving Hardinsburg. They took my clothes, shoes, everything."

"Did they give you something to wear, or are the curlies just flying?" Barbara responded, and Hedy laughed for the first time in a long while.

"Scrubs—from the hospital," said Hedy. "I'm looking good. Why are you still at the morgue? I thought it was pretty open and shut."

"I want to get this completely finished. A violent murder is rarely open and shut. I need to do this one up right. Besides I told the sheriff I'd have everything by 11:00 tomorrow, and I will. I've got everyone in here. They know it's your mother."

"Great," Hedy replied, mortified. "I don't guess you could have everything ready and be willing to come back here tomorrow by 11:00 instead of just calling it in?" Hedy held her breath.

"Was already counting on it. I'm not letting you make that drive yourself. I'm assuming that is 11:00 central time, so that gives us an additional hour," Barbara reasoned. There was that time thing again. It could work both ways. This time, it was a gift.

"I'm not asking you to say a word, but you can listen," stated Hedy. "This is the damnedest thing. I can't figure it out. Who would do this?"

"You're right. I can't say a thing, but it is astonishing in so many ways. The *Courier-Journal* has been calling," Barbara added. "It'll be front-page news tomorrow. Sunday, no less. They know too much all ready. Seems a lot of people down there want to be quoted. Plenty of loose lips from the uniforms too, even if they didn't add their name."

Hedy looked down and saw she was going ninety miles an hour. The BMW was so smooth she would have thought she was going fifty-five. Hedy was more worked up than she had let herself believe, and she eased her foot off the pedal. How many times had she made this trip? She knew every curve.

"I'll try to be home within the hour," Barbara said. "We are wrapping up. I'll get Miles to drop off the final report at the security house, and we'll have it for the trip back."

The car was quiet as Hedy went into the Fort Knox area. She started a list in her head. Cancel her work for next week. Whom would she call? She hadn't spoken to her boss in over three years, and she certainly wasn't calling her. No fake I'm sorries, and anyway, she was sure Rachel would use it against her—missing a week of work because someone had stabbed your mother was totally unreasonable.

Dorothy might be dead, murdered, but work was way more hurtful. It was a toxic environment, but the way the contract was written, she needed to have them end the relationship, not her. Not having her work was almost beyond Hedy's ability to comprehend. It was her life—well, besides Barbara, her son, Drew, his wife, Anaya, and their baby, Amy.

Drew, she thought. She should call him, but what time was it in Singapore? She looked at the dashboard and saw 2:15 a.m. That would mean it was 2:15 p.m. on Sunday afternoon. A good time to call.

Hedy had raised Drew almost single-handedly, and he had turned out to be everything one would want in a man. He had married a woman who was technically from Kuala Lumpur but had really been raised in Baltimore. She was Indian but as American as any child in the United States. They made a handsome couple, and little Amy was a beautiful mixture of cultures, races, and sophistication. At two and a half, she went to a school where classes were half in Mandarin and half in English. A full-time helper was so inexpensive that Amy had the luxury of another person loving her and getting her to school and classes seamlessly.

It was by accident that Drew had been transferred to the Singapore office, where much of Anaya's family was located. Some of the family lived right in Singapore, others in Kuala Lumpur, Johor Bahru, or Putrajaya, all within driving distance. They had been there three years, and while Hedy missed them terribly, she also knew it was the right place for them.

Hedy didn't know how Drew had managed it, but she could call a US number and reach him in Singapore without cost. It seemed a little shady, but he had assured her it was done all the time. Something about the Internet. She told the car to call Drew.

"Hey, what's up?" he said immediately into the phone. "A little late for you, isn't it? One of those fund-raisers or whatever?" Drew knew she and Barbara were active in a variety of causes they truly believed in, and he knew they socialized a great deal. A late call didn't surprise him. When he was in college, they had had a rule never to call each other before or after double digits. He wouldn't be up before ten and she would have been in bed by ten. The tables had turned.

"Got some news," she started. "I think it's bad news."

"Now you've got me," he said.

"Granny is dead. I'm just driving back from Hardinsburg now."

"Well, she was pretty old," he responded, "but I'm sorry." Drew had always been Dorothy's favorite, but he couldn't forgive her the childhood she had given his mother, and he only knew parts.

"She was murdered," Hedy continued.

"Murdered." The tone was one of shock, but there was little emotion. "How?"

"Someone shoved a piece of the rusty swing set into her neck. Severed her carotid artery, and did it so hard they crushed her larynx. I'm not kidding," Hedy said and got only silence on the other end.

"She did piss off a lot of people," Drew reasoned.

"It was cleanup day, and everyone was down there. They think one of us did it," Hedy said flatly. Drew knew exactly what cleanup day meant because he hated them. Hedy continued. "They don't think it's one of the husbands but one of us."

"You're kidding. You mean you are a murder suspect?"

"I am."

Hedy could hear Anaya in the background. He probably had the phone on speaker. "Tell her I didn't do it," said Hedy. "Seriously, I have no idea who did, but we were all over that backyard when someone was killing her in the living room."

"So she was still asleep?" Drew knew the routine.

"That's about it. Barbara came down herself, but of course she brought the chief deputy to actually work the scene. We've got the state police and everyone else who ever wore a uniform in six counties involved. You can read about it in the *Courier-Journal* tomorrow," Hedy continued, knowing Drew read both the *Baltimore Sun* and the *Courier* every day online.

"I don't know what to say," Drew said flatly. "Should we make plans to come home?"

"No, it's too expensive and too long a trip. Thirty hours. I'm having a hard time balancing work myself; I can't imagine what it would take for all of you to get away."

"Yeah, I'm in Shanghai next week, but won't there be a trial? Someone arrested?" Drew was slowly putting together the gravity of the situation. "How are you, really?"

"In my wildest imagination I cannot think of any sister who would actually kill her, so I don't know how I am. Patty had a seizure in the courthouse. We all have to come back tomorrow for questioning. The house is covered with yellow police tape. I have no idea how I am."

"Maybe I should come," Drew said, this time a little more urgently. "This is a tough thing. I mean, I know it's Dorothy and all, but murder, the aunts as suspects—it's a lot."

Hedy knew this kind of conversation surprised Anaya, who had grown up in a relatively normal family unit. Her mother had died when Anaya was only sixteen years old, but she was always surrounded by people who loved her and a big family that she knew would always be there. Murder of a mother, grandmother, was not something she was accustomed to calmly discussing.

"No need," said Hedy, "really, but thanks. I'm getting a lawyer. I thought I'd have Barbara suggest one from Louisville because she testifies in criminal cases all the time, but now I think it might be better if I get Bruce Edwards. He's local and knows the situation. He's good," Hedy reasoned and mentally made note to call first thing before one of the other sisters called him.

"Did anyone take anything? Could it have been a robbery?" he said, trying to make sense of the situation.

"What would they take? Anyway, all they have is a partial bloody footprint of a woman's shoe. I think that could be damming for whoever did it, but we all had on tennis shoes, and we all wear about the same size. I will say, this might be Breckinridge County, but I was very impressed with how they handled the investigation."

Hedy wasn't finished painting the picture. "Honestly, it was such a horrible blow to the neck it had to be someone who hated her and had hated her for years. Even the police were shocked. It could have been one of us, but why now?" There wasn't much more to say.

"I'm almost home," Hedy said. "How's Amy and Anaya?"

"We're all fine, but that really isn't the point," said Drew. She knew Anaya would have left the room. "I'm worried. Really worried. You'll call tomorrow? Don't call just at appropriate times. Middle of the night is just fine too. We want to know everything. I'll look at the paper as soon as it goes online."

Hedy was tired. "I'll let you know how it plays out. You have to admit she's gone out with a bang. Trouble till the very end."

# FOURTEEN

Sophie, Patty, and Paul pulled into their driveway exhausted. Patty had not fallen asleep even with the sleeping pill. That wasn't a good sign, and Sophie knew it.

"Take a shower," she said to Patty, who was still embarrassed about soiling herself and the seizure. She didn't speak, and she didn't even have her police radio on. It was stuffed deep into her jeans, which were way too big for her, but they fit her just the way she liked to dress. Patty made her way upstairs with her head down.

"I'm not sure how this is going to affect her, but it isn't going to be good. How will she answer questions? They want to do it alone." Sophie stopped and looked at Paul.

"She would be the most logical one to question," Paul said to Sophie. "She sat there all day rocking. She's an emotional mess, but she's still as smart as they come when she is fully present. Sometimes she can't find the right words to use, but she would have seen everything and everyone coming and going, sitting next to Lily painting those chairs."

Sophie was terrified. "I need to be in that room with her." She and Paul rarely disagreed, but she knew he felt Patty should be questioned alone like everyone else.

"You have protected her your whole life. She's been your life," said Paul, acknowledging the fact that he had always come second. "This is something we can't get around. If she has a seizure during the interview, they'll get us. It's certainly not the first, and it won't be the last." Reality was clear to Paul. Some things you had to accept. Sophie thought she could run from reality.

"Those are kind people down there, but there is protocol," Paul continued.

"What if she never speaks again?" Sophie knew the possible outcomes. She had talked with every physician who would review the case. She knew exactly where Patty fell on the Glasgow Coma Scale. She was always grateful that Patty had come out as whole as she had. She functioned, and while she would get words mixed up or have trouble putting together a sentence, she was very functional.

Sleep did not seem to be an option for either Paul or Sophie, but Patty was tucked in and snoring lightly. She loved her bright room with the rocker and shelves of neatly stacked paperback books. She hadn't read any of them, but she liked the way they stood tall and in order. Her police radio was on the night table.

Patty knew she had been very good today. Things had gone better than she had expected, and she smiled slightly, even in her sleep. She felt good. Strong, and for once, consequential. The seizure was bad, but she couldn't help it. They had wanted her to take off her clothes.

It was quick and violent, but Patty felt herself bow, her head and feet the only parts of her stiff body that were touching the bed. A low guttural sound emitted, and Paul and Sophie appeared at her door. The seizure was more pronounced than the earlier one. There wasn't much one could do, but Paul moved around the bed just as Patty began to vomit. He had her on her side so she wouldn't choke. Sophie stood in the doorway with her long nightgown hanging from her thin shoulders; she crossed her arms and watched as Patty rode the seizure.

It had never been proven that Dorothy hitting her in the head with the nine iron was the reason for this, but it certainly fit the pattern. The doctors accepted it as fact. They called the process in Patty's brain epileptogenesis. The hit on the head with the nine iron had resulted in blood seeping into a closed head and forming lesions. This caused an array of deformed cells in Patty's brain. Years after the initial blow, the cells hit a critical mass, resulting in her brain neurons misfiring and causing seizures. There was no cure. No going back to when she was bright and full of promise. Sophie wasn't as sure as the doctors, but there was never a seizure that didn't remind Sophie what Dorothy had done to Patty that terrible day so long ago. She wasn't angry for herself, but she was angry for Patty.

"It's OK," said Paul to Patty. "It's OK, you are just going to have to take another shower. You vomited this time." Patty didn't usually vomit, but this had been an unusual day.

Sophie felt exhaustion roll over her. "Get her to the bathroom, and I'll change the sheets," she said to Paul as he helped Patty out of bed.

The shower was running, and Paul made a quick dash to the other bathroom. He was always careful to give Patty her privacy. Sophie was careful to contain the vomit, but there wasn't a lot since Patty hadn't really eaten. Most of it was a thin brown bile substance. She wiped the plastic that encased Patty's mattress and wondered what the rest of the day would hold. They had to drive back to Hardinsburg and be interviewed. How could Patty go through this? She thought about giving her extra medication that would calm her. More seizures were almost certain. She felt so defeated. If she was overmedicated, they couldn't really interview her.

The sun was just beginning to rise, and the beauty of a fall Kentucky morning filled the room. Sophie retrieved sheets from the bottom drawer and pulled up the mattress just enough to snap the fitted sheet on the rounded corners.

She almost didn't see them, but the little cotton gloves were right where Patty had shoved them. They were covered in rust along with some pinpoints of blood. Sophie stared at the gloves, letting the implication flood over her.

Paul stood in the doorway looking at the gloves. "Is that rust?" They could hear the shower turn off.

In one swift motion, Sophie took the gloves in her hand and crossed her arms so they couldn't be seen. Tears welled in her eyes.

"What are you going to do?" said Paul in disbelief.

"I'm going to put these in our dresser drawer and finish making this bed," she answered.

"Sophie," Paul said, using his voice to help her grasp the implications, but Sophie was already down the hall.

Paul finished putting the fitted sheet on the bed, and Sophie unfolded the top sheet, the gloves safely stuffed in the back corner of their dresser down the hall.

"That is a good choice for you to sleep in," Sophie said to Patty as she appeared at the door. "Shorts will be good for tonight, and I'll put on another blanket."

Patty nodded and smiled. She walked over to the rocker and began her ritualistic movement. She did not speak.

Paul worked silently with Sophie until the bed was ready, and he gently guided Patty into the layers of cotton and bedding. "Do you think you'll be able to sleep?" he asked Patty.

"I'm going to give you another pill," said Sophie, shaking a little brown bottle and letting a round pill fall into her hand. "It'll be good for you to get some extra rest."

Patty was left in the room, which was beginning to lighten, but she was tired. She was so very tired, and she was happy. Happy that Dorothy was dead. It had worked.

"Where are her clothes?" Paul asked Sophie.

"I'm getting them now," came the reply. "See if her shoes are downstairs."

Paul picked up the tennis shoes, and there was no mistake that there was the slightest residue of blood on the heel. Sophie came down the stairs with the soiled jeans and simply pointed to small areas of blood. They were so small she could barely see them, but they were there.

"Patty killed Dorothy?" Paul said it out loud.

Sophie looked at him in anger. "Don't say that."

"How can I not say that? The gloves, the blood on the shoe, and the jeans. They thought it was one of us, and it was one of us." Paul could hardly comprehend what he was saying. "But Patty?"

Sophie was in full-blown denial. "I will not tell them what we have found. I will not do that." Her whisper was almost a scream. "I will not turn in my sister." Sophie buried her face in her hands, and she began to sob. "She's been through so much."

"I can't believe she did it so well," said Paul. "I mean, we never saw her go in and then out, she wasn't covered in blood, she did it all in one stroke. Who knew she was so strong? All she does is sit and rock."

"That's the point," said Sophie. "Nobody sees her. Nobody talks to her. She's always background. Her life was taken away. Do you remember what fun she was before she started having the seizures?"

Paul looked at his wife, and all he could see was pain. Years of pain. Sophie had been background when Patty was whole. They came after Lily, who was Owen's favorite, and they were completely abandoned. Eva and Hedy were so busy taking care of all the other children, they didn't realize they were robbed of their childhood. If Dorothy had not wanted the first child—and she had not—it was hard to imagine how she felt about numbers four and five, who arrived at the same time. It was overwhelming. By then Dorothy's illness had progressed, and soon the other girls started leaving the house, going to college. Patty and Sophie raised each other.

"We've got to be in Hardinsburg by 3:00," Paul started, wanting to force Sophie to look at things logically. "Holding back evidence is against the law. We could be charged with a felony. I'm no lawyer, but isn't there obstruction of justice or impeding a police investigation? Wouldn't we be an accessory to a crime?"

"What about Patty? What happens to Patty?" Sophie said softly.

Paul's rubbed his large hand over his tired face and shook his head. "She rammed a pipe in Dorothy's neck so hard it killed her. It was violent."

"It was efficient," said Sophie. "Efficient as hell." Sophie felt some pride in Patty's accomplishment.

"Are we sure she did it?" asked Paul.

"She did it." Sophie was resolute. "I know she did it." Sophie had known it from the moment she had spied the gloves.

"We should we call the others," Paul said.

"Have you lost your mind? I'm not telling anyone. We need to keep quiet and see how things play out. I won't wash the jeans or the gloves because that would be destroying evidence, but let's just keep it between us for right now. They would send her to jail," said Sophie.

"Yes." Paul agreed with conviction. "She just violently killed her mother, and she's upstairs sleeping like a baby. Who knows what's going on in her head? You might be next. Yes, they would send her to jail," reasoned Paul.

"Don't be silly. She's not going to hurt anyone else."

"This was planned," said Paul. "She made sure she had an extra pair of gloves."

"I keep extras in the car all the time. She goes nuts if they get dirty, and she doesn't have another pair. It's like batteries for the radio." Sophie was almost dismissive.

"You think she didn't plan it?" Paul responded.

"I think she had been planning it for years. She saw her opportunity and took advantage of it. She's wanted her dead just like the rest of us have wanted her dead," Sophie said as she stood up and retrieved a bag of coffee. "Do you want some? I'm starting the day right now because there certainly isn't going to be any more sleep."

The discussion was over. The ruling had come down. Sophie and Paul would be burdened with the evidence, and Paul would follow Sophie's lead. They both heard the Sunday newspaper hit the porch.

Paul was in some state that wasn't exactly fatigue or resignation but a mixture of both, with desperation mixed in. He stood up and went to get the paper.

"It's all right here on the front page," said Paul, starting at a photo of the pitiful little white wooden house. Police tape was everywhere. "It's a good thing they took the photo after you cleaned the flower beds and raked the leaves. It really could have looked much worse."

Sophie took the front section out of Paul's hands and sat down, staring in disbelief. "It's pretty detailed," she said. "Got all our names right. I think I'll send them a thesaurus, since they have used the word *violent* about a hundred times. Quotes from the neighbors are nice. More details tomorrow. I can't wait."

# FIFTEEN

Hedy could barely move, but she knew she had to. Barbara had already gone down to the security guard house at their condominium and picked up the final report. Barbara was well into reading it a second time. Hedy knew not to ask questions. Besides, what would she ask?

Neither Barbara or Hedy drank coffee, so there were no smells in the air that usually accompany a Sunday morning. Barbara's orange juice was long since consumed. Hedy felt her stomach growl. "Can we stop at Panera going out of town and get a bagel or something? I'm starving," Hedy said as she headed to the bedroom. "We can eat it on the way."

Barbara did not respond. She was concentrating on lab results and a stack of color photos that would turn anyone's stomach. There was no question how Dorothy had been killed, and Barbara could now see how the person who killed her had escaped being covered in blood. Other than the fatal blow, the old gal was in great physical shape. Heart a little enlarged, but otherwise, she should have lived for many more years.

"We have to be there at 11:00 their time, so that's noon for us. We should allow two hours, and then I want that Panera stop. So we'll leave around 9:30?" Hedy calculated. She wanted to make some business calls first and get her work responsibilities out of the way. It was already eight.

"Whatever," Barbara returned, barely listening and totally absorbed in the report.

Mike Dewitt was the second-in-command at the agency and one of the nicest people you would ever meet. He had been publicly and privately humiliated by Rachel Weiss for years, but he kept on because his salary was outsized, and besides, where else would he go? Mike always smiled, but he was the one who got to do the dirty deeds Rachel dictated: firing people, taking away benefits, describing how the agency was failing when in fact it was turning a high profit. The expectations were set so high, they weren't going to be met. Bonuses were rarely paid.

Hedy had decided to call him with the news that she'd need to cancel next week. He had five kids, and he'd be up on a Sunday morning, and, fortunately, he was in Atlanta, on eastern time.

"Mike, it's Hedy. I'm sorry to call so early on a Sunday," she said when he answered his cell.

"No problem, but is there a problem?" He was surprised to hear from Hedy.

"I've got a full schedule next week. Cedars Sinai, MD Anderson, and Vanguard, and I'm going to need to cancel."

"That's not good," he said. "Did someone die or something? The whole week?"

"My mother was murdered yesterday." Hedy was pleased to have a pretty strong excuse. "Someone jammed a pipe in her throat. If she had just died, I could probably get her buried and get back on the road, but it's a murder investigation."

"Oh my god. That's awful, Hedy. I really am sorry. Do they know who did it?"

"No, and actually, I am a prime suspect."

"That won't go over well," he said, not having to mention that Rachel would be disgusted because they both knew exactly how she would react. "She won't want the agency dragged into a murder investigation."

"I know," Hedy said. "I don't want to be dragged into a murder investigation either, but there isn't a lot I can do about it. It's front-page news here. Obviously I didn't do it, but they are focusing on me and my four sisters. No one else really had access to the house. We were all there yesterday when it happened. You can read about it online. The *Courier-Journal*." She knew he knew the paper. You weren't in advertising without being able to name every substantial newspaper in the country.

Hedy plowed on. "I'll e-mail you and cc Rachel as to whom I have meetings with and their contact information. I'm not sure how much detail you want. I'll reschedule as soon as I can. The Vanguard meeting is a little time sensitive because of the Tenet buyout. I'll send my research to MD Anderson, as they need to start executing the recruitment plan. I'll go over it with them on the phone. I think Jennifer should keep the meetings with the San Antonio Vanguard hospitals. She'll understand what to do. My meeting was separate, and I can reschedule. Cedars was just a training session. Janice will understand."

"Do you think it will drag out?" Mike asked cautiously.

"I have no idea. The thought of one of my sisters actually killing my mother is a little overwhelming. We are dealing with rural Kentucky. Everyone knows everyone else's business, so who knows what will come out and how fast?"

Hedy remembered another employee who was diagnosed with multiple sclerosis, and his job was eliminated in less than two months. He wasn't even really showing signs of the disease, yet he, along with his executive health insurance, was eliminated. Hedy felt a real dread in her stomach. She never regretted leaving her previous agency to join her current one, but the corporate culture she now endured was excruciating.

"Well, do what you need to do," said Mike, sounding as sincere as he could muster on a Sunday morning. "I'll wait for your e-mail with all the details, and I'll call Rachel."

Showered and looking much better than she had yesterday, Hedy was ready to head out the door. She had even washed the scrubs and had them neatly folded, ready for returning. They had plenty of scrubs around the house, and Hedy enjoyed wearing them—just not the ones from Breckinridge County Memorial Hospital. She wanted them gone.

Barbara had come out of her business coma and was slipping her wallet into her leather briefcase. "I guess we'll need to fill up, since you made the trip just yesterday," she said, looking up at Hedy as they stood in the foyer ready to leave.

Hedy nodded as they stepped out into the hallway. As she passed the two doors between her corner condo and the elevator, she noticed the Sunday newspapers had been picked up. She could just see her neighbors poring over the facts. Please, please, she thought, let me get out of here before we see anyone.

On the trip, Hedy remembered she was going to call Bruce Edwards and see if he would represent her. She pulled her phone out to go online and find the telephone number. Bruce had been a year ahead of her in school, and she knew him well.

"Are you sure you don't want a Louisville attorney?" Barbara asked. "I know plenty who have a lot of experience in homicides."

"I think Bruce is a better idea. He knows everyone. I just hope Eva or Lily haven't already called. It wouldn't occur to Sophie, I don't think."

When Bruce answered the phone, Hedy was quick to jump right into business. No one else had called. Yes he would represent her, but he advised against it.

"Why?" asked Hedy.

"Because it makes you look guilty. People down here don't get a lawyer until they've been charged. Last I heard—and it's the only thing anyone is talking about—is none of you have been charged. Do you think they'll charge you?" Bruce asked.

"I have no idea what is going to happen. We each have a two-hour time slot today for interviews. Mine is first at 11:00 am. I'm on the road now. I didn't kill her. I don't have the first idea who did. We were all there. It was cleanup day, when we try to beat back the wilderness called her yard." Hedy was reminded that she had been gone a long time. Bruce was right. Bringing in a lawyer this fast wouldn't be good. Hedy started to feel nervous. Would she eventually need to bring in Bruce?

"But if something happens, I can count on you," Hedy said.

"You called first, but I'm sure we can work something out if one of the other girls is charged. You really don't have a clue?"

"Not a clue. It's not that every single one of us hasn't thought about killing her," Hedy said with a small laugh, "but I cannot imagine who would have actually executed it."

"I wondered about James, your cousin, the hermit," Bruce commented. "He hasn't come out in forty years. I thought about him because this is so bizarre. Maybe someone just lost their mind and attacked her."

"Well, I hadn't thought about James in a while," Hedy confessed. "I guess he's still out in that shack in Union Star living off the grid. The thing is, we were all there. We swarm in and clean up the place, and then we get the hell out. We would have noticed someone, say, James, come and go."

"Not necessarily." Bruce was starting to sound like a lawyer. "I'm assuming there were eight of you, and at some point, everyone could have been looking somewhere else, just long enough for someone to slip in. James is a master of being invisible."

"They also have a partial shoe print, a sneaker, that has blood on it. Female." Hedy had forgotten that wasn't reported in the *Courier,* and Bruce was probably unaware.

"Whatever. Then maybe it's not James, or maybe he's wearing women's tennis shoes," Bruce said. "It's all a matter of reasonable doubt. It could be so many people. Remember the time Gladys's daughter accosted your mother and claimed she had made Gladys's life such a living hell she actually contributed to her death?"

Hedy remembered the event clearly, since she had gotten the job of driving to Hardinsburg and apologizing to the family. When the daughter accused Dorothy of the many transgressions, the two women were standing in a fast-food establishment. Dorothy had picked up a squeeze bottle of ketchup and shot the condiment into the daughter's face. In addition to the apology, Hedy had offered money, but that had been rejected. Now she couldn't even remember the daughter's name.

Gladys had cleaned for Dorothy on an irregular basis, and she had been treated poorly. First, it meant Dorothy had to get up by noon, so that put her in a bad mood. And second, Dorothy loved having someone she could be mean to. Gladys needed the quarter an hour, and she took the abuse.

"I like your style," Hedy said to Bruce. "Reasonable doubt everywhere." A local attorney was so much better than a high-powered one from the city.

"I'm sorry Dorothy's dead," said Bruce. "She was always nice to me. And funny. She could really be funny," he added.

"She did like you," said Hedy, "but I think you had a head start because she liked most of the Edwards to begin with. You were always kind to her."

"Let me give you my cell so you can call anytime. I'm not normally home, and this is the landline," he continued.

"You still have a landline?" joked Hedy. "What on earth for?"

"So people like you can look me up in the book and call. Do you know of a cell phone book? You've been out of Hardinsburg a long, long time, Hedy Anderson. As we say, 'you done good' if you like that sort of thing."

Hedy reached for her purse and started digging out a pen and paper. Lots of people liked living in a small town, just not Hedy. The call was making her remember how kind the people in her hometown generally were.

When Hedy had closed out the conversation, she asked Barbara, "Who are you meeting with at 11:00?"

"Bobby Clinton and Frankie Jones, the sheriff and state police guy."

"I'm meeting with them too, same time. This should be interesting," said Hedy.

"Naw. They'll want to talk to me first," said Barbara. "They think I'm just calling in the report, so I'll be an in-person surprise. You'll get to wait. I've got all the information they have been dying to hear. You're just a suspect. Low." She smiled and reached for a light pat on Hedy's hand. "You'll get through this. I promise."

Of course Barbara was right about whom they would want to see first, so Hedy was left sitting on a bench in the hallway of the courthouse.

"Gentlemen," Barbara said, extending her hand, and they quickly disappeared into the sheriff's office.

"There are a few surprises," said Barbara as she started the report. They didn't even bother to ask why she had come to Hardinsburg as opposed to phoning. "It's all pretty clear. Dorothy Anderson, a white female approximately eighty-six years old, died of a single blow to the throat. It appears a rusty pipe was the weapon. It was left on the scene. It was violent, crushing her larynx, and the external carotid artery had been severed as well as the jugular. Whoever did it was standing behind her in such a way that they did not receive much blood splatter. They probably would have gotten something on them, but it was a calculated blow that was perfectly placed to do the most damage while keeping them out of the blood pattern.

"She bled out quickly because the pipe entered on an angle. Remember, the assailant is behind her. If it had been a straight cut, the body would have tried to close the wound, giving her a little more time. That doesn't happen when it's on an angle. While that might be interesting, what really allowed her absolutely no time to seek help was the fact she had at least half a dozen different drugs in her system.

"It's all in the report, but it was calculated she had taken fifty milligrams of Ambien before going to sleep. To give you an idea, five milligrams is the usual dosage, and if you have a high tolerance, you might need ten. Fifty is taking it to the max." Barbara paused to let that sink into the minds of the two law enforcement officials.

"No doctor would have prescribed that much. We can't be completely accurate on the dosage because she took this much earlier in the day, but she probably also ingested 150 milligrams of Valium sometime during the day. You have an anxiety drug and a sleeping drug, plus a blood pressure pill and a diuretic. The last two had little influence over her death. There were also traces of Zoloft and over-the-counter meds such as Excedrin PM and Benadryl. Technically, she should have died from an overdose, but what that says is she has been building a tolerance for years." Barbara was careful never to use the word *I*. Technically, she had nothing to do with preparing the report or working the case.

"Your assailant looks to be right-handed, given the way the pipe entered the neck. The rusty pipe left at the scene matches the wound entry. We are having the rust from the pipe analyzed and the wound cross-checked, but the team investigating would be very shocked if anything unusual came back.

"This was a planned attack," said Barbara, almost choking on the words. "Someone had given this a lot of thought and done a lot of research. It was perfectly executed. Between noon and 2:00 p.m. would have been the time frame. It was fairly warm in the home, and the air conditioner was not on.

"It could have been a woman, but it would have needed to be someone pretty strong. The pipe almost severed the head."

Barbara looked up from her notes and saw both men staring back at her.

"So we don't know much more than what appeared as obvious yesterday," said Clinton, disappointed.

"Well, you can pretty much rule out anyone who is left-handed. We bagged a lot of blood to see if any is not Dorothy's, but that won't be back for at least a week," Barbara said. "It is what it is."

"Did you think about excusing yourself from the case given your relationship with Hedy Anderson?" asked Frankie Jones.

It took Barbara by surprise, but she did not hesitate to answer. How did he know?

"I didn't do the autopsy. My chief deputy did, and he did the report. The technicians ran all the tests. I simply called them all in and asked a favor for them to do it on a Saturday night, Sunday morning. You got better service because of my relationship with Hedy. I don't normally drive to small towns and give my expert opinion on a Sunday morning. I'm delivering you the report because I didn't want Hedy to have to make the trip again by herself. And, she's right-handed. I know you'll be able to rule out some of the suspects on that alone. I haven't told Hedy a thing. She wouldn't have asked anyway."

Barbara didn't blink. She had followed protocol to the last crossed *t* and dotted *i*, and she wasn't going to let them scare her. When she first started as the chief medical examiner, she kept such a low personal profile that people thought her antisocial. She, like so many other professional women, knew her job could be in jeopardy if she was exposed as preferring the company of women. But things had changed drastically in the last twenty years. She still owned her own home but lived mostly with Hedy. She didn't care anymore what people thought.

"Did you get anything off the partial shoe print?" Barbara asked. She was especially interested because she knew Hedy had been wearing a pair of plimsoll tennis shoes sold almost exclusively in Great Britain. She had gone with Hedy to a board meeting in London when she bought the shoes years ago. They were her favorites, and she wore them so often the toe was coming apart. They would be very distinctive.

"Like some of your tests, we won't have that back for at least a week. We are pushing hard too," said the sheriff. "Why do you ask?"

"I know you have all their clothes in custody and may not have noticed, but Hedy had on a very specific pair of tennis shoes she bought in London years ago." Barbara felt sure they wouldn't think of them as being that unique, and she was so sure Hedy hadn't murdered Dorothy she wanted them to take specific notice.

"Tennis shoes from London," said Clinton. "Now that would be different from your regular brands at Walmart."

Barbara felt she had made a mistake, and she felt bad immediately. She hadn't meant to brag; it was just she wanted Hedy cleared. Someone had rammed a pipe into Dorothy's neck, and they needed to find out quickly who had executed the fatal blow.

"I can have the body released," she said to the two men as she rose from the desk. "That is, unless you have any objections. I'm not sure what the family will want; I just wanted you to know we were finished with the body."

"I'm not sure," said Jones. "Let me call Post Four of the Homicide Investigation Department before you do anything."

"No problem. None of the family has asked for the body."

# SIXTEEN

Hedy was ushered into the office, and it was Barbara's turn to sit on the bench. It was Sunday, so things were quiet. When Barbara spied a drink vending machine, she dug into her purse looking for coins. She was used to vending machines that took dollars, even credit cards, but apparently the courthouse in Hardinsburg hadn't changed machines in twenty years.

"I'm happy to buy you a drink." The voice rattled Barbara a bit. It was Joe Cross from the *Courier-Journal*.

"No, thanks. But I will take a quarter. I've got the first fifty cents."

"When was the last time you could get a can of soda for seventy-five cents?" Joe noted.

"I guess I don't have to ask why you are in Breckinridge County this beautiful Sunday morning," Barbara commented as Joe handed over a quarter and she slipped the money into the little slot. "You know I'm not going to talk to you. We'll be issuing an official statement on Monday. It comes from the local coroner. I faxed it to him this morning and left others with the sheriff and state police."

"Extra speedy, huh, Barbara? The woman was just killed yesterday afternoon, and you delivered the report yourself. When was the last time you did that?"

"We don't get a lot of homicides in Kentucky," Barbara said. "Only about ten percent of the deaths each year are homicides, and this one was particularly interesting."

"Especially considering it is the mother of your partner." Joe looked at Barbara hard, eager for a reaction. "And I hear she is a suspect," he added for punctuation.

"It was all done according to the book." She wasn't going to take the bait. "I didn't do the autopsy or have anything to do with the lab results. I was just a delivery girl, and Hedy didn't kill anyone."

"The chief medical examiner, a delivery girl. Even I have to laugh at that one," said Joe. Barbara and Joe had always gotten along well. He covered the shootings and ugly stuff that happened in Louisville, as well as big stories out in the state, such as this one. She had always been very careful to give Joe accurate and timely information that could be easily understood, and she always answered his calls.

"But let's talk about what you really want to discuss. How is it that you are so interested and informed about my personal life?" Barbara asked Joe. "It's not as if we are out marching in the gay pride parades, although we may start." She was over hiding.

"Surely you don't think it is a secret that you and Hedy are a couple and have been for...what? Fifteen years?"

"Longer than most marriages," Barbara said, tilting her head just a little and smiling. Barbara took a slight breath because she really didn't want to have to go into this, and the last twenty-four hours had been stressful enough. "You know this is all off the record, just a couple of friends talking." She smiled.

Joe nodded in agreement.

"I guess I thought for a long time it was private, but these days, I don't care. Things are changing. Same-sex couples can get married in what, seven states now, and the Second Circuit Court of Appeals just upheld Edith Windsor's New York court victory, ruling that she didn't have to pay inheritance tax when her partner of forty years died. They had gone to Canada and gotten married. Of course, it'll go to the Supreme Court next year, don't you think? The Defense of Marriage Act is ridiculous. We'll look back on this the same way we now look back on *Loving vs. Virginia*, when in 1967, they invalidated the laws prohibiting interracial marriage.

"Do you want to add into some story that Hedy's son married a woman of Indian descent? They have a child labeled Eurasian. It means a child of mixed ancestry. Is that part of the story too?"

Joe lowered his head. "Actually, I didn't know Hedy's grandchild was part Indian. Of course it doesn't matter, but it is of some significance that Hedy and you are together, her mother is murdered, and you are involved in the investigation as the chief medical examiner."

"I'm not involved. I'm really just here to support Hedy. It's been a tough couple of days." Barbara rarely showed any emotion, but she would do just about anything to spare Hedy's life story being splashed across the local newspaper.

"It's no secret that a lot of the most powerful women in Louisville are lesbian," Joe kept pushing. "And I won't even go into the powerful gay men. You have your own exclusive dinners and a secret handshake for all I know. Judges, doctors, EVPs of some major corporations. I want that story," said Joe.

"I can't help you there. A lot of the powerful LGBTs don't want to talk. We like having our private dinner parties and secret handshakes. Every big family name in Louisville has more and more of their family members coming out of the closet, but a newspaper article on them? That's a lot.

"It's not always been easy for Hedy professionally," said Barbara. "I'm working in a morgue, so I'm generally left alone, but Hedy directs health care for the largest recruitment advertising agency in North America. Health care means hospitals, and hospitals mean religion. She really has to fly under the radar.

"Remember, this is off the record, Joe. But once, when Hedy was pitching a huge account—it was long-term care or something, and the big decision maker was a born-again Christian. When Hedy started talking to her about the very talented team she had put together to work on the account, the woman actually said, 'I can't have some-one on the team named Horowitz. I assume she's Jewish?' Hedy was stunned. Prejudice comes in lots of forms.

"Of course, Hedy's next thought was that the woman really wouldn't want to be working with her either, but Hedy passed. She regrets to this day not saying something to the woman, but it was twenty years ago, and she assigned someone else to the account. They got less talented people because of their bigotry. Served them right." Barbara was on a roll.

"Once, when they were putting a pitch team together, the client asked for family photos of the team they'd be working with. It was a very large, very religious account, and Hedy had herself photographed with her best friend, a gay man and his dog. She regrets that to this day." Barbara wasn't finished.

"Hedy had a brief marriage, and that gave her something she cherishes more than anything else in this world, and that is her son. Having a son, being divorced, helped her pass all those ugly early professional years. Does that make sense to you? That she was forced to hide, feel shame?

"Hedy didn't know she was gay at the time. You are told all your life you should like chocolate cake, and chocolate cake is all right. You can live with chocolate cake. You can even marry chocolate cake, but then one day you taste carrot cake, and you immediately know carrot cake is what you really want. Who you really are. You've been told carrot cake isn't good for you, but carrot cake is all you can do, all you can be.

"Leave it out of the story, Joe," Barbara said quietly. "I promise you right here, today, that I'll do almost anything to help you any way I can. If you want to write a story about powerful gays in Louisville at a later date, I'll try to help, but leave it out now. Hedy doesn't deserve anything more."

Barbara felt as if she were making a deal with the devil, and then she started to wonder if people actually knew just how many gays were running Louisville and the rest of the world. It might not be so bad to make a public statement. Courage. She so admired those with courage. She'd written many a check, but they had mostly stayed in the background.

"I'm going out to hunt down the coroner," said Joe. "Maybe he'll give me a sneak preview of the report. I know everything is off the record, but I'm going to hold you to that promise. I'll leave the relationship part out unless someone else starts reporting it," he continued.

Barbara thanked him. "I won't forget the promise," she added.

Joe hooked up the seatbelt, checked the rearview mirror, and took off in his sensible Volvo, a father of four. The sun was shining, and it was a beautiful late October day. Lily and Howard rolled up to the courthouse, with what seemed to Barbara's distant observation to be no conversation. Lily looked especially dour.

"Did they interview you too?" Lily asked Barbara as she sat down on the courthouse steps in the mild sun. It felt as if Barbara didn't deserve to be part of this exclusive club of suspects.

"No, I just delivered the autopsy and lab reports. Hedy doesn't need to do this alone today. Do you all get to be interviewed together or separately?"

"Who knows?" said Lily is a dismissive tone. "I think it's separate. I hate all of this. Can't we just bury her?"

"I think they want to know who murdered her," said Barbara, who had joined Lily on the steps. "Little fact that needs resolving."

Barbara found Lily to be the hardest of the sisters. It wasn't that she was mean, it was just she never showed much emotion. She had learned to shut down as a child, and she could shut down quicker and easier than any of the others, even Hedy. It had worked in her childhood, but it didn't work so well now, and she didn't even see it.

"Well, I didn't kill her," Lily said. "I was painting the damn chairs. I have no idea what they are going to ask me. It's not like I have anything to add."

Howard was unusually quiet. Normally he was the one to hug and welcome everyone. "Well, I was breaking down the murder weapon. How would you like to be in that position?" Now the three of them sat on the steps in amenable conversation about a gruesome topic. Being with the Anderson sisters took some getting used to.

"Did you kill her?" asked Lily, turning to Howard.

He looked at her. "Not worth going to jail over, but if they are dusting for fingerprints, mine are all over that stupid swing set," Howard answered.

Hedy appeared at the door and started down the steps. She sat just a step below the other three. Barbara knew not to reach out to her physically. She could see Hedy was more than a little vulnerable.

"How'd it go?" asked Lily. "I mean, it's Bobby Clinton and Frankie Jones. This isn't big-time police work. Did they scream in your face and call you a killer?"

"It's tougher than you think, and they are better than I thought. Eva and Don are somehow off the suspect list," Hedy said with surprise. "I have no idea why, but they aren't even coming in today unless they are called to fill in some information the rest of us don't provide. What is so special about them?"

Barbara knew it was because they were both left-handed, but she couldn't say anything. She had told both the sheriff and the state police officer she knew they were the only lefties in the bunch.

"Well, good for them," said Lily, "but what did they want to know?"

"Where we all were all the time. Who could have slipped in and out without notice. Who was in the front yard, who was in the back. Who had access to the swing set after it had been broken down. Frankie got the fingerprint report while I was there, but it sounded like Howard's were the only ones on the pipe. Most of us aren't even in the system."

Hedy turned to look at Howard, who was already sweating. "I guess you have to be in the system because of being bonded by the bank?" Howard was a banker in Owensboro.

"Yes, the bank. Up to now, I've stayed out of the criminal system." Howard was clearly upset. He hadn't been reared in this dysfunctional environment, and he wasn't handling it as calmly as the sisters. It was a strange situation. No one seemed to think any one of the group had killed her, yet they were the only logical choices.

"They seem to be trying to find a motive. Like why now? Was there an insurance policy? Did she have cash? Did any of us need money? Did we know of a will? Did anyone change their clothes?" Hedy took a breath.

"They wanted to know a lot about why I had planned her murder all those years ago. That was a stupid statement in hindsight. I told them more about our childhood than I thought I would or even could.

"I told them about looking at a photograph of me at six and how sad I thought I looked. Of course, it was me looking at little Hedy when I was an adult, but I could clearly remember how much guilt I felt about why she hated us, about how much responsibility I felt, and how much failure was running through me. I remember feeling so alone. That there was no one to protect us. Our father couldn't or didn't. The nuns kept us alive sometimes, but they didn't call anyone. The doctor treated us, but he sang hymns next to Dorothy in church each Sunday. Not our grandmothers, aunts, uncles. No one. It was the fifties and sixties. I remember Drew being about the same age when I looked at the photo, and I thought about how different his life was. How it wasn't fair to be that sad and responsible at six. And so abandoned."

Hedy looked up quickly, realizing the officers would be coming out to get the next interviewee soon. "I told them about the time Sophie broke her leg and walked on it for four days just so she wouldn't have to tell Dorothy. That it was black when we finally had her pull down her knee socks. I'm not sure they believed me."

Barbara could listen, but it was oftentimes difficult to hear. She reviewed child abuse cases all the time, and every time, she could see Hedy's face in the report. Most of the time, she saw shaken baby deaths, and they were different from the way the Anderson girls were abused. She looked away, not wanting to think about the abuse—emotional and physical. She didn't want them to see her cry.

Frankie Jones stepped out of the door. "We probably shouldn't be letting you all sit together and chat, but we really don't have holding cells."

"Thanks," said Howard with a touch of sarcasm. "We don't know who killed her. We can't even come up with a simple explanation. You don't have to worry about us chatting up and creating a story."

"I did want to mention to the group and get it affirmed that Don and Eva are the only left-handed ones among you. The murderer was right-handed."

Everyone nodded. "Well, that makes sense, then, why they are off the hook. Oddly enough, they have two right-handed children," said Hedy.

"Yes, and Sophie and Paul are both right-handed and have two left-handed children," Lily added.

"Genetics," said Barbara. "Funny how it works."

# SEVENTEEN

Lily walked in alone. She hadn't heard officially that they wanted to interview everyone individually, but it made sense. Howard remained sitting in the sun.

Barbara and Hedy said they were heading back to Louisville after a stop at the funeral home to make arrangements for the body to be transported. Barbara would have the body released to the Trent-Dowell Funeral Home in Hardinsburg, and Hedy would sign for the release. They could decide exactly what to do later.

"You were the first to arrive?" the sheriff asked Lily.

"I was. I needed to go to the bathroom and did. Slipped in and out without notice."

"Did you know your mother was asleep?"

"I assumed she was, as that was her habit. She slept on the couch in the living room most of the day. She had a hard time getting to the grocery before it closed around eight thirty at night." Lily was simply reporting the facts with no emotion.

"She would roam all night. Read various newspapers she subscribed to, watched the television. She felt she was more informed and brighter than anyone in the county. She took a lot of sleeping pills. She drank a lot of instant coffee. It was all pretty gross."

Both Bobby Clinton and Frankie Jones were struck at how unemotional the Anderson girls were in the interviews. Their mother had just been practically decapitated, yet there was not a tear or even a sign of distress. Individuals were generally distraught when being interviewed, a combination of fear, grief, and worry about answering the questions correctly. Hedy hadn't blinked, and Lily was even colder.

Did they all do it together? Clinton mused to himself. Are they covering up for one or all of them? It was going to be a challenge to get them to break.

"So only Howard was here with you when you first went into the house," Jones said, going back to the point of Lily being there before everyone else.

"The swing set hadn't even been touched by that time, so he couldn't have killed her the five minutes we were there alone," snapped Lily. "Howard didn't kill Dorothy. Hedy was right behind us."

"His fingerprints are all over the pipe."

"He broke the swing set down," she answered calmly. "Of course they would be. Were there other prints?" she asked, turning the interview around. Confident. Controlled.

"No, and that makes us believe someone might have been wearing gloves," said Jones. It was slight, but he saw a change in Lily's face. The mention of gloves had struck a nerve. "There were small white pieces of fabric caught in the pipe. It was so rusted, they left a trace of fabric. So they weren't latex.

"Did any of you wear gloves?" he pushed.

"Actually, I'm not sure," Lily responded, but the edge had softened just a little. "I was just trying to think. I know Eva and Sophie worked in the flower beds in the front yard. Eva wears gloves sometimes when she is gardening, but you said it had to be someone right-handed. Eva is completely left-handed. I guess Sophie could have been wearing gloves. I really don't remember. I was in the back painting the chairs. Patty was rocking next to me."

Lily knew Patty always wore gloves, but they really weren't focusing on Patty. Lily started thinking. Had Patty been there by her the whole time? Could she have done it? Her gloves would have left a small trace of white fabric. No one would have noticed her being gone for a period of time. Patty was permanently in the background, little less than a distraction.

"How long would it have taken someone to kill Dorothy?" Lily asked. "I mean, ten minutes, twenty minutes?"

"Depends on how prepared they were." Jones liked the line of questioning. "Why are you asking?"

"I know I said I didn't care who did it, but I do," Lily said softly. "It is really hard for me to think that one of my sisters or any of the husbands would do such a thing, and I understand why we are the prime suspects. I mean, if you were just someone from Hardinsburg and you wanted to kill her, doing it in front of eight people in the yard would seem pretty risky. You could easily pick a better time."

She continued slowly, carefully. "The back door is pretty much left open. Anyone who knew her habits could come in and do whatever. I can say with certainty that if one of us had been gone for more than twenty minutes, we would have noticed. Most of us were in the back, but Eva and Sophie were in the front, together, so they would have known even more profoundly if they were alone. Paul was on the ladder, and Don was right with him. Hedy mowed the whole backyard and filled a truck with leaves. We worked steady. We got it done.

"It's not a joke that we have all wanted her dead," said Lily without emotion. "She was very cruel to us. We spent our childhood days trying to survive and hide it from everyone. She did things most people would never even think about doing." Lily was talking openly now. It was as if she had been given permission to open the floodgates.

"Let me tell you what she did to Hedy once," she said with emphasis and a little hit on the desk with her finger. "Hedy won a 4-H competition, and she got to go to Chicago. It was a pretty big deal. She was representing the state, and she was going to take the bus to Chicago for a national convention. Everything was paid for. She had worked hard to get enough clothes together for the week, and you know how you keep your suitcase open the night before you leave so things don't get crushed? Well, Hedy did that, and somehow, she didn't hear Dorothy coming up the stairs. We normally slept on the floor so we could hear. If she decided to beat us in the night, hearing her come up the steps helped us react more quickly." Lily didn't look at the men directly, but rather looked slightly away, as if she was reliving the night.

"Dorothy had opened a can of beans, and she came in and poured them into Hedy's suitcase. Then she took a wet cloth and snapped it in Hedy's face and said, 'Now, you little bitch, see if you go now.'

"Do you know what Hedy did?" Lily turned and looked at the men. "She got up and washed all her clothes in the bathtub. Dorothy wouldn't let her use the washing machine. She ironed them dry. Then she closed the suitcase and walked up to where she was meeting the Greyhound bus that used to stop at Harrington's Drug Store. She never said a word, but she got on that bus and had a great time in Chicago."

Lily stopped looking at the men and simply crossed her arms. "I've thought of nothing else but who might have done this," she said. "I wish I had an answer that would unlock the $64,000 question.

"What she did to Hedy was terrible, and she did those things regularly to all of us. We all reacted differently. Our aunt had gotten Eva a prom dress, and Dorothy took that dress the afternoon of the prom and scrubbed it in the mud. The difference between Eva and Hedy was that Hedy got on the bus, and Eva simply said, 'I never thought I'd get to go anyway.'

"So who did it? I have no idea. My big question is why now? If we were going to kill her—any of us—we should have done it before she ruined our childhoods."

There was nothing but silence. Where should they go now with the questioning? Lily looked up with a sad face. "I'm glad she's dead. I loved my father, and she tormented him every day of his life. He didn't leave us alone with her. He didn't just walk away. He didn't save us either, but he was there, and oftentimes he would take us, if just for an afternoon, and then we didn't have to worry about her beating us with her shoe.

"Are you finished with me?" she asked abruptly. "I really don't have much more to say. I've told you everything I know. I painted the chairs. I watched everyone work all day cleaning up her yard. She didn't deserve us. I'll cooperate in any way you want me to, but I won't be sorry she's dead. I am totally right-handed."

The sun was just right as Lily walked out of the sheriff's room and into the pleasant weather. Howard was sitting alone on the steps. He was a mess, and she didn't understand why. She certainly didn't think he had done it, but emotionally, he was ready to break.

"How bad was it?" he asked her quietly.

"I was honest," said Lily. "More honest than I've ever been in my entire life."

Howard didn't know how to respond. What had Lily not been honest about? Did she know something he didn't?

Clinton motioned for Howard to come in and be questioned. "They aren't going to hurt you," Lily said to Howard as he got up. "Just tell them what you know. You didn't kill her." Lily was certain about that. Howard didn't have the nerve.

Lily looked straight ahead without seeing anything but Patty rocking on the chair beside her while she painted. She wore gloves. Those little white ones that seemed to calm her. Patty had been especially fidgety in the afternoon. She had been gone for certain times. Lily had assumed she had gone to check on Sophie in the front or Hedy's progress in the back. It didn't seem important at the time.

It all seemed logical. Patty had taken that pipe and rammed it into Dorothy's neck. Patty. Lilly was still sitting on the steps putting the pieces together when Paul, Sophie, and Patty rolled into the parking space by the courthouse. Something had happened. They all looked terrible. Sophie had clearly been crying. Paul was tight.

"Have you already been questioned?" Sophie asked as she got out of the car. No greeting.

"Yes, Howard is in there now," Lily said calmly. Somehow she felt peaceful. She felt sure she knew exactly what had happened. She had been honest about her childhood, and she knew Howard was probably excusing himself to go to the men's room to throw up during the interview.

"Does everyone go in alone?" asked Sophie. "We can't let them interview Patty alone." The words tumbled out of her mouth.

"I'm not sure they will give you that option," Lily responded. "They are sort of in charge."

"Patty had another seizure last night, and it was a bad one." Sophie had come prepared, and it was perfectly clear to Lily that Sophie knew Patty was the one who had done the deed.

"Do you want to talk?" Lily said to Sophie.

"About what?" Paul and Patty stood a few feet away by the car.

"Eva and Don are no longer suspects," she started. "The murderer was right-handed. Whoever did the crime wore gloves. White gloves. Now, do you want to talk?"

Patty let out a sound that was not human. Paul lowered his head. They all knew, and now they knew Lily knew.

"Get in the car," said Sophie to Lily. "Please. We haven't even talked to Patty about it," Sophie whispered. Paul was helping Patty into the back of the car. Lily got up and slid into the other side of the back.

"I'm going to leave the courthouse," said Paul, putting the SUV into reverse. "I don't want them to know we are here, and we are a little early." He drove toward St. Romuald because he knew the parking lot should be empty on a late Sunday afternoon. Catholics got things finished early. It didn't take more than three minutes to drive there, and no one spoke.

"Patty, did you kill Dorothy?" Sophie said in her kindest voice when they had come to a stop. She had turned in her seat so she was looking directly into Patty's eyes.

"Yes," she said and smiled. "And I did it well."

"Why did you do that?" asked Lily. "You know this will put you in a lot of trouble."

"I don't care that I'm in trouble. I wanted to do to her what she did to me. I wanted to do more. I didn't just want to hit her in the head, I wanted to kill her, and I did." Patty's fist was squeezed tight, and her teeth were gritted.

"I thought about it for a long time. I can't drive, so I had to do it when Sophie brought me down here. I knew cleanup day would be perfect. Everyone would be here. I had a knife with me yesterday, but the pipe looked better. I thought it would tear a bigger hole in her neck, and it did." She smiled again.

"She's dead. I'm going to tell the policeman how I did it, too," Patty announced with a little triumph.

"No, you can't do that," said Sophie, and both Paul and Lily turned and stared at both of them. It was hard to know what would be appropriate.

Paul said, "We found the gloves last night with the rust and the spots of blood. There was more blood on her jeans. Sophie doesn't want them to interview Patty, and she doesn't want to tell them we have the evidence that pretty much proves she did it." It was clear Paul didn't completely agree.

"What will happen to Patty?" Sophie cried. "Would they send her to jail?"

"I don't know, but we've got to take control of this and not let Patty confess this afternoon to Bobby Clinton and Frankie Jones," Lily said with force. "We all need to get together and discuss exactly what we want to do."

"We are supposed to be at the courthouse in exactly eight minutes for our interviews," Paul said, looking at his watch. "If we don't show up, we will be arrested." You could almost feel the fear.

"No," said Lily calmly. "You are going to drive me close to the courthouse, and I am going to be sitting there alone when Howard comes out. I am going to tell them you called, and Patty has had a seizure. A bad one. You were on your way, but you had to go to the emergency room. I'll make it Baptist East if I have to name a specific hospital. You had just gotten on the Watterson Expressway coming in for the interviews. You've been too busy to call until just now. You knew I would already be in Hardinsburg. You want to reschedule for tomorrow. Ten o'clock."

Paul looked at Lily and didn't know what to say. He knew she could pull it off.

"Call Hedy and get her back down here. You drive to Eva's, and we can all talk this through. Howard and I will come straight to Eva's once I'm finished polishing off Bobby and Frankie. Hedy told me this morning she had already called Bruce Edwards, so he's on call for legal advice."

Paul put the car in gear and began driving toward the courthouse. No one said a word. Lily jumped out at the corner and began walking around the back, where everyone had been sitting all day.

"Where have you been?" said Howard, a little irritated. "I've been out for ten minutes. They want to get on with the interviews." Howard saw Paul's SUV drive off, passing the courthouse. He turned and looked at Lily who smiled. "I went for a little walk. Who knew you'd get out early?"

Frankie appeared at the door. "Paul and Sophie not here yet?" he said. "You've all been so punctual."

Lily pulled her phone out of her pocket. "Sophie just called. Patty has been having seizures all afternoon. They need to reschedule for tomorrow. They are so sorry, but they haven't been able to stabilize her at the hospital."

She wanted to avoid identifying the hospital, just in case he called all the hospitals to verify whether a Patty Anderson had been admitted. "You know how upset Sophie is about not being here. I told her you would understand." Lily knew Bobby had a soft spot for Sophie. "I guess all this has really brought it on for Patty. Sophie said she'd try to do it over the phone, or they could be here tomorrow. Ten o'clock?" Lily should have been Oscar nominated, and Howard watched in disbelief as she went on. He knew she was lying. He knew he had just seen Paul's SUV. He remained mute.

"It has been a long day," Bobby said to Frankie. "Ten tomorrow would be OK with me."

"They will have probably gotten Patty stabilized or admitted by tomorrow, so both Paul and Sophie could get away. Hedy also is in Louisville and could take over. Tomorrow would be good," Lily ended.

This needed to work. Lily waited with a knot in her stomach. The silence was deafening as the two men looked at each other. They had a brutal murder on their hands and little to go on. They were awaiting some lab results, and they weren't being pushed by the family for answers. Were they doing enough? The coroner's report wasn't going to be released until tomorrow.

"Hedy is getting the body released to Trent-Dowell," said Lily, filling the air with something official and cooperative. "The body will be back here sometime late tonight or early tomorrow, depending on when they can get to Louisville."

"OK. Tomorrow we'll have more labs back," said Frankie. "I put a real rush on it."

Blood. Patty was O negative, the universal donor. Less than 10 percent of the population had that type of blood. It was just a matter of time until they matched her blood to the weapon. She hadn't done as well as she imagined, Lily thought.

"Are we OK to go?" Lily looked up at the men. "Thanks for making it not so bad today. None of this is easy."

# Eighteen

Howard got into the car just as Lily was putting on her sun glasses and crossing her legs in the front passenger seat. She needed to stay focused as the two men watched them pull out. Howard calmly turned to her as he backed the car into the street and said "What the hell is going on? I saw Paul's SUV passing the courthouse."

"Yes, you did," said Lily. "They are not at the hospital, and we are not going home. Please drive to Eva's, as that is where everyone is meeting. Patty killed Dorothy, and she's happy about it. She wants to tell the policeman all about it." Lily put an emphasis on the word *po-lice-man*.

"Patty?" Howard said in utter disbelief. "Patty?"

"Patty," Lily repeated. "Had a knife with her yesterday, but when she saw the pipe you put in Don's truck, she thought it would rip a bigger hole in Dorothy's neck. So she went for the pipe. Unfortunately, the rust caught some of the little white material off those gloves she always wears. She even left a little blood. A nick on her finger from the ragged pipe. It's just a matter of time until they figure it out, not to mention Patty's urgency to confess. And those lab results that are coming back tomorrow will show that the right-handed killer had O negative blood, a rare type that just happens to run in Patty's veins."

Howard kept his eyes on the road. He tried to process what had just happened. His wife had boldly lied to two police officers investigating her mother's brutal murder. His sister-in-law had rammed a rusty pipe into her mother's neck and killed her, and she was happy about it. And he was cooperating with it all by driving away.

When they pulled into Don and Eva's, they were immediately met by Sophie. "How did it go?" she said nervously. "Did they buy it?" She was almost irrational.

"Hook, line, and sinker," Lily said proudly. "You have an appointment at 10:00 a.m. tomorrow. That's how long we have until we do something. I didn't have to name the hospital, so they'd have to call them all if they wanted to check the validity of the story. It wouldn't take too long, but it would at least slow them down a little." Sophie stared at Lily and seemed just a little calmer.

"Hedy and Barbara had stopped at Trent-Dowell to make arrangements for both getting the body back here as well as the funeral, so fortunately, they hadn't gotten too far," Sophie said. "They actually should be here in about ten minutes. Hedy is calling Bruce Edwards, and he'll be here about the same time. Hedy wasn't surprised, just sad."

Patty was rocking, unconcerned. She was not speaking and had not spoken since Sophie had reiterated she shouldn't be thinking about confessing. She was angry and tired of being told what to do. She pulled her police radio out of her pocket and listened as she rocked. She held it tight to her ear. No one else would be able to hear. They didn't deserve to hear anyway, she thought, sinking into an ugly mood.

Hedy didn't knock when she and Barbara arrived, but rather just walked into the kitchen. "Is Bruce here?" she asked.

"Not yet," Eva responded.

"I thought maybe he'd beat us here. He's more than willing to help, but I'm a little nervous that all of our cars are here and Lily has just lied to the police. Aren't we a little obvious? They know our cars by now, and then you add Bruce's?"

"I think we have to take the chance it's Sunday afternoon and they are waiting until tomorrow for tests. I don't think they'll be driving around hunting us," Lily said.

"Don't be so sure about that," Bruce Edwards said as he opened the back screen door. "It looks like a party. This murder investigation is the only thing anyone in town is talking about. My phone has been ringing off the hook. People calling wanting to know if I know anything," he continued. "I guess I should be pleased that everyone assumes you would call me."

Eva, Sophie, and Hedy all nodded their heads. "I've stopped even listening to the messages," Eva said. "People have been driving by. I got a green-bean casserole this afternoon," she said, pointing to the counter.

"My mailbox is full, and I'm not touching it. Unless it's one of you, I don't answer," said Hedy.

"I'd suggest moving the cars. What would we do if they were driving around and knocked on the door?" Bruce cautioned. "We'd have no time, no plan, and they could easily charge Lily. Let's start with simple lying to a police officer and then add aiding and abetting, obstruction of justice. I could go on, and it wouldn't be just Lily, although that was a bold move you pulled off."

Don turned to Howard, Paul, and Barbara. "Each one of you drive your respective car, and we'll drop them off parked at the Walmart, the grocery, and the hospital, and I'll pick you up as we go. Then we'll all come back here. Bruce, pull yours into the garage. We'll put the door down, and mine and Eva's will be the only ones visible."

No one disagreed, and the plan began to play out. When Bruce reentered the house, he sat down across from Patty. Eva, Hedy, Lily, and Sophie were scatted, seated around the main living area.

"Patty, listen to me," said Bruce. "I am your lawyer. Do you know what that means?"

Patty looked up. "I have grand mal seizures. I have trouble forming words and conversation gets jumbled in my head, but I'm not stupid. I'm intellectually much slower than before the seizures started, but I know what's going on. I know what a lawyer is. I have good days and bad days. Today is a good day. I understand everything. I killed her, and I'm glad I killed her."

Bruce sat back and took a deep breath. "Why did you kill her, Patty? And, since this is a good day, you know I can't tell the police or anyone else anything you tell me. Lawyer-client privilege."

"Are you sure?" she said, turning over the words *lawyer, client,* and *privilege* in her mind. There was a lot she didn't understand.

"I'm sure," he responded, slightly relieved she wasn't as intellectually crisp as he had first thought. He saw no other options than to plead that she was either not guilty by reason of insanity or guilty but mentally ill. Neither would have a pleasant outcome.

"First, I want this to be perfectly clear: I am your lawyer and your lawyer only. I'm not Hedy's lawyer or Sophie's lawyer or anyone else's lawyer—only yours."

Patty liked that. "They tell me what to do a lot," Patty responded childishly.

"They love you, Patty. They just want to do what's best for you."

Barbara and the men entered the room quietly and began to listen. Barbara knew she shouldn't be hearing all this, but she couldn't leave Hedy to deal with this alone. She would excuse herself tomorrow totally from the case and turn it over to her chief deputy. She was grateful that she was being included as an equal.

"Now, tell me why you killed her," Bruce said in a calm, straightforward manner. He hadn't had a lot of similar cases and was listening to every word, taking notes on a yellow legal pad. As a lawyer in a small community, he did everything—divorces, expungements—but not a lot of criminal defense.

"I killed her because I wanted her dead. She was mean. I've been listening to the police radio a lot and started thinking how I might kill her so it would really hurt. I also didn't want to get caught. I don't care about that anymore. I know I'm going to get caught. I'm going to tell them I did it."

"Why are you sure you will get caught?" Bruce asked.

"I heard Sophie talking to Paul. They found my gloves. The ones I shoved under the bed. I knew they were dirty with rust and some blood. Then, Lily said I left bits of my gloves on the pipe. I have to wear the gloves." Patty had dropped her head in defeat.

"I thought I stood just right," Patty said with tears starting to form in her eyes, "but I guess I did get some blood on my clothes. I failed at keeping out of the blood splatter. You can read about it on the Internet," she continued. "They didn't take my clothes, but I know Paul and Sophie have them."

No question of premeditation. She planned this murder, Bruce thought, and then he mentally moved to a guilty-but-mentally-ill plea.

"I don't want to get anyone else in trouble," she said. "The others are being interviewed, and I did it. I'm glad I did it."

"Why did you do it now?" Bruce asked.

"Because I had the opportunity. I can't drive, so there had to be a reason for me to be there. If I could drive, I would have driven down to Hardinsburg and killed her in the night and walked away. Just any old night. I have a knife," she said as she reached into her pocket and pulled out a folding 4½-inch knife used by hunters. "I got it at Walmart for ten dollars."

Sophie tired to think when she might have been able to get away long enough to buy a knife at Walmart. Where had she gotten the money? She involuntarily shook her head.

Bruce reached for the knife. "May I take this, Patty? You don't need it anymore."

Patty nodded and handed over the knife.

Expressions around the room ran from shock to tears. There was no doubt Patty wasn't getting out of this in one piece, but then, she hadn't been in one piece since she was hit in the head with the nine iron.

"Everyone was working fast," began Patty. "They wanted to finish and get out. Lily didn't talk to me, she just painted. She was in a bad mood."

Lily put her head down. She had been in a bad mood; she and Howard had argued the whole drive to Hardinsburg. She hated clean-up days, and she really, really wanted a divorce but didn't know how to go about it. How do you end a thirty-six-year marriage? The kids were gone. She should have spoken to Patty, but she hadn't. She just hadn't.

"Everyone is nice to me, but they don't know me. They don't even see me," she continued. All eyes were on her now. "I know I am a burden to Sophie. I've kept her from having friends, and I'm never going away like the kids. They both went to college and have a life, but Sophie and Paul still have me."

"Hedy's bad," she said, putting her hands up to her mouth. "She sleeps with Barbara. Do you know what I mean?" she asked Bruce.

"I know what you mean, but that doesn't make Hedy bad," he said.

Hedy thought what conversations had been held behind her back over the years. She was pretty tired of it. Patty considered her bad, so it must have been great gossip. Barbara caught her eye and smiled. Things were better now.

"When I saw Howard put that piece of pipe in Don's truck, I almost jumped up, I was so excited, but then I thought I had to be calm or Lily would notice. It was so much better than my knife. It was longer, too, and I felt better about keeping clean. Blood splatter." She loved the words *blood splatter*. They were exciting.

Patty continued without any interruption. "Lily was pouring the paint when I got up. She didn't notice. I picked up the pipe and walked in, and there she was on the couch. She had the underwear on her head. I walked around the living room, and she didn't wake up. I stepped back at an angle to avoid the blood, and I rammed it in!" Patty almost yelled, and she moved her arms just as she had on Saturday. "I kinda wanted her to wake up and know it was me, but she didn't," Patty added calmly.

"Then I thought she might wake up and hit me," said Patty, smiling, "but she didn't. She opened her eyes, but she couldn't get up. I didn't move. Maybe she did know it was me. There was a lot of blood, and she gurgled a little.

"It worked. I felt so good. I waited until I knew she was dead, and then I walked out. It wasn't as hard as I thought. I should have done it sooner," Patty added.

"Then what did you do?" Bruce questioned. He knew the Anderson girls had not had a perfect childhood, but he used to run in the same crowd as Hedy in high school. It couldn't have been too bad. How had Patty gotten this far off track? Why wasn't everyone in shock?

"I sat back down and rocked," Patty said simply. "It wasn't long until Lily told me I'd have to move to the picnic bench so she could paint the chair I was sitting in. When I got up, I went to the car and changed gloves. I knew there was rust on them."

"Did you tell anyone else you had killed your mother?" he asked.

Patty shook her head no. "They probably would have been mad. Well maybe not mad, but it was a mess in there."

"Did the police talk to you?" he asked.

"One asked me about my police radio, but no, not too much. Do you know what it's like to be invisible?" Patty asked Bruce. "You are there, but it's like you are not really there."

"No. I don't know what that is like," Bruce admitted.

"It's uncomfortable," she said. "Sometimes I think, what if I took off all my clothes? Would people notice? I hate it most when they talk to me like I'm a baby. I'm not a baby! I understand. Now can we tell the police what happened?"

# NINETEEN

Bruce looked around the room. He had known almost everyone in this room for his entire life. He also found it a little strange Barbara Collins was actually sitting cross-legged on the floor. She was the chief medical examiner of Kentucky and quite well respected.

"Can any of you tell me what's going on?" said Bruce to the crowd. "Your sister killed your mother with a pipe shoved with such force it crushed her larynx and severed her jugular. I got the report from the coroner," he said, explaining how he knew the details. "I told him I had been retained by the family. It's Breckinridge County." There was no need for explanation.

"It's odd, isn't it?" Barbara spoke up. "It's hard to get used to their reactions." No one expected Barbara to do the explaining, but no one else felt ready to offer anything. Besides, they weren't sure what he was asking. Patty had pretty much explained what she had done.

"As a medical doctor, my professional opinion would be severe post-traumatic shock syndrome. The husbands not so much, but the girls—you have no idea what they lived through until they got out and away to college. The husbands have been around it

142

long enough that they accept most of it as normal. Like so many abused children, these girls did what they had to do not to expose what was going on. I see it often in my line of work, but I've rarely seen it this severe, and remember, I work in a morgue. Dorothy was exceptionally bright and unbelievably cruel and mentally ill. Quite the combination. Sometimes Hedy will make a statement about something that happened in her childhood, and it takes my breath away. She doesn't know that whatever she's told me is wildly inappropriate."

No one said anything, so Barbara continued.

"They really don't care that she is dead. Don't expect tears. They are only concerned about what is going to happen to Patty. They all feel responsible. Could they have stopped Dorothy from hitting Patty in the head with the golf club? They don't know what the center is because they were reared so far off the charts. They don't even notice that their reaction to this violent murder is not natural."

"But I was there," said Bruce. "Hedy was as normal as the rest of us. Sophie was a cheerleader, and Patty one of the smartest in the school. Who knew this was going on?"

"Lots and lots of people," said Hedy. "Lots and lots of people who betrayed us every day." Her statement was without emotion, and she wasn't looking for pity. She had worked too long in therapy. She had worked very hard to know a center even existed.

"The nuns knew it. Lily came close to having parts of her fingers amputated from frostbite because we walked to school every day regardless of the weather." Hedy spoke without interruption.

"Remember that really bad cold spell when it got down to something like minus six degrees? Well, by the time we got to the graveyard at St. Romuald, all Lily wanted to do was go to sleep. We didn't have gloves. Eva and I dragged her into the school, and the nuns worked on saving her hands all day. Johnny Flood was called, and he came to the rectory that day and worked on her fingers. His wife just happened to be there to drive us home at the end of the day." Hedy didn't have to explain that Johnny Flood was, at the time, the family physician practicing in Hardinsburg.

"I can't tell you how many times Johnny Flood sewed us up, set a bone, gave us pills for pain, and then sent us home. He knew. But he sat in the next pew with Dorothy on Sunday. She never got up before three any afternoon except for Sunday. She never missed a mass. All was forgiven." Hedy continued.

"We were all covered in bruises, and while we tried to cover them up, child abuse was obvious. We all thought everyone knew how to roll into a ball to keep from having your fingers broken. Your back can take a blow much better. The kick doesn't seem as hard.

"The nuns did nothing. Dorothy thought the Catholic church was her salvation. It didn't matter what she did the rest of the week; she showed up for mass every Sunday, and she confessed her sins. She told us she had to beat us. It was for our own good." Hedy was cold in her explanation.

"I don't think I need to provide you with more stories, Bruce," Hedy said. "I could go on for days. We lived in hell, and our father drank a case of beer every night. I don't blame him, but when you get down to it, he didn't save us either. Let's talk about Patty. We have until 10:00 a.m. tomorrow."

Bruce had never seen Hedy like this, and it took him a moment to soak it all in. He slowly rose from the chair where he was sitting across from Patty and felt the roomful of eyes following him.

"Eva," he began, "do you have a Diet Coke or maybe ice water?" He was thirsty, but he was also buying time.

"Tomorrow they will be certain Patty is guilty. The blood lab test. The white gloves and the fact that she wants to confess. It will be better that she does confess. Turns herself in at 10:00 a.m. . We can all go in together. She will need each of you for different reasons." Bruce was thinking as he was speaking.

"The way I see it, we have a few ways to go about this," he continued, taking a drink of the ice water Eva had handed him.

Bruce was going over the details in his mind. He needed more time to research. He also needed criminal attorneys from Louisville. "She can claim a lack of competency to stand trial because she is insane. That would be not guilty by insanity. I'd have trouble making a jury or anyone else think she's insane," he said, motioning to Patty, who was rocking and not completely engaged.

"There's extreme emotional disturbance, but nothing drastic happened at the time of the murder, so I wouldn't suggest that. I think I would suggest guilty but mentally ill. That is a hard one to prove. It's only used in about one percent of murder cases and has won in only about twenty-five percent of that one percent. I think it is our best bet, though, and I think it is the appropriate plea. Everything changed after the John Hinckley trial," Bruce said, referring to the young man who attempted to kill Ronald Reagan when he was president of the United States. "Hinckley was found not guilty by reason of insanity. The verdict outraged the nation," said Bruce.

"Let me explain the difference between insanity and mentally ill," he began. "Kentucky is one of a few states that actually has the guilty-but-mentally-ill plea. Michigan was the first to recognize a need for a bridge between being totally sane or totally insane. It's actually a big difference that she is in Kentucky," he continued.

Everyone was listening intently. "In 1979, an eighty-year-old woman was brutally killed by her deranged daughter in Louisville.

I remember the case because I was just out of law school and clerking in Louisville. It was a big deal. The mother was strangled. The family supported the daughter even though they also feared her. You all don't fear Patty, do you?" he asked, and everyone was quick to say no.

"There is little connection between the earlier Louisville case and Patty's with the exception that a daughter killed her mother. The original case did not have child abuse, and the only plea option at the time was not guilty but mentally ill. The daughter took that plea, and she was found not guilty. She stayed less than two years in a psychiatric facility, and she was eased back into society."

"That's what we want for Patty," said Sophie hopefully, but Bruce shook his head.

He began to explain. "Because of that case, the Kentucky Supreme Court took the unusual action to recommend a guilty-but-mentally-ill statute. That means today, Patty has the option of pleading guilty but mentally ill," he continued.

"The difference is that if we go that route, Patty would be found guilty. The other woman was found not guilty. It's a fine line between mentally insane and mentally ill. Kentucky has made the distinction. It doesn't seem fair in this case, but it is what we have to work with today. I don't think I can convince anyone she is mentally ill."

"But Patty would get out, right?" continued Sophie, trying to keep the differences straight.

"No she would be guilty, and guilty to murder means life in prison, minimum," Bruce continued. "But I really think it's our best bet because she would be allowed treatment as opposed to being put into the general prison population. She'd be in a psychiatric hospital, but I want to make it very clear she will be in jail or the hospital for the rest of her life."

There was a unanimous gasp.

"Don't they let you out when you are no longer a threat to yourself or others?" said Sophie in near hysteria.

"No. If she pleads guilty—even mentally ill—she will be found guilty. She'll go to the Kentucky Correctional Psychiatric Center in LaGrange and be treated. If and when she gets better, she'll then go to Pewee Valley and the Kentucky Correctional Institution for Women for the rest of her life." He needed for them to understand exactly what was going to happen.

Sophie let out a small cry and left the room. They could hear her vomiting in the bathroom through the closed door. Bruce winced but continued because there was a lot to be decided.

"We will want to plea bargain. I'd hate to see this go to trial, although if I can't get a plea, we'll want it tried right here where people knew Dorothy. There would be a lot of sympathy, but they have a strong case, not even counting the fact  she wants to confess.

"Hopefully, they'll arraign her tomorrow, and if we go in with a guilty-but-mentally-ill plea, she will immediately be sent to the Kentucky Correctional Psychiatric Center for evaluation. That will take thirty days. It's the law." Bruce was well into his lawyer mode. "It's a locked psychiatric facility, and while it's a pretty good one, it's not all that nice. The people there are very mentally ill."

"She will be evaluated by either a psychologist or a psychiatrist. I'm not sure what they have there now. Let's hope she has some bad days because, let's face it, she's pretty sharp when she wants to be. She will need to demonstrate that she has the lack of capacity to appreciate the nature and consequences of her actions and of the proceedings. That she is not able to keep up with the ramifications of the trial," Bruce continued, almost breathless. There was so much to consider.

"If the rest of you don't know the center, as Barbara put it, Patty doesn't either. Not to hurt, but you surprised me—no, have shocked me today—and I've always thought you were the best of the best," Bruce continued.

"Thanks, I think," said Hedy. "But we are just a bunch of broken eggs. Humpty Dumptys."

Bruce smiled at the Hedy he knew. Quick witted and honest. "The mental health professional will come back with an evaluation. You will not be able to bring in your own professional to dispute anything unless we go to trial. I don't think we want to do that," he continued.

"We can strengthen our case with supporting evidence. Has she spent time in Central State Hospital or Our Lady of Peace? Any psychiatric facility? Does she receive Social Security for being mentally disabled? Does she see a mental health professional regularly? What medications does she take? We will also want each of you to make a statement on why she is incapable to stand trial, and, if possible, be interviewed by the psychologist or psychiatrist at the prison." Things were starting to sink in for the sisters. "They are pretty short handed out there at LaGrange, but maybe the professionals will make time because this is going to be such a big case," he continued.

"We might want to call Dr. Flood to testify. He's retired now, but maybe he'll man up. I don't think any of the nuns or priests are around, but you could see if they are in retirement in Owensboro and would be willing to make a statement," Bruce said.

The girls all started talking about whom they could call. Sophie had all her health records of when Patty had been in Our Lady of Peace, her therapist, and her medications. She did receive Social Security checks for disability. Hedy would research and see what nuns might still be alive and willing to testify. Hope began to rise in the room.

"Is the best possible outcome that she is going to the hospital but not ever getting off the hook?" said Paul to Bruce. "Is there any way she could just get off?" Paul was angry and had been most of the time he had known Dorothy. In fact, he hated her and what she had done to the girls.

"She won't get off the hook," said Bruce bluntly. He needed everyone to understand. "If she is found guilty but mentally ill, she will be indefinitely confined and released only to the Women's Prison when she is no longer mentally ill and not dangerous to herself or others."

"Indefinitely confined," Paul repeated. "So she goes to jail, just a jail for crazies, and that is our best option." He was angry and sarcastic at the same time. "Dorothy took her life away once, and now she'll spend the rest of her days locked up."

"I know, Paul. It's not fair, but she killed her. You don't want her in a regular women's correctional facility. She wouldn't last long. It was premeditated. She had a knife. She's happy she's dead. She wants to confess. I'm just giving you the facts."

The room became quiet.

"There's no other way?" Sophie started to cry harder at the realization.

"Can you possibly see any way that they are not going to be able to prove that she is guilty?" Bruce countered. "This is a case we cannot win. I am hoping I can get to Stanley Dowell, who will be the lawyer for the commonwealth, and talk him into a plea bargain so we can be spared the agony of a long, drawn-out trial. And then get the judge to accept it. Kenny Nall won't be easy to convince. This is a big murder case. People will want to know all the ugly facts, and he loves attention."

"I'm not so sure we need to go in with a guilty plea," said Lily. "Aren't we just accepting the worst and making it easy for everyone? Couldn't we at least try to convince people that she was justified in killing her?"

"How was she justified?" said Bruce calmly. "Dorothy was asleep. It was premeditated."

"I know she did it, but Dorothy deserved it," Lily said calmly. "Couldn't we buy some time by going in with a not-guilty plea?"

"This is first-degree murder. It's life or the death penalty. Don't you want her in a hospital as opposed to jail? Where would we get twelve jurors to say she didn't do it when she wants to confess?"

"I did it," said Patty, coming to life. "Listen to me. I did it. I want everyone to know I did it. Nobody else was there for us. I killed her, and I'm glad."

Bruce sat down, fatigued. He turned to Patty. "If I told you to plead not guilty just for tomorrow, could you do that?"

"No. I don't want to lie," said Patty. "I'm not going to lie about the best thing I ever did in my life."

"We've all lied before," said Hedy to Patty. "Like the time she hit you in the head we told the nurse you fell down. Everyone knew it was a lie, but we did it," Hedy continued. "Sometimes you lie just enough to buy time, especially in legal situations. It's not really lying."

"I did it," Patty insisted. "I am guilty."

"I don't think she is going to say not guilty," said Lily, uncrossing her legs and standing up. A single eyebrow was high and communicated what everyone was thinking. "If she is going to plead guilty, we want to control the outcome as best we can."

"I can medicate her," offered Sophie. "Bruce could do the talking for her."

"No," screamed Patty. "I'll spit it out."

"Do we have a choice, Bruce?" Hedy brought things around.

"I haven't had the time to do enough research, but I think guilty but mentally ill is the way to go for lots of reasons."

"It still doesn't sound good," said Sophie, defeated. "She'll be in jail for life."

"There has to be some way around this," said Hedy. "You have to do something. If that woman who killed her mother got out in two years, why shouldn't Patty?"

"Because now we have the guilty-but-mentally-ill plea," he said, resigned. He wasn't getting through to these women. "Patty has a plea that fits her crime. Epilepsy is not generally considered a mental illness. I'm already reaching."

"It's unfair," said Hedy. "Completely unfair. Patty was justified, and the other woman wasn't justified. She gets to go back to society, and Patty will rot in either the hospital or jail?"

"The laws are revised all the time. That case was in the seventies," said Bruce. "That woman was granted convalescent status. If Patty pleads guilty but mentally ill, I can try to work a deal, but the convalescent leave status doesn't trump the murder charge. Regardless, she will be convicted of murder. If Patty ever received convalescent leave status, that would just send her to the woman's prison in Pewee Valley, not back into society. The other woman was found not guilty."

"Does she have to turn herself in tomorrow?" asked Eva. "That'll give you more time to research if there are other options."

"Sophie, Paul, and Patty are scheduled to be interviewed tomorrow. I don't want to suggest perjury. If they don't know who did it already, they soon will," he answered. "Perjury could be the least of what everyone could be charged with."

"Can't I plead the fifth?" asked Sophie.

"The fifth amendment only comes into play when you are the person charged. Besides, no one has been charged." Bruce was worn out mentally.

"What happens if we just don't show up?" Sophie continued, searching for some way out.

"You'll be subpoenaed," he said simply. "They are going to put all this together. Do any of you have O negative blood?" he said. "The coroner told me they found O negative blood on the pipe. Dorothy was A negative."

murdered. Dorothy Jackson Anderson was struck in the throat and died within minutes of that single blow. I know the coroner has earlier provided you with the details surrounding the death, so I won't repeat them. Those details were a result of an autopsy and investigation conducted by the deputy chief medical examiner, John Hamn." Clinton paused, making sure he had explained who had done the autopsy.

Hedy wanted to step down and kiss him for this gesture and thoughtfulness.

"We have made an arrest. Patricia Anne Anderson of Louisville, Kentucky, Dorothy Anderson's daughter, voluntarily turned herself in to my office this morning around 10:00 a.m. She is currently in the Breckinridge County jail awaiting arraignment, which we expect will take place this afternoon. She has been charged with first-degree murder."

The last sentence was met with a collective gasp, as the journalists were fully aware the murder would have been premeditated.

"We consider the investigation closed and will now let the judicial process proceed," ended Clinton as he turned to Hedy. "The family will make a short statement,"

Hedy stepped from the family and took her place between the sheriff and the state police. In a clear voice, she began. "As a family, we are deeply saddened by the tragic events that caused the death of our mother, Dorothy Jackson Anderson. We are in complete support of our sister, Patricia, and will do everything we possibly can to aid in her defense. We ask that you respect our need for privacy at this very difficult time." Then she turned and went back to stand next to Barbara. She would not say she was sorry her mother had died violently, and she would not let them see her cry, although she was on a thin edge.

"We will take a few questions," said Clinton, knowing they were going to keep digging until they got what they wanted.

"Will you be seeking the death penalty?" came the first blow.

"That has not been decided," answered Frankie Jones. "The Commonwealth Attorney will make that decision based on information that will follow, but the charge is first-degree murder."

"Did she have any accomplices? Are you expecting any other charges?" someone asked.

"No, we believe—and the evidence supports this—that Patricia Anderson acted alone," said Jones. "We have completed our part of the investigation."

"Do you know when the court is expected to arraign Ms. Anderson?"

"Court is scheduled to begin at 2:00 p.m. I'm not sure where this case will fall on the docket," the sheriff answered. He did not go into the calls and pleas for the arraignment to happen so quickly.

"Dr. Collins," said the reporter for WHAS-TV in Louisville, "What is your official capacity, since the sheriff did not introduce you?"

"I am here as part of the family. Hedy Anderson Miller and I have been partners for over fifteen years." The response was like any other she would have given to the press. Clear and concise, but it caught them by surprise, and they didn't have time for any additional questions. They had been given a lot of information, first from the coroner's report and then the sheriff. She owed them nothing more.

"Thank you for your time," the sheriff said as he turned and went into the courthouse with the family following behind. They walked to the conference room.

"Well, that went about as well as it could," said Bobby. "Bruce is talking with the Commonwealth Attorney right now. You can stay here for as long as you like, but it's hours till Kenny will call session. I think now is as good a time as any to try to get away for a while.

"When we take a woman to LaGrange, we have to have a female ride along with us. I'm going to get Mary Theresa ready to go with me. I'm going to drive her up myself," said Clinton. "I think it's very important that we get it done today." It was clear that Bobby Clinton wanted to afford Patty every possible consideration. This was not a normal murder arrest.

"May I see her?" asked Sophie.

Bobby Clinton shook his head no. "The first time you'll get to see her is when she is brought into court. Prepare yourselves. She'll be handcuffed and in an orange prison suit."

Sophie slid into a chair, grateful he hadn't mentioned a turtle suit.

When they walked into Eva's house, the picnic table on the back patio was covered in dishes of food. Fried chicken, corn pudding, yeast rolls. It was common practice to bring dishes with a death, but this was no ordinary death, and the acts of kindness hit the sisters particularly hard. How had the town reacted so quickly? They automatically went to pick them up and carry them into the kitchen.

Paul reached for a yeast roll. "I always loved these rolls. David Hayes's mother makes them. I hate to feel so good about eating them."

"Little bright spots," said Hedy to Paul. "I'm grateful for anything that gives me any kind of relief. Eat one for me," she said as she passed him in the kitchen. "I'm calling Trent-Dowell and buying us some time. I'm just going to tell them to put her on ice. It can be months, as far as I'm concerned. How long can you keep a dead body?" She turned to Barbara.

"Depends if you freeze them or not," Barbara responded unemotionally. Barbara couldn't believe she was answering such a question so casually, but she was sort of a newbie to this family. All the other in-laws had been around for more than thirty years, and she had only put in fifteen.

"Do you think Trent-Dowell has a freezer?" asked Hedy.

"Probably, but do you really want to do that? I'm sure they can keep the body until some of this calms down," Barbara said. "She was refrigerated in Louisville, and they just picked her up today."

"Interesting," said Lily. "I heard gases form, and their eyes bug out." Lily made her eyes as large and as possible and let out a little giggle.

Barbara stared in disbelief.

"They do, but hers won't. Things have been taken care of; let's change the subject." Barbara drilled the answers to Lily. She looked at the food and felt her stomach rumble. Barbara had not grown up in the South, and this kind of food was something she and Hedy would never eat. It looked fabulous.

"I'm eating," Barbara said as she rummaged for a plate and fork.

"I talked with Ann Rhodes at Trent-Dowell," said Hedy as she walked back into the main room where everyone was eating. "They can hold her for just about forever. I was thinking about really pushing it out, but you have the presidential election coming up November sixth. St. Romuald is a polling location," she explained.

"I wanted to do it on a Saturday, when school was out, so that would mean November third. You know how they sometimes make the kids go to a mass if there aren't a lot of people at a funeral? I just didn't want to fool with it. Then it hit me. You have Halloween on October thirty-first, or All Soul's Day, November first. What do you think? Put her down with the ghosts?" Hedy smiled to the group as they enjoyed fried chicken and an assortment of side dishes.

"Let's do it on a Saturday," Eva said. "Kids won't be there. I'm sure Bobby will send some officers to close off the area. I'll make sure the priest knows we want a simple prayer and then into the ground. Let's get it over with."

"November third it is," said Hedy. "Ann has already written the obit they're going to post on their website. She's sending it over on e-mail for us to take a look before she posts it. It's not like she didn't know who the survivors were. I'm going to fill in some dates like when Dorothy was born, etc. She said the press from everywhere had called about how many sisters, names, dates, addresses, what she knew. She was pleasant, professional as always."

"Some of the press is milling around outside," said Don as he looked out the window. "I thought you did a good job, Hedy, but I guess they didn't hear that part about our need for privacy."

"I don't know if I can go," said Sophie. No one had noticed she hadn't taken part in any of the conversation.

"I think you will be the one Patty will be looking for," said Paul to his wife.

"I'm defeated," she said slowly with her head down. "I feel so responsible."

"We all feel some responsibility," said Lily, "but it's not our fault. We were dealt a shitty hand when it came to our mother. The court will see that and give her a plea. I'm sure of it."

"And then what? Bruce acted like it was a victory that the woman who killed both her parents was institutionalized for twelve years. Can you imagine Patty being locked up in a psychiatric facility for the rest of her life?" Sophie was despondent.

"She will be indefinitely confined until she is not a threat to herself or others," said Barbara. "Then she will go to a woman's prison. Let's hope for a long hospital stay."

"I can't," Sophie mumbled. "I can't hope for that."

"You've got to be the strongest of all," said Hedy. "You have the knowledge, the records, her trust. She'll need for you to be strong."

# TWENTY THREE

C linton had made sure the front row in the courtroom was reserved for the family. Media and locals filled the rest of the space until not another body could be pressed into the room. They all filed in and sat down quietly. They weren't sure what to do. They stood when told and then sat back down when the judge appeared.

Patty had not only been handcuffed, but she also wore leg chains. "You are kidding me," whispered Hedy. "Is that really necessary?" She felt as much as heard Sophie gasp. Patty looked for her immediately, and Sophie smiled back. Patty looked small in the orange suit that hung off her shoulders. At least it wasn't a turtle suit. She kept her head down.

It took only minutes. The charge of first-degree murder was read aloud. Bruce had Patty coached on how to act. She was completely withdrawn.

"How do you plead, Ms. Anderson?" said the judge in a loud, clear voice.

"Not guilty, your honor," said Bruce quickly. He put his hand over Patty's and then turned to her. "Trust me on this, Patty. I would never hurt you, but this is the best way right now."

Patty whipped her head around and stared at him. She hated him at that moment. She started to cry. "You lied to me." She spit out the words. If the judge or the Commonwealth Attorney had heard the exchange, they did not respond.

"Don't touch me," she said, drawing a line.

The Commonwealth Attorney covering the counties of Meade, Breckinridge, and Grayson, normally practiced in neighboring Grayson County on Mondays, managing the Breckinridge County case load on a different day. For him to be in Hardinsburg on a Monday was unusual, but he had made the trip and rearranged his schedule so Patty could be taken to LaGrange that day. This was the sign Bruce had been waiting for. There was some sympathy for Patty.

"Your Honor, may we approach the bench?" said the Commonwealth Attorney, clearly steamed. What was Bruce pulling?

As they headed to speak with the judge, Patty shook her head. She had been told she could plead guilty. She was supposed to trust Bruce, but he had lied to her.

It was as if all the family was silently sending Patty a message. Keep your mouth shut. They held their breath. Barbara smiled, knowing that Bruce had come to the same conclusion she had. There was no need to simply acquiesce to a guilty plea. Adding "but mentally ill" did little other than guarantee an initial stay at the Kentucky Correctional Psychiatric Center. If she pleaded guilty without even attempting to bargain, she was sentencing her herself to life.

Patty was an adult, and this was a felony. It trumped the county attorney and lessened the pull Bruce might have in arranging a plea bargain. Stanley Dowell, the Commonwealth Attorney, was a no-nonsense guy who went by the book. Everyone knew this was a terrible case. This was now national news, and he wanted to make sure he didn't come across like some country bumpkin.

"Judge," began Stanley Dowell, "Bruce Edwards indicated—no, told me to my face—that Patty Anderson would plead guilty but mentally ill. I wouldn't have pushed this through today if I had known he would be entering a not-guilty plea."

The judge looked over at Bruce. "That was the initial agreement," began Bruce, "but a lot has come to light since I spoke with Mr. Dowell." Bruce was choosing his words carefully. "There is currently a very similar case in New York. A young man, nineteen years old, stabbed his mother to death as he was coming out of an epileptic episode. He has been charged with her murder and sent to Rikers Island while the courts look at the extending situation."

"I haven't heard that she had a seizure on the day of the murder," said Dowell. "I don't see the similarities. I'm not even sure we should use epilepsy as a mental illness. I was giving you the benefit of the doubt. She rammed a pipe into her mother's neck." Dowell continued to whisper, which was the usual way at the bench, but his whisper was forceful.

"The night prior to the alleged murder," Bruce began, knowing he couldn't plead not guilty and admit to Patty actually killing her mother, "Patty Anderson experienced cluster seizures. She had twelve in an hour, which is on the high end of a cluster. It sometimes takes days for the individual to come out of the effects. Violence is often accompanied with cluster seizures, similar to the nineteen-year-old in New York." Bruce knew the men were listening intently.

They didn't know any more about epilepsy than Bruce had before this case.

Bruce wanted to be careful to pull the New York-versus-Kentucky card. These men did not want to look incompetent nationally, and being compared to New York was a little threatening.

"Patty will waive her right to a speedy trial, if, as in New York, her epilepsy and mental capacity can be evaluated at the Kentucky Correctional Psychiatric Center," Bruce offered. "The New York case is not on all fours with this, but the accused individual in that case has been incarnated now for months while everyone is working together, attempting to find an agreement that is a fair and just punishment. That is all I am asking." In other words, Bruce was buying time.

The judge spoke up. "In the New York case, what is the socioeconomic status of the parents?" The question was blatant. Were these people rich and buying their son's freedom?

"The parents never married, and he was raised virtually alone by his single mother, who was a schoolteacher. She, of course, is now deceased. His father, with whom he had little contact growing up, is a tenured professor at Columbia University. The father and stepmother are involved and supporting their son. Patty's family is more than supportive. There are a lot of extenuating circumstances," Bruce said, aware that both the judge and Commonwealth Attorney knew Dorothy Anderson.

"I'll accept the plea," began the judge. "But without bail, and she will be taken immediately to Kentucky Correctional Psychiatric Center for a thirty-day evaluation. I also want to order that she not have any visitors during the evaluation. I want the professionals there to judge her without the input of her family. I want to know what Patricia Anderson is all about, not the rest of the Andersons."

Bruce was a little surprised at the order to keep Patty from seeing her family. A family that had been nothing but supportive.

"Speedy trial or not, I don't want this dragging on for months. I don't care what they do in New York. In Kentucky, we apply the law equally," he continued.

There was nothing Bruce could do, so he nodded in agreement and then turned to the Commonwealth Attorney. The judge directed the question. "Everyone in agreement?"

Stanley Dowell knew when he had been bested. He had hoped for a guilty plea, and he wasn't going to get it today. "I have my reservations," he began. "Bruce, don't tell me one thing and then grandstand in front of the media."

Bruce continued to look at Stanley Dowell without uttering a word. Grandstand in front of the media? Bruce would rather be in his office alone. It was Stanley and Judge Kenny Nall who loved being in front of the national media.

"I'll agree," said Dowell slowly and quietly, and the two men returned to their tables.

"Do you understand the charges against you?" asked the judge, and Patty answered a "Yes, sir," in a quiet, clear, defeated voice. She was not able to take on Bruce and these men. She felt invisible. Tears rolled down her bowed head.

And it was over. She would be sent to LaGrange for an evaluation. The judge informed the attorneys and everyone in the courtroom that it would take thirty days for the evaluation to be completed and that no visitors would be allowed. He would review the report when it came in, and he would schedule a meeting as quickly as possible after reviewing the documents.

Journalists began leaving the room and whipping out their cell phones. Television personalities were running to their cameraman, flipping their perfectly coiffed hair. Another accused person came in, and Patty was taken away, looking back only quickly. She turned to Sophie, who was crying. "Bruce lied to me," she said to Sophie, always her savior.

"It's the best thing for you," Sophie said quietly. "It's the best," and she smiled as they took away her twin sister.

Bruce closed his portfolio and looked back at the family. "Do you want to meet in my office? I want to explain some things."

The group, guided by Bruce, walked in a tight knot, bumping against one another while questions sailed toward them. "Did your sister kill your mother?" came one unusually crass statement.

Once they were in the office, Bruce said, "I had to enter a not-guilty plea. I need time and facts to bargain. I am not sure if I can get the charges reduced to manslaughter or actually find a way to work the not-guilty-but-insane plea. The last thing we want is to go in immediately with a guilty-but-mentally-ill plea. If she is found not guilty, in any way, she can work her way out of the system. John Hinckley now enjoys six-month stays out of the hospital with his mother. Guilty but mentally ill is still a guilty plea and a life sentence. I had to take the chance of surprising Patty and hoping she'd go along with it. I think it's for the best. We can always plead guilty but mentally ill. I'm sorry I had to surprise everyone, but it took me a while to think everything through."

Sophie took an audible breath. Everyone else nodded with optimism.

"I certainly don't speak for the family," Barbara said cautiously, "but I had come to the exact same conclusion. I just didn't know how you were going to keep Patty from screaming out guilty."

"That was my worry too," said Bruce, "but I thought if I blind-sided her, she wouldn't have the strength to challenge me in front of everyone while in court. I'm grateful it worked. It won't matter what she tells the psychiatric center people. We still have at least thirty days to work out the best agreement for her. Lots of people knew about Dorothy."

"Just didn't do anything about it," said Hedy.

"Our job now is to build as strong a case as we can and bargain for leniency based on child abuse and the diminished capacity of Patty," Bruce said to the group.

"Let's get back to Louisville," Paul said to Sophie. "We have a lot to do."

Bruce's office was across the street from the courthouse, so it was easy enough to slip into the appropriate cars and escape. When the family arrived at Eva and Don's, the television crews were set up in the yard.

"Jeez," said Don as Barbara pulled into the driveway. "Leave us alone."

"We are getting out of town," said Hedy. "We all know our assignments. Let's just keep in touch with one another. E-mail, phone, conference calls. Thirty days will go by quickly." They were all bunched in the garage.

"Thirty days will make it November twenty-eighth," said Barbara, looking at her iPhone. "But with Thanksgiving, I'm sure the deadline will be set at Friday, November thirtieth. Bruce can confirm that, but I'd work on that time frame."

All the sisters made quick getaways, leaving the film crews without much to cover. They would be splashed across national television without anyone understanding the real situation. It didn't seem fair.

Hedy's phone rang just as they pulled onto US 60. It was Mike DeWitt from the agency.

"It's all over the news, Hedy. National news. We've been swamped with calls from your clients."

"Is that good or bad?" Hedy answered.

"Mostly bad. Health care accounts don't need to hear that you have a female partner who happens to be the chief medical examiner of Kentucky. Health care is religion. Obama may have come out for same-sex marriage, but a lot of our clients don't want to hear all that on national television. Besides, it's so unseemly. A pipe rammed into your mother's neck?"

Hedy was getting steamed. "Do you think I like it, Mike? Is there anything about this you think I like?"

"No, and I'm sorry. This really must be tough."

"Tough is an inadequate word," Hedy spoke slowly. She didn't want to blow up, even though that was exactly what she wanted to do.

"Did your sister really do it?" Mike knew it was terrible to ask, but he couldn't fathom that one of his colleagues actually was on national television saying she supported her sister who had just killed their mother. He worked almost daily in New York, even though his family was in Atlanta, and even to him this was a little over the top.

"Yes. She absolutely did it," answered Hedy. "She will probably be imprisoned in a psychiatric facility for the rest of her life."

He turned to business. "Hopkins is balking on the budget. I thought you had that one nailed down."

"I did have it nailed down, but I cautioned Jim that our products were not compatible with their Applicant Tracking System. I told him it was just a matter of time. We shouldn't be selling certain products to them if they've already made their decision about their ATS."

"It's just not good, Hedy," Mike continued. "We need to keep them happy. When are you back in Baltimore? We need to figure a way around this ATS thing," he continued.

"Yes, we need to sell them what they need and back off trying to sell them things that aren't going to work in the long run," Hedy responded. Hedy wanted to add that she'd get back to Baltimore as soon as she wiped the blood off her hands, but she held her tongue.

"Rachel wants more of their wallet." She had heard it a thousand times.

"I know what Rachel wants," Hedy said. "I'll call Bonnie and see what's up after I talk with Jim and see exactly where things are. I'll get to Baltimore, but I will need to take some time off to prepare for my sister's defense."

"Really?" Mike asked. "How much time? Don't you have lawyers?"

"Stacks of them, for which I am paying," she said to let him know she was carrying an extraordinary financial burden. "But they can't track down the nun who taught us in first grade so she can testify to our child abuse."

"Why not?" said Mike.

"You sound like Rachel when she told you to come home from China. Let's not go there. I'll get to Baltimore." She wasn't going down without a fight. Everyone knew all the moving parts.

"That'll be good. We've budgeted that money. The investors want clients with names like Johns Hopkins."

"And more of the wallet," she said sarcastically.

Hedy closed out the conversation and tried to think what was important to her. It wasn't Mike's fault. He was just carrying out orders. He had a family, tuition, and a mortgage. Hedy thought about Sophie, Patty, Lily, Eva, and their childhood, and somehow nothing was adding up. She felt as if her arms were not attached to her body and that everything around her was falling apart.

"Is there anything I can do?" said Barbara as they sped along, eating up the miles between Hardinsburg and Louisville. They normally kept their professional lives very separate.

"Same stuff. Rachel wants more of their wallet, and I'm supposed to do it even though I've got a sister who is being transported to the Kentucky Correctional Psychiatric Center for murdering our mother. I'm not sure where to start."

"Forget the job for right now, and let's concentrate on getting everything together for Patty's evaluation," Barbara said.

"That would be the kiss of death," said Hedy as she turned off the connection of her iPhone to the car. "I'm going to call and see when Bonnie at Hopkins can meet and work around that," said Hedy, in effect putting her job before Patty.

Sophie was equally worked up as she and Paul made the same trip to Louisville. She called the Kentucky Correctional Psychiatric Center to see if she could visit and was met with a resounding no. Not during the evaluation. It was the judge's orders. Sophie knew that, but she thought maybe the message had been missed.

"But it says on your website that she can have visitors," countered Sophie.

"First, the judge said no visitors during evaluation. We just got the paperwork. Second, you'd have to be put on a list by the inmate, and then you'd have to be cleared. You can't just be walking in here like's it's K-Mart," said the woman with sarcasm.

Sophie thought she must be someone who goes home and kicks the dog. Sophie was also told she'd be called if they wanted to interview her personally.

"What about her regular prescriptions?" began Sophie.

"Now don't be bringing any prescriptions in here, either. We have a sign twelve feet high warning people not to bring drugs into the facility," said the guard in a strong Eastern Kentucky twang. Sophie closed her eyes. She had worked hard on at least minimizing her accent. "You'll be arrested, the pills will be confiscated, and you won't be allowed on the visitors list ever. Do you understand?"

She didn't understand. "These are not illegal drugs," said Sophie, feeling the blunt force of the correctional system. "How will they know what medications she needs to take?" she continued in a much more pleasant tone than she felt.

"We take care of all that" was her simple reply.

"But I have worked with the doctors here in Louisville for years to get her medications just right," Sophie tried again.

"We got good doctors here," came the reply. "Don't be driving in here with some pills," she cautioned. "You'll regret it. This is prison. Your loved one is an inmate charged with first-degree murder."

Loved one! she thought in disgust. Do they have written instructions on how to address people in this situation? If she thought calling her a loved one was helping, she was wrong.

This was Patty, not some thug who murdered people. It had taken years to get the medications worked out. The seizure medications interacted poorly with so many other drugs. Prozac had helped with her depression, but they had gone through four or five other drugs before finding what she could tolerate. Why wouldn't they just let her explain? She felt dread creep over her, knowing what would happen to Patty without the drugs.

Sophie had no idea the psychiatric part of the prison system was connected to a general prison that covered more than 2,400 acres of bucolic Oldham County. There were over two thousand beds in the system. The Internet showed photos of fields where the inmates grew their own vegetables and attended classes for earning a general education degree. It talked about respecting the inmates, but she was getting the feeling that wasn't actually the truth. The long list of rules let her know this was not what Patty was accustomed to. Sophie had never given the prison system much thought. It was not in her world of playing tennis and going to work as an RN in a sophisticated hospital in Louisville.

Working her iPhone furiously, Sophie learned that you also can't call inmates. They are sometimes given the privilege of making a call. If a call was made, Patty would not only have to get permission to make it, she would have to do the dialing. She almost never used the phone, and never by herself.

Only immediate family and three friends were allowed on the visitors list. Visits were possible on Saturday and Sunday and public holidays, but in this case, they would be allowed only after Patty's evaluation. It seemed you could send money to the inmate only via US mail, to the prison, in the form of a money order. They could then purchase things at the canteen. No letter could accompany the money order. Visitors couldn't wear coats, were subject to searches, and got only two-hour visits. You needed a picture ID and had to carry a clear plastic coin purse so they could easily see the contents. Only two keys were allowed to be brought into the visitation area, and they had to be on a key ring.

Sophie wondered about the reasoning but figured a working system had evolved over the years. Where do you buy a money order? Find a clear plastic purse?

She put her iPhone down and turned to Paul. "I can't see Patty until after the evaluation, and then just on Saturdays and Sundays."

Paul didn't respond, knowing that had been part of the agreement from the judge, but he pressed on, cognizant that his wife was not accepting reality and that her introduction to the prison system had been a shock. He couldn't even think what it would be to Patty.

"They won't let her keep her police scanner or wear her white gloves," said Sophie to Paul after reading the complete website of the Luther Luckett Correctional Complex. "I'm not sure when the meltdown will occur, but it's going to be soon."

Paul knew what they had been given at the county jail when they went to pick up Patty's personal belongings. The scanner had been on top of the clothes he had carefully packed, along with the gloves.

"She seemed pretty good in court," Paul said to a slumping Sophie.

"I thought she might slug Bruce," Sophie said, turning to face her husband with a small smile.

"It was a well executed move on his part," Paul continued. "One that may have saved her life."

"Why don't you start a list?" he continued, knowing she needed to keep busy. "The medical records from Our Lady of Peace. Her current doctor and therapist."

Sophie sat up and pulled a paper and pen out of her purse.

Paul was glad they had taken away the police radio and gloves. They needed her to be as unglued as possible. This evaluation would be everything.

Paul was thinking how he was going to approach Johnny Flood, the retired general practitioner. How much would he be willing to admit to knowing? What about the records? How far would they go back? Would he consider that the family might be accusing him of malpractice? Paul needed to let him know quickly that all they wanted was for Patty to be found incompetent to stand trial for a murder she happily admitted to committing.

# Twenty Four

Mary Theresa Starks did not want to make the trip to LaGrange, and Bobby Clinton didn't want to push her; he knew the trip was exhausting and unnerving for her. She was the only female officer, so he asked his wife if she would join him. It didn't have to be an officer, just a female in case Patty had to go to the bathroom or something. Kathy had accompanied him before, and the county would reimburse them for dinner in Louisville. Patty would be in the back of the police cruiser behind a Plexiglas wall.

As he helped Patty into the back of the car, she asked about her police scanner. The media was all around filming as he held her head. "Not now," he said to Patty, who looked straight into the cameras.

The drive was pleasant enough, and Patty didn't speak. She rocked. This wasn't much different from when she rode with Paul and Sophie. They didn't talk to her a lot either.

Kathy Clinton had asked her if she needed a drink or the bathroom, but Patty had declined both. Her hands were cuffed, but in front of her, so she just sat in the back and watched the fall colors that were beginning to fade. Leaves floated down.

Bobby was second-guessing himself about the turtle suit. It was protocol for psychiatric patients, but they were so uncomfortable and degrading. Patty didn't seem like a suicide risk, but was he letting his childhood memories cloud his judgment?

The Kentucky Correctional Psychiatric Center was a part of a very large complex with high walls and barbed wires curled along the top. The roadway into the prison was almost what one would call a boulevard, with a lush, green strip running through the middle.

Clinton had made the run here a few times, but he always had to think exactly where to go to drop off a prisoner. He had never brought one to the psychiatric center, which was a separate facility from the main prison.

"Identify yourself," asked the guard.

"Robert Clinton, sheriff of Breckinridge County. My female escort is my wife, Kathy, and I have an intake psychiatric patient, Patricia Anne Anderson," he replied crisply.

"We've been expecting you," said the guard. "All over the news."

"I know," Bobby replied while the guard checked Patty's name off a list.

"Go to that building on the right. Wait for them to come out to the car. I'll call and let them know you are here. It'll just be a minute."

Two male nurses and an attendant were waiting outside the facility with a stretcher when they pulled up.

"She doesn't need a stretcher," said Kathy. "She can just walk in."

"Kathy, they don't know Patty like we do, and they have a certain way of doing things. I'm sure they have a reason. Let's just help her go along with protocol." After Bobby handed over all the paper work, he open the door and helped Patty out.

"Didn't cuff her in the back?" asked the male nurse. "Isn't she the one who rammed a pipe into her mother's neck? No suicide safety smock?"

"It's a long ride from Breckinridge County," said Bobby. "I wanted her to be more comfortable."

"We'll need to restrain her on the stretcher. Arms and legs," came the reply.

Bobby turned to Patty. "You need to get up on the stretcher. Kathy and I can help if you like."

"I can do it," she replied. "Well, these handcuffs," she said.

Bobby reached over and unlocked them. Kathy held her arm. The nurses and attendant immediately surrounded Patty as she moved onto the stretcher, their muscular arms at the ready. They clamped both her legs and arms immediately. Patty started rocking.

"She's not dangerous," Bobby said to the hospital attendants.

"I don't know what you call dangerous in Breckinridge County, but ramming a pipe into your mother's neck and almost decapitating her in one blow counts as dangerous here on the psych ward."

"You only know what you hear on the news," Kathy snapped. She was usually so reserved it surprised Bobby, and he turned and looked at his wife in disbelief.

"The old woman deserved it," Kathy added, and she walked off to the police cruiser. Bobby almost laughed. He knew many people were privately thinking the same thing, but up to this point, he hadn't heard it said out loud. And from Kathy, of all people.

Patty's rocking became more labored because she couldn't move her arms and legs. Her therapist had taught her how to self-soothe. She needed to be able to move her arms.

The bright lights of the hospital shocked her, and she felt that slow sickness start to wash over her when a seizure was about to happen. The seizure took over, and she started to choke. "Release her arms," said the nurse. "We have to roll her over on her side. She will choke." He was almost screaming. Patty continued to convulse.

People were all around, and when she finally stopped, she was exhausted. They had given her several shots, and she felt herself slipping away. She closed her eyes and let the tears roll down her face. The seizures had been under control for so long, and now she was failing. She felt the fog descend.

Patty woke up in a room that was small and white, with bars on the windows and doors. Everything was old and painted so many times you could see the layers. She couldn't reach out of her sleep, and she felt as though she were underwater. Her arms and legs were secured, and a small woman sat in the corner.

"Couldn't leave you alone," she said. "I've been watching you all night because you can't be having those seizures while you are restrained."

Patty clawed at her drowsiness. She wasn't sure where she was, and then she remembered. The hospital. Not Our Lady of Peace, but somewhere else. The prison. She remembered hitting Dorothy with the pipe. She was confused as the woman got up and left the room.

Within minutes, another woman, one in scrubs, walked in. "Do you know where you are?" The woman worked quickly, releasing Patty's hands and feet. She didn't need the restraints now that she had come through the night.

"The prison hospital," said Patty as she fought against the fatigue. She began to move around.

"Do you know what day it is?" The woman was preparing a shot.

"No," said Patty, trying to remember. Everything was running together. She knew these were important questions. "Thursday, maybe."

"Tuesday," the woman answered.

"What is your name?"

"Patty Anderson," she said, feeling a little better.

"Who is the president?"

"Obama," came her reply, and she started to pull up.

"That's good," said the woman, who looked like a nurse. "Do you think he'll be reelected?"

"Yes," said Patty. "I'm voting for him."

"I don't think you'll be voting for anyone, honey. We don't run patients into the polls on election days."

"How long will I be here?" asked Patty as she started rocking. Patty liked to vote.

"It all depends. I'm giving you this shot to keep you calm," she said as the needle went in. "A social worker will be in this afternoon." Patty felt herself slipping back into darkness. The nurse seemed far away, and she couldn't form the words she wanted. She didn't want the shots. Why hadn't the nurse asked her?

When the social worker appeared at the door, Patty had partially come out of her drug-induced sleep. She also felt the affects of the seizure, and she felt more groggy than usual. She sat up and looked at the social worker, who had a file and clipboard in her hand.

"Why are you here?" asked Patty. She wasn't sure what was happening.

"I'm here to ask you some questions," said the woman warmly. "It's called intake. We just talk, and I make some notes."

"I don't believe you," said Patty without a lot of emotion. She was too tired, too drugged.

"What don't you believe?" said the woman as she started to write.

"What are you writing down?" Patty wanted to know, even though she knew she didn't have a choice but to speak to this total stranger.

"I'm writing things down like you are female, Caucasian, look to be in reasonable health."

"Well, OK, now you can leave," said Patty.

"No, I need to ask you some questions," the woman said again. "I don't want to have to put down that you were uncooperative."

"I want to be cooperative," responded Patty.

"Good. Let's start at the beginning."

"What beginning?" asked Patty, confused. "The beginning like Adam and Eve, or the beginning of when I killed my mother?"

The woman almost laughed but knew that wouldn't be professional. At least this intake interview wasn't going to be the same old routine of yeses and nos. "I think let's start at the beginning of you. Where were you born?"

"St. Joseph's Hospital in Louisville," said Patty calmly. "Pretty much everyone else in Breckinridge County was born at the hospital there or at home, but Dorothy insisted on coming to Louisville. You know, everyone was incompetent at home. She was too important for anything less than a Louisville hospital."

"And Dorothy is your mother?" said the social worker.

"You know Dorothy is my mother," responded Patty, a little irritated. "Why would you be asking me these questions if you didn't know Dorothy was my mother?"

"How far did you go in school?" said the social worker, returning to the questions on the form.

"High school," said Patty, looking down at the floor. "Just high school."

"Did you want to go to college?"

"Desperately," said Patty, "but the seizures came on and got really bad. I had the grades and was accepted to the University of Kentucky, but that summer, I had to go to Our Lady of Peace."

"Have you thought about going back to school?"

"Yes, but I can't," continued Patty dejectedly. "I can't drive, and I'm already so much of a bother to Sophie. She has two kids, you know, and they did everything in school. Swimming. Soccer. It has been hard for her."

"What about the bus?" the social worker pressed.

"I have trouble focusing," admitted Patty. "More school for me is pretty unreasonable at this point." Patty felt herself drifting off. The effects of the last seizure hadn't left her system. When she didn't have seizures regularly, her mind was still sharp. When she did, she could almost touch the dullness.

"Have you ever been married?"

Patty shook her head no and started staring out the window. "I had a boyfriend in high school, but then the seizures came."

"What about sex?" asked the social worker.

"What about sex?" answered Patty.

"Have you ever had sex with another person?" The social worker wanted to be politically correct.

Patty laughed and put her hand over her mouth. "No. No. Not anyone. Not even like Hedy." And Patty's eyes darted back to the woman. "You know, like with another woman."

"Do you have feelings of wanting to have sex with women?" she asked without any emotion.

"No," said Patty, dragging out the word. "No. Hedy does, though."

"And Hedy is your sister?" the social work asked, and Patty nodded.

"Let's focus on you," said the social worker.

"Focus on how I killed Dorothy. Isn't that why you are here?" Patty started feeling better, and she wanted to talk about killing Dorothy.

"OK. Did you kill her?"

"Yes. I rammed the pipe in her neck," said Patty with a gesture indicating some force.

"Had Dorothy ever sexually abused you?"

"No. That was about the only way she didn't abuse us," answered Patty. "Why are you so into sex? I don't even think about sex."

"It's all part of the questions on the form. We ask everyone the same questions so we can compare," said the social worker. Maybe she had been at this job too long, she thought for a moment. She knew she was so focused on getting through the questions that she wasn't really listening to what Patty was saying. Patty made you want to talk to her.

"What do you want to talk about?" said the social worker, putting down her pen and clipboard.

"I don't know, I guess," said Patty. "No one ever asks me what I want to talk about."

"I want to know what you want to talk about," responded the social worker. "What about killing your mother?"

"It was great," said Patty, smiling. "She died quickly. I hope she knew it was me."

"How did you decide exactly how you were going to kill her?" asked the social worker, knowing this question wasn't anywhere on her intake form.

"I thought about a lot of ways," said Patty calmly. "When I haven't had a seizure for a while and I can focus, I look on the Internet."

The social worker did not respond but gave Patty a look that encouraged her to keep speaking.

"I read where a farmer in North Carolina had to bury 250,000 chickens all at once. He buried them in a mass grave, but he didn't do it right, and the gases built up with the rotting birds, and then they exploded and shot dead rotting bird parts all over his neighbors' farms."

The social worker simply looked at Patty. "I don't see the correlation." She didn't know whether to laugh or make notes. Wouldn't you put lye or lime or something on them to prevent exploding birds? the social worker mused silently as she wondered about the validity of the story. She'd have to look it up on the Internet.

"It made me think I'd like to shoot Dorothy all over town. I searched how to buy dynamite, but you have to have a federal explosives license. You can buy the pipes for dynamite on eBay, but I don't have a credit card. And then I'd have to mix up the chemicals. No dynamite up her butt."

"So cutting her throat proved a better idea?" said the social worker, resuming her note taking. She couldn't wait to turn this one in to the doctor.

"It did," said Patty, "but I got caught."

"Yes, you did," confirmed the social worker. "Are you sorry you killed her?"

"No. Not at all," said Patty.

# TWENTY FIVE

B ruce, along with everyone else around him, was doing nothing but working on Patty's case. It continued to be in the news,
and the Louisville law firm was peppering him with requests and research. Other lawyers were in contact with the Kentucky Correctional
Psychiatric Center. The psychologist wasn't going to see Patty until
she'd been in the system at least two days. It hadn't been good. She'd
had a seizure, was on twenty-four-hour watch, and was being kept
drugged. The only good thing was that Sophie couldn't call and in-
quire, and Bruce wasn't about to tell the family.

Paul was meeting with Johnny Flood later in the day at Bruce's office, and Hedy had found only one nun who remembered the girls and
was willing to talk. She was on her way to Owensboro and the retirement home. The nun would give at least a verbal statement that Bruce
would have transcribed, and it would be included in the report. Hedy
was taking a small camera just in case she agreed to be filmed. Film
would be more powerful. Bruce had been notified that every sister and
husband would be interviewed, so names needed to be filled in against
the open slots of available times. Thirty days wasn't a long time, and he
didn't have a raft of paralegals to do the mundane.

Johnny Flood walked into the foyer, and Bruce waved him into his office. "Never thought it would come to this," said Johnny to Bruce. "I've been practicing medicine for over fifty years. I found their records." He held up a couple of thick paper files.

"We've got to show abuse," Bruce spoke quickly.

"Not on my back you aren't" was the response.

Paul had entered the office but was being questioned by the receptionist.

"Send him on back," said Bruce into the phone. "Get Sally to transcribe, but don't send her back until I call for her." Some convincing was needed.

Paul shook Dr. Flood's hand and sat down. "Thanks for agreeing to be interviewed," said Paul. He was nervous because things didn't seem warm.

"It's been almost fifty years. What do you want from me? I couldn't be sure they were abused. Kids fall down all the time. I looked at the incident when they brought Patty in. They said she hit her head. I didn't make any more notes."

Paul could see Johnny Flood didn't want to cooperate. "Johnny, my sister-in-law is on trial for the murder of her mother. A mother who beat her nearly every day of her life. She has seizures resulting from a trauma to the head." He knew he had to be careful. "Her mother hit her in the head with a nine iron.

"Hedy drove up to the back door, and your nurse let them into the treatment area because they came to the back door. Hedy couldn't have been thirteen years old at the time. She shouldn't have been driving, but they were desperate. You didn't ask how they got to the office because you didn't want to know," Paul continued.

"Patty was out cold. Hedy could barely see over the steering wheel. You knew it wasn't regular. All I am asking is that you confirm they turned up at odd times, with odd problems that most likely was child abuse. Dorothy got away with it for years. I understand it was different back then, but how long does Patty have to pay? Do they all have to pay? Please help us with this. Patty isn't going to get any better. In fact, she'll get worse, but having her in a psychiatric ward is much better than having her in general prison population." Paul was close to begging.

The air stood still. No one spoke.

"It was the worst case of child abuse I have ever seen," said Johnny back to Paul. "What she did to those girls physically was awful. Neglect. Lily almost lost her fingers. My wife would drive them anytime she saw them walking to school late in the cold, rain—all kinds of weather."

"Thank you," said Paul. "Just give us a fighting chance."

"You had to wonder what happened to Dorothy to make her so mean. So unhappy. Hedy once came to me to get her committed, and I told her it would be next to impossible. And it would have been. There was no cooperation. She was so mentally ill."

"Can I get Sally in here to transcribe your recollections?" Bruce asked Johnny.

"Sure. I'm an old man. I did the best I could. Those girls just kept managing. I thought when they got out, everything would be OK. Let's make this straight."

Hedy was just getting into Owensboro when she called Lily. "Since you're here in town, how about you go with me to the nuns' retirement home?"

"I'm trying to fill in the appointment schedule for each of us to go and be interviewed by the psychologist. Bruce just sent me a list of the available times. What day do you want?"

It was only Wednesday, and she had done little else than work on Patty's case. "Do you have a spot tomorrow?" Hedy replied, knowing she was going to have to keep the clients happy while working on her sister's defense. When would she get to Baltimore?

"Two in the afternoon. I'll put you down," said Lily. "Don't forget the funeral is Saturday."

"How exactly could I forget?" Hedy said. She was exhausted. Another trip to Hardinsburg. "So you don't want to join me and the Ursuline nuns?"

"Correct," Lily replied. "Getting these appointments is totally time consuming. I thought it would save some money if I took it off Bruce's plate."

"You can't imagine how much I appreciate that," said Hedy, trying not to think about the mounting legal bills. "I'll be sure to be there at two," she repeated to confirm the agreement with Lily.

The official name for the retirement facility was the Motherhouse of the Ursuline Sisters of Mount Saint Joseph, and it was fifteen minutes outside Owensboro in Maple Mount, Kentucky. Hedy had found Sister Mary Joseph on the Internet. The nuns had both a website and a robust Facebook page. Throwback Thursdays was a big favorite and reflected the changing clothes of the nuns over the years. Hedy remembered Sister Mary Joseph in a stiff white headpiece and black robes, with a rosary by her side. She was a little overweight and always smiling.

The grounds were beautiful, and a little leaf posted at the entrance reflected the date of 1874. Hedy was a little nervous. She was sure everyone had heard the story of Dorothy's death and why Hedy was coming to visit. She had a little recording device in her purse, both video and simple recording. She wasn't sure what she would be able to capture.

"You must be Hedy Anderson," an older woman greeted her as she walked into the Motherhouse.

"Well, it's actually Hedy Miller, but yes. I'm here to see Sister Mary Joseph."

"We know, and we are so very sorry. You and your family have been in our prayers."

Hedy thanked her. The Catholic Church made her skin crawl. She knew she had broken just about every rule of the church, and Hedy considered those rules as nothing more than creations by old white men trying to keep women in their place. Divorce. Birth control, not to mention homosexuality.

Sister Mary Joseph, now much thinner, was wearing relaxed slacks and a simple white blouse and sweater. "It's you, Hedy," she said. "You were in my first first-grade class. I remember you well."

"Thank you," said Hedy, a little surprised.

"You were so bright," she continued, and Hedy thought of the green tint. Was she laughing behind her back? It never went away.

Hedy pulled deep and attempted to reassure herself she knew there was no green tint. "What did you grow up to be?" she inquired as she walked over and sat on a small green sofa, gesturing for Hedy to follow.

"I work for a New York advertising agency. I work in health care, with hospitals all over the country. I enjoy my work." Hedy felt about six again as she eased into a chair across from the sofa.

"Sounds exciting. I always knew you'd do well."

"You know why I've come," Hedy said.

"Yes," the frail nun replied. "I was surprised that Patty did what she did. I was surprised by the whole thing, and then again, I wasn't," she said sadly. "It was just that you all had gotten out. Why did she do it now? Her life will never be the same. Patty and Sophie were in the last class I taught at St. Romuald. They moved me to St. Denis in Louisville after that."

"I think she was just tired of carrying the burden. You know she developed epilepsy and suffers from severe seizures. The doctors have speculated that it was caused when Dorothy hit Patty in the head with a golf club."

The old nun lifted her hand over her mouth in horror. "We all knew it was bad," she said simply. "But Father Ben told us it was none of our business. That the family takes care of its own, and we were to stay out of it."

"Really? You spoke with him?" said Hedy. Her face flushed at the thought of him turning his back on five little girls. "Birth control is a sin, but look the other way when a child is being beaten," said Hedy with a little more attitude than she meant toward this nun who had tried to help.

"We did what the priest told us to," she said. "It was a long time ago."

"I know," said Hedy. "I'm sorry. But you knew there was abuse?"

"Of course we did. All of you were always bruised and all so smart. I remember one day in first grade, Lily was furious because Eva had packed her a cheese sandwich. She turned to me and said, 'She knows I loathe cheese sandwiches.' How many first graders use the word *loathe*?"

Hedy laughed. Lily still hated cheese sandwiches.

"As you know, Sister, we have to prepare an evaluation of Patty so maybe the judge will allow her some leniency. We need desperately to show child abuse."

"I read in the paper that she pleaded not guilty. Are you sure she did it?" asked the nun.

"She killed her," responded Hedy simply. There was no reason to try to cover up the truth with this nun who was cooperating. "She was advised to plead not guilty just so we could try to get a plea bargain out of the Commonwealth Attorney. Otherwise it's life for Patty. She could be tried for the death penalty, though that doesn't seem logical at this point."

"What about Dr. Flood? We had to call him more than once to come down to the rectory," the nun said. The comment took Hedy a little by surprise. She couldn't remember him coming other than for Lily's hands.

"He's giving a report as we speak," Hedy assured. She was hoping for a good report from the nun, who looked competent and spoke so adequately. "How is it that you remember all of us so well? All our names? You must have taught hundreds of children over the years."

"You all were special, and you were in my first class. You remember. I didn't teach Eva, but of course, she was around. And the abuse. It's haunted me for years. That we did nothing. Our hands were tied."

Hedy didn't know what to say but realized she needed to be getting this on film.

"I just never thought it would end up like this," said the nun, lowering her head. "The newspapers and television said it was quite brutal."

"It was," said Hedy sadly. "I need you to tell the story, and I'd like to videotape it. It will become a part of her evaluation." Hedy held her breath that the nun would not back out.

"You don't have to worry." Sister Mary Joseph reached over and patted Hedy's hand. "I've wanted to make this right for years. It really has haunted me. We should have been stronger. I made some notes to help me remember," she said as she pulled a small paper out of the pocket.

Hedy turned to set up the small camera and tripod. The nun sat up a little straighter as Hedy trained the camera on her face.

"How do I look?" she asked.

"My name is Sister Mary Joseph Fletcher, and I was assigned as a first-grade teacher at St. Romuald in Hardinsburg, Kentucky, beginning in 1956…"

Hedy was emotionally spent when the nun stopped speaking after forty-five minutes. She had recalled things Hedy either had never known or had forgotten. Things that had been inflicted on her sisters that were never discussed. Eva had carried the load, keeping things even. Sophie and Patty were always together. Their beatings had gotten worse, but Hedy had been unaware. She had escaped.

She was crying when she thanked the nun and had packed away the camera.

"No, thank you for giving me this opportunity to at least be able to say we tried. We wanted to help. It was different. I remember such poverty. Kids with nothing but biscuits for lunch and having to leave school to help with the farm work. But you girls stood out. I hope this helps Patty."

The drive back to Louisville was difficult. It was long, and she was exhausted. She didn't have the strength to remember so much that she had pushed away. Scenes popped into her head, and she pushed them back. It was too much.

Hedy called Bruce to let him know the nun had cooperated and that the video was strong. He let her know Johnny Flood had also given a powerful statement, but without accepting any blame for not doing more when Patty had been hit in the head. He didn't know about the bleeding.

"It was a closed head injury, and they had been there so often, it was just one more time," Dr. Flood had closed out the conversation.

# TWENTY EIGHT

The body of work supporting Patty's defense was coming along well. Bruce felt good about it, but he still hated the goal of simply getting Patty committed indefinitely to the Kentucky Correctional Psychiatric Center. What he had read indicated that even if she made progress, it was unlikely she would ever be released, and even then, it would just be to a women's prison. Her illness was progressive, and she would get worse. He needed to build a case that would allow her home visits and to eventually be turned over to Sophie and Paul. How could he convince Stanley Dowell?

Today was Saturday. Almost 10:00 a.m. He went to look out of his window, and he saw the hearse pass through downtown Hardinsburg. It was followed by two cars. There were no little purple flags on the cars that read Funeral; it was just a line of people who had been crushed. A family broken. He noticed other people pausing at the sight.

Bobby Clinton had arranged to have the entrance to the St. Romuald complex blocked off. Orange cones were rolled to one side, accommodating the passage of the three vehicles. The weather had turned a little chilly. A tent had been set up, and the priest was waiting.

Impeccable as always, the family that composed the staff of the Trent-Dowell Funeral Home stepped out and began opening the back of the hearse, allowing the coffin to be released into the sunlight.

The family began to step out of the cars. Barbara was driving, with Hedy in the front and Don and Eva in the back. Lily and Howard had pulled up adjacent with Sophie and Paul. No one said a word, and they were all dressed in black. They walked to the tent but did not take any of the seats that had been arranged around the gaping hole in the ground.

Lily looked up at the priest and said, "We're ready," as the coffin was being placed over the hole. There were no flowers even though people had sent them. They had been dispatched to the retirement home.

"Lord, please accept this woman, Dorothy Jackson Anderson. Please forgive her, her sins, and may her family find comfort." He then took out a small cylinder and tossed holy water onto the coffin as it was slowly lowered into the ground, and the family turned their backs to the process.

"Thank you, father," Sophie said to the priest she did not know.

"Your mother came to mass regularly," he offered.

"I know," said Sophie. "I know. It gave her comfort to think that she could be forgiven all her sins. But being forgiven is one thing, and leaving behind what those sins did to other people is something else altogether. We are trying to forgive her," Sophie explained.

"If you need to talk…" he began.

"Thank you," replied Sophie. "We all appreciate what you are of-fering." She walked away and joined the others on the asphalt parking lot. She looked over at the old but well-maintained church with its brick facade and stained-glass windows. A lot had gone down in that church.

Hedy looked at the priest's house, the same one that had been used as an examination room when Dr. Flood came down to treat the girls. She remembered clearly the priest who had told Sister Mary Joseph to stay out of it, and she turned away because she could not endure the rage that was rising in her throat.

The funeral director nodded his head to the group, and they nodded back. He got into the hearse as the sounds of dirt being thrown over the coffin began, and he drove away, leaving the small group.

"What now?" asked Lily. "At least we have her in the ground."

"We probably need to move on from here. The sheriff's deputy can't go until we go," said Don. "Let's go to the house. I know everyone is exhausted, but we can review where we are with the information Bruce has asked for."

They nodded in agreement and exhaustion and got into their cars. There were a few older people standing on the sidewalk along the road that ran in front of the church. They held rosaries, and Hedy tried to think of how she should acknowledge their presence. Thank them for coming? Pray for their sister? Understand why they did not hold a mass and open funeral for their mother, a devout Catholic who had gone to this church her entire life? Hedy was beyond making decisions. She was grateful that Barbara just kept driving.

"That went well, Eva," Hedy said as they entered the house.

"I can see you were very specific with your instructions," said Lily to Eva.

" He wanted a mass, and he wants to counsel us," Eva said.

"He offered that to me too," said Sophie. "Like that will ever happen."

"Not knowing how Patty is, is killing me," said Sophie.

"I told you Bruce said she was cooperating," replied Paul.

"When Dr. Terrell interviewed me," Hedy said, "he said she was having good and bad times."

"I wish I knew what that meant exactly," Sophie said, sitting down. "They won't let me advise them about her medications."

"But you've provided all her medical records. Dr. Terrell is surprisingly competent," Hedy said, taking a seat across from Sophie. "Did you know he went to undergraduate at Vanderbilt and Wash U for both his master's and doctorate? Pretty impressive."

"So why is he practicing at a prison?" Sophie asked. "Doesn't make sense. How is he repaying his loans?"

"Doesn't look like he has a lot of loans. Pretty well dressed," said Hedy. "When are you scheduled to be interviewed?"

"Next Tuesday at ten. I can't wait. Seriously. I want to see all this for myself." Sophie was miserable at her lack of knowledge.

"I have given Bruce the Social Security papers we filed for her disability payments, and her therapist sent all her records to the prison psychiatrist. Her medical doctor sent in all the work we have done getting her meds just right, and he has sent copies of her tests, labs, etc., etc. There isn't anything more on my list," Sophie said, knowing she needed to stop thinking about all the things she didn't know.

"I got the video from Sister Mary Joseph to Bruce," said Hedy. "She really laid it out there. Did you all know Father Ben knew about the abuse and told the nuns to stay out of it?"

"Well, sometimes Dr. Flood would see us over at the rectory," said Lily, "but no, I didn't know that. Priests. I guess we should be glad we weren't being sexually abused."

"That's a little harsh," said Sophie.

"Please, let's not go into the Catholic Church. I know you are still drinking the Kool-Aid," Lily shot back.

"I'm still drinking too," said Eva, "so let's just leave it there."

"I got Johnny Flood to give a pretty detailed report," said Paul. "Bruce was there, and he is having it transcribed. I really was pleased with what he had to say once he got going."

"Have you all written your own statement?" said Hedy to the entire crowd. "I'm finding that really hard."

"I don't have the first clue where to start," said Sophie. "Leaving us alone in a playpen all day, not feeding us, killing the family dog in front of us, not sleeping in beds, telling us we were stones around her neck."

"That is just it," said Eva. "I think we have to focus just on Patty. What she did to Patty. This trial is not about us, it's about Patty."

"It's about all of you," said Paul. "You have to paint a whole picture."

"I agree with that," said Barbara, who was getting bolder about her interactions with the family. "This is a case of very serious child abuse. You all don't even see it as clearly as it should be viewed. Write your story. Write how you felt, how you feel. Write what happened to Patty, but don't forget you were all harmed."

"We have until November tenth. One week. Bruce has to file everything with the court by November thirtieth," said Eva. "We'll need to get on it because he has to have time to keep adding to the case. Our statements need to be in the bag early."

Slowly, without discussion, everyone got up. "I'm back on the road on Tuesday," said Hedy. "I've got to go to Baltimore, then on to Boston. I'll be writing on the plane." She picked up her purse and headed toward the door thinking about how many reports she had written on so many planes, but none would be like this report. "Thanks, Eva, for always having the door open. I'm glad today is over."

"She's buried and gone," said Lily with resignation. "Next we have to do something about the house."

"Have you considered a match?" Eva asked.

"I found a company in E-Town that will come over and clean crime scenes, when people commit suicide or if there is a fire. I'll call them and get them to at least clean out the living room," said Howard. "We use them at the bank when we are closing estates. They do a good job."

"Has the house been released?" asked Barbara, knowing it probably had not.

"Not yet," said Eva. "Bobby says he'll call me or Don when it's clear. I'm not sure what's taking so long."

"Sometimes you have to go back in to check a last-minute detail," said Barbara. "Kind of like when families want to cremate a body quickly after a murder or wrongful death. Lots of times, we have to hang onto them. Once the body is gone, or the house is cleaned, it's gone forever."

# TWENTY NINE

Dr. Terrell looked up and smiled when Patty presented at the door. He hated seeing her in the suicide safety smock. She hated it too, but he had no choice. She had asked him to let her die.

"Hi, Patty. How are you feeling?" he said while guiding her into the room. The nurse turned and left them alone.

Patty didn't respond. She just looked at him. Her eyes were wild. Her hair disheveled. He was worried. "Have they been giving you your medications?" he asked her.

"I think so." It was difficult to maneuver in her new fat outfit. It stuck out from her body like a big puffy envelope. It was sleeveless, and she wasn't allowed anything else on. The neck bunched up under her chin when she tried to sit down.

"I don't like this thing," she said.

"You told me you wanted to die," said Dr. Terrell.

"So you are killing me with this suit?" she responded, and the doctor smiled. Hadn't lost her spunk.

"Some patients try to kill themselves. The suit prevents that," he reiterated.

"I'm not going to kill myself, but the suit may," she said.

Dr. Terrell was observing her carefully, trying to ascertain whether the appropriate medications had taken affect. It would take a bit to be fully effective. He had gotten the facility medical doctor to write the scripts exactly as her regular physician had prescribed. Sophie had done a good job getting her medications on target.

"I want my police scanner and my gloves," she said to the doctor. "I think I have the right to my own property."

"Well, you don't," he replied. "You are in prison."

"Because I killed the bitch?" came the response.

Dr. Terrell sat back. Patty had never exhibited any violent emotion. In fact, she had worked very hard at trying to do well in their sessions. Trying hard was a common reaction.

"She deserved it." Patty's mood was turning black.

"Did you know what you were doing was wrong?"

"Yes. I knew it was wrong." She wasn't helping her case. "What she did was wrong. Isn't there something about an eye for an eye? She took my eye, and I took hers."

Finding Patty Anderson insane was going to be problematic, even though Dr. Terrell was trying hard to do just that. He liked her. She didn't deserve this, but then, she did ram a pipe into her mother's throat and caused her death.

"What day is it, Patty?"

"I have no idea," she said. "How would you keep up? I don't know when it is day and when it is night. I have a lunatic for a neighbor, and she screams all the time for her baby. If I can't have a police radio or gloves, then she isn't going to get a baby."

"Who is the president?" If he could justify that she couldn't aid in her defense, he could stall things.

"I don't know because I don't know what day it is. Did Obama win reelection?"

Dr. Terrell winced. The "don't know" was good, but asking about the election was not. "Yes. He was reelected."

"Well, then Obama will still be president," Patty said simply. "Is today Wednesday? I missed voting?" she said miserably. "I always vote, even in the primaries."

It was obvious she knew national elections were held on Tuesdays. "Today is Friday."

"Have you been eating?"

"No. The food is disgusting," she replied. "I want my police radio." She started to rock, although it wasn't so obvious in her oversized padded suit.

"Do you have a nail file?" asked Patty.

"Why would you need a nail file? I can have someone clip your fingernails if they are long or broken," he responded.

"My nails are fine," said Patty. "It's my tooth. I need to file it."

"Your tooth?" asked the doctor in amazement.

"I think I cracked it when I had that seizure, and I want to file it down. When we chipped a tooth, Eva would file it down so we wouldn't have to tell Dorothy. She hated having to take care of things like a chipped tooth, but when it is cutting your tongue, you need to file it. My tongue is bleeding," she responded.

"We will take you to the dentist," responded Dr. Terrell. "I don't want you to file your teeth anymore. Do you understand?

"Besides your tooth, is everything else OK?" he asked.

Patty looked at him with disgust. "What is OK about all of this? I'm not OK. My tooth hurts, and I want my police scanner."

"I'll see what I can do about the radio" was Terrell's answer, although he knew it was never going to happen.

"How do you feel about your mother's death?"

"Good-bye, Dorothy. Sleep tight. Pay for your sins," Patty responded. "You know I killed her."

"Yes, you have told me," answered the doctor.

"Bruce lied to me," she said. "He told me I could plead guilty, and he said not guilty right out loud."

"He did that for you so he could get you some help."

"This kind of help?" she said, looking down at the suit and then the room. "I wanted to tell everyone I had taken care of the problem. Everyone was in a bad mood that day because they had to be down there. Hedy was in her own world with the mower. They don't ask me to do anything. I'm just like a pet rock."

"Well, you weren't a pet rock that day," answered Dr. Terrell.

Patty smiled. She looked around the room and did not speak, just remembering.

"Patty, what do you think is going to happen to you?"

"I'm going to jail," she responded calmly. "I don't think I'm going to like it because the food is so bad. But if I can have my police scanner…I can't really read much anymore. The words get jumbled. What's the difference? Will I get my police scanner? I'll give up on the gloves. This whole place is full of germs; what difference does it make?"

Dr. Terrell looked at his patient and tried to understand where she was mentally. He had interviewed every sister and husband, and even the chief medical examiner, and they were all much more concerned about Patty than Patty was about herself. He moved her closed file slightly on his desk. He had done little else than learn about Patty Anderson.

"Will I get my police scanner?" Patty asked again, a little more urgently.

"There are a couple of ways I've thought of," Dr. Terrell said. "If they sell them in the commissary, you can buy one there."

"Why would I want to buy one when I have one?" she asked.

"Because we don't allow personal property to be brought into the correctional facility," he continued. "There are rules. They don't really sell police radios in the commissary. It would have to be special ordered, and that could take some time and convincing. I've been thinking if I prescribe one for you, I may be able to get the warden to allow one on the property. I'd still have to order it, but through the pharmacy. I'm looking into that."

"Really?" said Patty. "Thanks."

"How have you been feeling?"

"What do you mean?" Patty answered.

"Do you think about Dorothy? Are you sad?"

"Why would I be sad?" she said and began rocking a little more pronouncedly.

"She was your mother, and she is dead."

"I killed her. I wanted her dead," replied Patty, again looking away at nothing specific. "Do you have any cigarettes?"

"Do you smoke, Patty?"

"I used to," she said. "And I was thinking a cigarette might be nice. Sophie made me stop. It was really hard when she took them away."

Dr. Terrell could only imagine what it must have taken for Sophie to get Patty to stop smoking.

"Did you smoke a lot?"

"Yes," she replied. "I did, all day long. Sophie said they would kill me. That would be OK now," she said.

"Do you think you'll die soon?"

"No. Why would I die now? I'm in jail. I can't even have my police scanner. I don't know what's happening in Chicago."

Dr. Terrell was amazed at Patty's ability to carry on such a conversation. She was childlike in so many ways, but then again, she could be quite logical. How deep was her disability? When she was not in a fog from drugs or a seizure, she was mentally very sharp. But could she assist in a trial? Would she help in her defense when all she wanted was credit for killing Dorothy?

"Do you drink alcohol, Patty?" asked Dr. Terrell.

"I want to sometimes, but Sophie says I can't because of all the drugs I take. She drinks wine, but almost always after I go to bed. Some days Paul will have a beer when he gets home from work. I don't like beer. I feel bad that Sophie has to wait until I go to bed."

"Are you mentally ill?" he asked her directly.

"You mean like Bruce said I had to say? Guilty but mentally ill?"

"Well, sort of. But do you think you have a specific mental illness?" Dr. Terrell said, trying another approach.

"They used to call it madness. Someone was mad. I think I am mad," she said.

Interesting, thought Dr. Terrell. "Mad as in angry or mad as in mentally ill?"

"She made me so angry all those years that I think maybe I went a little mad," said Patty.

"So you think you are mentally ill," he continued.

"I want to be accepted," she said slowly. "I want to matter. I don't know about the label. I know I used to be smarter, but I can still be worthwhile."

"How do you want to be worthwhile?" he asked, genuinely enjoying the exchange.

"Sophie always lets me go with her when she goes to Whole Foods. I love the grocery," said Patty, throwing up her hand, smiling at the thought. "Sometimes I get to test taste if they have a table out. Cheese and stuff. So one day this little boy went for too much cheese, and his mother slapped him. He fell backward, and he dropped the extra piece of cheese. I wanted to slap her, but Sophie moved me away. The cheese was wasted, and he could have enjoyed it. I could have told her what happens when you hit a child."

It was hard for Dr. Terrell to respond. He smiled, and Patty knew today was a good day.

# THIRTY

Bruce had an appointment with Dr. Terrell, and he was beyond anxious. He had built a strong case for Patty with various statements and other similar cases, but none of it would really matter if the doctor did not provide corroborating evidence that Patty was in a diminished state mentally when she killed her mother. Could he pull off a not guilty by reason of insanity? It was mid-November, and time was running out.

LaGrange was a two-hour drive from Hardinsburg. It had turned cold, and the sky was gray; Bruce had lots of time with his thoughts. Thanksgiving was next week, and he wondered about how Patty would celebrate. How any of the girls would celebrate. They had provided everything he had asked for and more, but the family was an emotional wreck. The media wouldn't leave them alone, and they had all become virtual prisoners looking at the calendar and counting off the days until there was a resolution.

Hedy was traveling five days a week and working past midnight most nights in a hotel room. Sophie had turned inward, and Lily had turned to stone. Eva was left with the entire county looking at her with a strange combination of horror, fascination, and judgment. Bruce felt nothing but dread. The weather reflected everyone's mood.

"Identify yourself," said the guard as Bruce pulled up in his Lexus. He pulled out his driver's license and handed it to the guard. "You're on the list," the guard said, and he took down the number on Bruce's license. "Park in one of the visitor spots and go into the administration building. He'll meet you in room 412. Elevator straight ahead once you enter."

Bruce pulled into the first visitor spot and gathered his briefcase. He also tried to gather himself. He had done nothing but this case for weeks. He was consumed, and he was exhausted.

"Bruce?" said Dr. Terrell as he looked up from his desk.

Bruce extended his hand. "Thank you for seeing me, Dr. Terrell."

"Call me Jack." He motioned for Bruce to take a seat. He was nothing like Bruce had thought. He was good-looking and thin, with a wicked smile. Maybe he was a runner. Well dressed, thought Bruce as he unbuttoned his suit jacket and sat down, grateful he had opted for one of his best suits as opposed to a more casual look.

"Patty is amazing," said Dr. Terrell immediately. "I like her a lot."

"She was really amazing before the seizures manifested," said Bruce. "We went to the same high school. She was a little younger, but a real standout then."

Dr. Terrell took note of the fact Bruce only referred to her being something special in the past tense. "Do you know her now?" he asked, looking directly at Bruce.

"Not so much, now. I know the other Anderson girls better. I stayed in Breckinridge County, and most of them moved away. I was in Hedy's social group in high school, and we've stayed in touch. I'd see her at the airport." Bruce smiled slightly.

"Patty believes people don't see her because of her diminished capacity."

"Well, she might be right," said Bruce, thinking about how he never spoke to Patty directly when he would see Sophie and Patty. "She pretty much quit speaking," he added in defense.

"She speaks now. A lot," said Dr. Terrell.

Bruce did not respond. He got the feeling he was to blame for something.

"Patty wants to admit that she killed her mother. She looks at it as probably her greatest achievement," began Dr. Terrell. "She also would like for people to hear her story. She wants a voice. She wants for people to understand more about child abuse. What happens when you hit a child. She doesn't see jail as much different from her life in her bedroom at Sophie's. She thinks if she is in jail, it will be better for Sophie. That she has been a burden."

Bruce looked at the doctor without comment. He wasn't prepared for these observations.

"I disagree with her on her assumption that jail will be about the same because she also likes the products from Whole Foods," added Dr. Terrell with a slight smile. "She has no idea what kind of people are behind those walls. Jail will be a shock for her."

"Will be a shock," Bruce said with a sinking feeling of defeat washing over him.

"I have looked at every possible way I could come back and recommend an insanity plea. First, she won't agree to it. She wants to plead guilty. Second, she's not insane. A little slower than she was, but even her current IQ falls into the normal category. I appreciated you sending me all the records. Her sisters supplied even more. In fourth grade, she tested 133. I administered a test here, and she came in at 93. I'm sure I don't have to tell you that 133 is genius level, and 93 is the low end of normal but within normal range." Dr. Terrell wasn't even looking at notes. Patty had been the most interesting case so far in his career, and he knew every detail.

"But isn't there some way she can stay hospitalized?" Bruce started pulling at straws as he saw his plan beginning to fall apart. "There is a case pending in New York where a nineteen-year-old stabbed and killed his mother when he was coming out of an epileptic episode. It has been months. I spoke with the attorney, and he says everyone is working together to get the boy a plea arrangement where he will receive private hospitalization out of state. Patty is on Paul's insurance, and it will cover in-hospital treatment. There are a number of good facilities."

"Is that what Patty wants?" asked Dr. Terrell. "Or have you only consulted the family?"

"Patty isn't capable of making her own decisions," replied Bruce. "Her family has her best interest at heart. They would do nothing to hurt her."

"How do you know what Patty wants?" Dr. Terrell countered.

"She wanted to plead guilty," said Bruce. "That very first court appearance. If we had done that, we'd be in the sentencing phase right now, not looking for alternatives to get her the best possible medical care."

"So you blindsided her and pleaded not guilty when she had specifically said she wanted to plead guilty. She even agreed to the mentally ill part, even though she's not mentally ill and she doesn't want to be labeled mentally ill."

Bruce looked at the doctor, unable to decide if he just wanted Patty behind bars, was working in her best interest, or was just some government thug who wanted to make a name for himself in a high-profile case.

"Look, I have to do something in thirty days," said Dr. Terrell in an open tone.

"She has waived her right to a speedy trial," said Bruce, jumping in before the doctor could go on. "Just like the New York case. If everyone agrees, maybe we can work out a plea agreement."

"I have a court order for thirty days," Dr. Terrell said, restating his deadline in the case. "You can waive her right to a speedy trial, even though I don't think she would agree, but I have thirty days."

The doctor paused and wondered how he could phrase his next question without seeming rude to Bruce. "I'm going to ask you again. Do you know what Patty wants?"

"I'm assuming from you she wants to go to jail," said Bruce.

"I don't think she realizes what going to jail means," said Dr. Terrell, "but what I do know is that she wants to be heard. And she wants to take credit for killing her mother. I've tried to imagine if we can go in with some kind of plea bargain that takes into consideration something akin to battered wife syndrome. Battered person syndrome. There have been many defenses built on battered wife/person/husband syndrome, and Patty certainly fits the description. But again, I'm not sure Patty will go for that. She does have the ultimate say. She is not mentally ill."

"There is another case where a forty-seven-year-old woman stabbed her neighbor," began Bruce, happy that the doctor was at least thinking of something other than a straight-up guilty plea and a life sentence. "She received surgery in the form of a temporal lobotomy, and she fully recovered from her seizures. They downgraded the murder charge to manslaughter and she has remained in a psychiatric facility, but she will eventually get out because there was no murder conviction."

"Patty's situation is different. First, she wants to plead guilty to murder, and second, her lesions are inoperable," Dr. Terrell said simply. "She will not get better. She will get worse. If I test her IQ again in a year, she may be in the eighties. But she can surprise you. She is very clever still, on good days. That good mind doesn't go away when she is clear from drug effects or a seizure."

"Are you sure it's inoperable?" asked Bruce. "Maybe that diagnosis is no longer the case. Lots of progress has been made."

"She hasn't been examined for that specifically lately, but I've looked at her records. There is nothing to indicate she would benefit from, or even maybe survive, a temporal lobotomy. Her initial trauma was very severe."

Bruce wondered how Dr. Terrell could say he liked Patty so much. Everything Bruce proposed, the guy shot it down.

"I ordered an MRI, and amazingly, it was approved," said Dr. Terrell. "High-profile case, I suppose. Patty has constant spiking. That means there is an ever-present high possibility for a seizure at any time. She has kept the seizures mostly at bay because Sophie has been standing over her and working constantly on the right combination of drugs. It worries me that she won't get the same care here, and certainly not in jail. If she were here, I could watch over her—and I would—but I'm not sure we can get a ruling that will allow her to stay here. She's really not mentally ill."

"In the New York case," Bruce began again, "the defendant's attorney says they are almost ready to release the young man because his epilepsy is not being controlled."

"I would agree with that for Patty," said Dr. Terrell. "She has a high probability that it won't be controlled in confinement. But in the New York case, wasn't that man coming out of a seizure?"

"Yes," said Bruce, happy the doctor was at least listening. "He really didn't remember his actions, but the mother had called 911, so the phone was open, and the operator heard and recorded everything."

Dr. Terrell nodded, trying to connect Patty's deliberate actions to that of a young man who was coming out of a seizure and completely unaware.

"Patty had cluster seizures the day before the murder. Twelve in an hour," said Bruce. "Sophie thought maybe she wasn't fully out of them or maybe she had a complex partial seizure where she lost consciousness during the crime."

"She remembers the crime well," said Dr. Terrell. "She planned it. I'm surprised about the cluster, but she wanted to make Dorothy pay. She looks at it as an achievement for herself and for all of her sisters, even though they basically marginalize her." Dr. Terrell needed to keep Bruce focused on the facts, not just on finding a magic bullet that would somehow cleanse Patty of a horrendous homicide. A homicide for which she wanted to take credit.

"There are enough cases of violent episodes associated with epilepsy that with some help, I can make a case for at least reducing the charge," said Bruce. He wasn't getting any help here, and Dr. Terrell's assessment was just going to make things more difficult.

"I'm not sure Patty will go along with anything less than a guilty plea," said Dr. Terrell.

"Do you think that is a good thing?" asked Bruce. He had about had it with this guy.

"I'm not sure what to think," began Dr. Terrell. "What I know is that Dorothy took away her life at an early age, and the family, while meaning well, have reduced her to a kind of imprisonment. They take great care of her. They love her, but they ignore her."

"And in pleading guilty, she will improve her situation?" said Bruce in indignation.

"No. But what I am trying to tell you is that I haven't come up with the right answer for Patty either. I don't think you have heard me," said Dr. Terrell. "I am on Patty's side. I want what is best for her, but she rammed a pipe into her mother's neck and killed her in a bloody, horrendous way, and still no one is listening to her story. What does she have to do to be heard?" said Dr. Terrell, looking directly at Bruce.

"I have interviewed every single family member, and they all have her best interest at heart. What they think is her best interest. What happened to Patty is incredibly cruel, but we live in a society where you cannot kill another human being without consequences."

"That's exactly right," said Bruce. "At least Dorothy got closure. Patty has had to live with her own death every day. No University of Kentucky. No quick mind. No children. No lover. No individuation from her twin. No life. Only a bedroom, white gloves, and a police scanner. She knows her life was taken away."

# Thirty One

Bruce sat in his car in the visitor parking spot at the Kentucky Correctional Psychiatric Center and stared off into space. He knew he needed to start his engine and drive away. The guard would be knocking on his window in minutes.

He looked up and saw Dr. Terrell open the big door of the Administration Building, and he almost skipped out. He walked fast, and the gray weather did not seem to bother him. Bruce grabbed the door handle and swiftly left the safety of his car. "Dr. Terrell," he said into the air as the doctor turned in his direction and stopped his sprint across the yard.

When the men met in the middle, Bruce was quick. "I have realized that I was wrong," he said. Dr. Terrell was surprised but registered no emotion. "You are right. I have spent hours and hours on this case, and I have never interviewed Patty. Not even once did it occur to me to make an appointment with her. I was working so hard with the family, it was as if she was not a part of the discussion. I don't know what she wants," he continued, and Terrell simply looked at him without a response.

"Have you thought about meeting with her?" responded the doctor slowly. "You know she is right here."

"I'm not sure about the rules," began Bruce. "Do I make an appointment? Drive back? Go through you? May I interview her during the evaluation?"

"A defendant always has the right to her counsel," began Dr. Terrell. "It is usually by appointment, but it's not as if you have to wait for the weekend and regular visiting hours. You are her lawyer. She has a right to counsel."

"It's two hours each way, and I'm running out of time," was Bruce's response.

"Let me see what I can do. Come on back with me into the office," said Dr. Terrell, again taking off in a near sprint. Bruce followed.

"There are special rooms for attorneys to meet with their clients," said Dr. Terrell as he returned the black phone to its resting place. Prisons were slow to make changes. Landlines were still commonplace.

"She doesn't want to see you," said Dr. Terrell, and Bruce slumped. "I am going to speak with her. I may have to be present. She will be available in about twenty minutes. I will go in first, and then I will bring you in if I'm successful."

Bruce sat up and gave up a small thank-you.

"I really do want what is best for her," said Dr. Terrell, knowing Bruce probably didn't believe him. He really understood all the sides of the situation. Well, with the exception of Dorothy. He would have liked to interview her.

"Do you want something to drink?" asked the doctor, as if this were a social call. He needed to cancel a group session. He thought no one in the group would mind.

"Water would be great," Bruce replied, but he was deep in thought.

Dr. Terrell took note and got up from the desk. He returned with a plastic bottle.

"Somehow I expected a cup of water and not a bottle," Bruce said.

"I bring them in myself," answered Dr. Terrell. "We don't get much of anything here. Budget cuts. The only way I get any money is if I testify that funding something or finding more money will mean safer streets for the general population. The legislators don't care about the people in here. It doesn't matter what they need. I've learned over the years."

"I looked you up," said Bruce, almost embarrassed. "Vanderbilt and Wash U? Why aren't you in private practice?"

"When I first took this job, my partner and I were in debt. School loans. He's an attorney. It was the best-paying job at the time. I enjoyed the work. I don't know, I'm not a religious man, but it really did become my calling. I've heard just about everything. Patty isn't the only one."

"But a gay man in a men's prison?" Bruce said, trying to imagine.

"Oh, I've heard it all. Catcalls just walking across the prison yard. How they'd like to open me up like a ripe watermelon. I don't want to be crude, but you just keep walking. Not much different from growing up in the Deep South at a military boarding high school. Torture. It's about time," said Dr. Terrell, looking at his watch. "Let's walk over and hope for the best."

Everything was institutional, from the highly waxed tile floors to the overpainted windows sealed shut. Bruce had never been inside a maximum-security prison, and he was overwhelmed at its sameness and despair.

They paused and looked into a small room that was nothing more than a glass box that held three orange hard-plastic chairs and a table. Dr. Terrell nodded to the guard, and he motioned for Bruce to take a seat just out of eye's range. He opened the door, and the guard brought in Patty. They sat across the table from each other.

"I don't want to talk to him," she said, simply sitting down and crossing her arms, rocking. She had been released from the suicide suit and was in simple prison clothes. They hung on her small frame.

"He is here to help you," said Dr. Terrell.

"Like pleading not guilty when we had agreed guilty but mentally ill," she said.

"He knows you want to plead guilty."

"Why should I trust him now?" she asked.

"Because I am telling you I have convinced him you want to admit to the murder and be heard. He is your lawyer. He is here. He will be representing you in court, and you should take this time to tell him what you want."

Patty looked off into space. She was torn. She knew Sophie and Hedy and everyone else was paying a lot of money for her to have a good lawyer. How would she get what she wanted?

"Will he be doing all the talking in court?" she asked. "Like before? Will I be able to speak?"

"Do you want to speak in front of all the people who will pile into the courtroom? Remember how it was before? It will be worse." Dr. Terrell was trying to paint an accurate picture of how it would be. "Most people talk through their attorney."

"Most people's attorney say what was agreed to be said." She was adamant and completely rational. Much higher than a 93 today, Dr. Terrell thought. He needed Bruce and Patty to speak.

"I will stay in here," said Dr. Terrell, "and I will help Bruce listen to you. It won't just be you he has to agree with, but me too."

Patty looked at the man with pained eyes. She had had so few people she could trust. So many had let her down. "OK. I'll talk to him if you stay. Sit on my side," she said in a small voice.

"Let me get him. I'll be sure to sit next to you," Dr. Terrell said, and he left the room.

Bruce tried to smile when he saw Patty. She had lost weight. Gray roots were showing through her dark hair. Sophie would never have allowed that. Patty looked up at him with a combination of hurt and anger.

"Hi Patty," began Bruce. "I'm sorry it has taken me so long to see you, but I've been working every minute on your case."

"Why?" she responded. "How hard is it to plead guilty and close the books? Did they bury her?"

"Yes," said Bruce with some relief as he looked across the small table separating him, Patty, and Dr. Terrell. "It was on November third, a Saturday, and the weather was very nice."

"Too bad," said Patty. "Did all the kids come in?"

"No. It was just your sisters and their husbands and Dr. Collins," Bruce said cautiously, not wanting to scare Patty into not talking to him. "They didn't have a mass or anything, and the police blocked off all of St. Romuald so no one else could attend. It was very quick, according to Eva. They didn't even allow the priest to say much of anything."

"Good. That would have made her so mad. No big mass and a church full of people. Thanks," said Patty, easing a little physically.

"Thank you for seeing me," began Bruce, "because I need to work out with you what we are going to do."

"Plead guilty. I killed her," said Patty. "It's not like they don't know I did it. I'm guilty. I took the pipe, and I killed her. I'm glad."

"Are you glad about how you are being treated in here?" asked Bruce. "The food, the clothes, no police scanner or gloves?"

"Dr. Terrell says he is going to get me a police scanner," she replied, now knowing Bruce knew she hated the food and the clothes.

"I said I would try. No guarantees. My guess is that they won't allow it," Dr. Terrell said gently. "Sometimes they don't listen to me. You have been charged with murder, and that is a capital offense."

"Do you know what it means to be charged with first-degree murder?" Bruce said to her gently.

"That I killed the bitch who took away my life. We slept on the floor. We didn't eat. We didn't have clean clothes. The kids made fun of us when we came in the same outfit all week. She beat us. She killed the dog."

Bruce looked at Patty. He had never heard her speak this much. She was not as confused as he had thought. There was no question he couldn't get a not-guilty-but-mentally-ill plea if she spoke this clearly.

"What do you want?" said Dr. Terrell, trying to refocus the discussion he knew needed to go on between his patient and her attorney. Her voice in court.

"I want to plead guilty, and I want the *Courier-Journal* to write a story about why I did it," she said in a clear voice.

Both men simply stared at her.

"A story in the *Courier-Journal*," said Dr. Terrell in surprise. "You've never told me this before."

"You never asked. And maybe *People* magazine. I looked at those when I would go see Dr. Levy. It's hard for me to focus enough to read a lot, but I can some," she said. "I want to plead guilty, and I want to tell people like that ugly mother in Whole Foods not to hit their children. I can show them what happens."

Patty looked down at the table, and then she looked up and said, "And Diane Sawyer. She's from Louisville. I want that the most. Diane Sawyer."

Bruce had never considered this angle. "But if you plead guilty to murder one, then the judge has to send you to prison for life or even give you the death penalty."

"OK," she responded. "If I get to tell my story. Hedy is some fancy advertising person. She'll know who to call."

I know who to call, thought Dr. Terrell, shocked that he could still be surprised. The media would fight for the inside scoop of this story. "So you want to make a difference to the children who are being beaten and not helped," he summarized, and she nodded.

"But do you really want to live the rest of your life behind bars? Not here. Not with me, but at a place called the Kentucky Correctional Institute for Woman? It's in Pewee Valley, closer to Louisville. You probably won't get your medications regularly like you have been getting here, because I won't be around. You won't be my patient. The state will decide they are too expensive, and you will have seizures. A lot of seizures."

Patty thought about the seizures. She liked it when they were controlled.

"What about the food? More bologna sandwiches on white bread?" she asked.

"On good days. No Pepperidge Farm rye bread and tuna from Paul's. No candy from Cellar Door on holidays." Dr. Terrell knew exactly what to say.

"But I have to plead guilty," she said, knowing she hated the white bread that almost stuck to the roof of her mouth. She wanted her police scanner. "I killed her. Everyone knows I killed her, and I want news stories about what happens when you hit a child."

Why hadn't he talked to her before? thought Bruce. This changed everything. She was logical and certainly could help in her defense, even if it was a guilty plea.

"I thought we might have a chance to go with a not-guilty-by-reason-of-insanity," began Bruce as Patty began to rock and shake her head no.

"I won't testify that she is mentally insane," said Dr. Terrell. "She is completely lucid about the murder. She wants to confess and have the story reported in the news. It is a murder-one case. Where do we go from here?"

Patty looked at Dr. Terrell, and she smiled.

"I assume you can see why it has been so difficult for me to write my report," Dr. Terrell said in earnest to Bruce.

"What if we go in with a guilty plea to manslaughter?" said Bruce, wondering how he could get the prosecutor and judge to agree with a reduced charge.

Terrell looked up and smiled. "Ten years minimum sentence, no discretion by the judge, and he could sentence her to more. But if you could work it, she could be out in something like eight years. I'd have to call the parole board to be sure," said Dr. Terrell in a rush, but that would allow her to plead guilty.

"But it was murder, not manslaughter," said Patty in defiance. "I killed her, and I want to talk about it."

Bruce fumbled for his briefcase. "Let me read to you what the law says manslaughter is, Patty," said Bruce, pulling out papers. He shuffled them and then put them down on the table, pointing his finger to a section. "Here is what the law says: Manslaughter is when a person's 'intent is to cause serious physical injury or death,'" he said. "Serious injury or death." It was a eureka moment for Bruce. The family would be disappointed, and the defense would be outraged.

"You would still have to go to jail," said Dr. Terrell to Patty, "but they would sentence you to a jail term, and then you would be eligible for parole. I know you can get your story in the *Courier-Journal* and *People,* maybe even Diane Sawyer. I would want Bruce to argue that there are mitigating circumstances. The epilepsy. The child abuse or battered person syndrome. And get you into the Kentucky

Correctional Psychiatric Center—here—with me. Where I can control your medications."

Patty could tell the men agreed. She wasn't sure. "Can you tell me again what manslaughter is and why it is better if it is still murder?" she said to Bruce.

"It is a lesser charge, but it still covers murder," he said carefully. "It means you had a reason to kill Dorothy and that you just weren't mean and one day thought, 'I want to do something mean, so I am going to kill my sleeping mother,'" he said, knowing what Patty was looking for.

"Because you had a reason to kill her, a very good reason, the court will sometimes agree with you and say you're not a bad person, but a person who has been hurt by the person you killed." Bruce knew he was stretching things, but he felt he had to sell this.

Patty wouldn't be the only person he would have to sell this to. Wait until Kenny Nall and Stanley Dowell heard his proposal. Not to mention the family. They were looking for a magic potion that would make all this go away.

Patty looked at Dr. Terrell, and he nodded his head. "It's still not good," he said, looking at her. "You will have to go to jail for a long time. We don't know if the judge will give you the minimum or the maximum or even if they will take the manslaughter plea, but you will be pleading guilty to killing her, and you can tell people why they shouldn't hit their children or be mean to them."

"Do you know there is an orphanage in Louisville called St. Joseph's?" said Patty, seemingly completely off the subject.

Have we lost her? thought Bruce with more than a little bit of desperation.

"Yes, I know that," replied Dr. Terrell, listening to every word.

"Dorothy always got the *Courier-Journal,* and they would have ads about a picnic every year. I remember reading those and thinking how wonderful it would be if we could just have gone to the orphanage." Patty smiled at the thought.

"I guess I have to take manslaughter," said Patty, returning to the small, ugly room and the two men trying to help her. "But it has to be guilty."

# Thirty Two

This time, Bruce had no trouble starting the engine of his car and pulling out onto the highway. He had two hours of driving and some tough work. He was exhausted in so many ways. How was the family going to take Patty's decision and understand fully that it was absolutely hers to make? He pulled the car off to the shoulder and found his phone. He attached everything needed to make a hands-free call. He had gotten better at managing his personal things since his wife had died of breast cancer four years ago. He still missed her so much it hurt physically. She had been so young.

"Hedy, it's Bruce Edwards," he said when Hedy answered on the second ring.

"I know. I have you programmed in. We don't take calls unless we know who is calling," said Hedy. "Where are you?"

"Between LaGrange and Louisville," he said, not having to add anything. "Where are you?"

"Just leaving the airport," said Hedy as she ran her company credit card into the parking lot machine, which would pay and release her into the general space of Louisville. Seventy-eight dollars. She had been on the road six days. "Orlando, San Diego, Los Angeles, and Chicago," said Hedy into the phone. "I'm exhausted."

"Oh, I was hoping I could talk with you about Patty's case. I've just spent time with her and Dr. Terrell," he said carefully.

"How is she?" asked Hedy immediately.

"About as good as I have ever seen her," he began. "She is thin, hates the food, and wants her police scanner, but she's very lucid, and her medications are managing the seizures well. Dr. Terrell is really looking out for her."

"Wow. That's good news, I guess. What's up with the case? Where are we?" she asked.

"That's what I wanted to talk with you about," said Bruce. "She has some things she won't budge on."

Hedy was just edging onto the Watterson Expressway, heading home. "If you are between LaGrange and Louisville, why don't you go to dinner with me and Barbara so we can have a civilized conversation? We were going to Volare tonight. Half-price bottles of wine and a nice menu. Italian, but American too. Steak, whatever." She had no idea what Bruce liked to eat.

"You sure?" said Bruce, thinking about the last time he had gone out to dinner. Since Katie's death, he sometimes just didn't eat, or he fixed a sandwich. All of a sudden, he wanted to go desperately.

"Totally sure. We need to catch up, and not just on the case. I know the kind of effort you have put into helping Patty. We all really appreciate it. We can talk about the case, but I'll buy dinner if you stop the clock and just relax a bit."

"It's a deal," said Bruce as he thought about all the hours he had not charged Hedy—and still the bills were mounting, especially with the Louisville criminal team that was charging every minute. "Do you want me to meet you at the restaurant? What's the address?"

"Actually, you are probably already in Louisville," she guessed. LaGrange wasn't that far away. "Why don't you come by the condo? We'll probably get there about the same time. Put the address 1400 Willow in your navigation system. The guard will let you in. This will be great."

"Sounds good," said Bruce.

The guard, thought Bruce. Hedy is not living in a fourth-floor walk-up. He smiled as he once again pulled off and fumbled with technology. It didn't take long, and he was on his way to an address called 1400 Willow Ave.

The condo was located in the Highlands section of Louisville—the most lovely part of the Highlands, with sweeping lawns and million-dollar homes in the Cherokee Park Triangle. He could feel himself relaxing as he pulled into a parking space along the circular drive. He looked up and surmised twenty or more floors. High-rises were not part of the Hardinsburg skyline.

"I'm here to see Hedy Miller," said Bruce as he stopped at a small single room that held monitoring cameras and a guard. The attached sign explained visitors had to receive clearance before the doors to the building would be unlocked.

"Are you on her cleared list?" asked the guard as he typed in Hedy's name and waited for the names of her cleared guests to appear.

"No," Bruce said, "I'm sure I'm not, but I just spoke with her. She said she'd be here any minute. Coming in from the airport," he continued, waiting in the little room that was both neat and crowded with flower deliveries and other packages. First-world problems, he thought, getting your packages and flowers.

"Let me call Dr. Collins. I know she's up there. What's your name?"

"Bruce Edwards. I don't think Dr. Collins is expecting me," he said, hoping Barbara would remember his name.

"Dr. Collins," this is Kenny. "There is a gentleman here, Bruce Edwards. He says Ms. Miller is expecting him. Should I let him up?" The guard nodded his head and smiled. "Yes, ma'am."

"She says come on up. It's the sixteenth floor. The elevators are around the back of the lobby. You'll see. Make a left when you get off," he said while punching a button that released the front doors. "Tell Ms. Miller she needs to stay home more," he added affectionately. "She works way too much." Kenny smiled.

Bruce headed for the building, and he caught sight of Hedy's BMW as she whirled into the driveway and waved. She could tell Bruce had managed the guard house, so she punched the garage door and went up into the second-floor entrance.

"Well, this is a nice surprise," said Barbara, standing in the entry-way of the condo waiting for him to exit the elevator. "I know Hedy is on her way home."

"She's here," said Bruce. "I saw her as she entered the garage."

"Oh good," said Barbara. "I'm starving. Are you going to dinner with us?" She was warm, and she led him into an open space. It was as if there were no walls, and the condominium was larger than many homes. The huge bay window, complete with seats, looked out over Louisville, and he caught sight of a UPS plane making an approach to Louisville International Airport. He watched in fascination as it descended with the clouds as a backdrop.

"This is quite the place," said Bruce, looking around.

"It's all Hedy's. I just hang out here. I have a home on the other side of the park," she said, and Bruce thought about what that home might look like. "I've got way too many stairs," said Barbara, "and no one to accept my groceries and dry cleaning." She smiled as they entered the home, and Bruce took a seat looking out over the city of Louisville.

"I am going to dinner with you."

Hedy pushed open the door, dragging a black roller-board suitcase and an obviously heavy backpack. "Sorry I'm late. An accident on Grinstead."

"I don't know why you insist on going the long way home," said Barbara.

"Because I have no sense of direction, and there are signs that point me home on the long way. Give me a break. It doesn't save five minutes, and you have all those lights on Eastern Parkway."

"But rarely an accident," Barbara replied easily. "Look who I found hanging around looking for you."

Hedy dropped the backpack on the floor and released the piece of luggage. "Thanks for coming, Bruce." She reached down to give him a little kiss and embrace. She was comfortable doing that in Louisville, but it was not something either of them had grown up with. It surprised Bruce a little.

"How about some dinner?" she said. "I know you just got here, but I'm starving, and I assume you have a drive back to Hardinsburg tonight. We'll make it an early night."

When they arrived at the restaurant, Hedy got out quickly and smiled at the valet. She didn't need a numbered tag. He knew her car. They were regulars, and she wanted to get into the building quickly. The media was always around. They would protect her in the restaurant.

Hedy looked back at Bruce as he and Barbara followed her. "Let's go to the bar. It's Friday night, so they'll have some good music. Do you mind?"

"Sounds great to me," said Bruce as he followed her to the corner of the bar. They would be able to talk easily.

"A bottle of Fire Road?" said the bartender as he spied Barbara and Hedy.

"I think we are starting to get a bad name," said Barbara as she nodded a yes to the bottle of wine.

"Always a good name," the bartender responded. "I think those are reporters in the corner," he said as he tossed out some paper napkins. "They've been waiting here for about an hour. Nursing a beer."

"Ugh," responded Hedy. "I guess that's what you get when you have favorite restaurants. Our habits are so obvious. We come here a lot on Fridays."

"Josh says we can ask them to leave," the young man continued, referring to the executive chef and part owner, as he twisted open the top of the sauvignon blanc.

"No need yet," said Hedy. "They haven't done anything to ruin our night so far."

"And you, sir?" The bartender looked at Bruce.

"This is my high school friend Bruce Edwards," Hedy said to Shawn, one of their favorite wine pourers. She didn't want to name him as her sister's lawyer.

"What do you have on draft?" asked Bruce as he nodded the acknowledgement of the introduction. He was amazed at Hedy's easiness. She had always been so intense in high school. He'd had no idea what she and her sisters had dealt with.

When the cold Peroni had been placed before him with just enough head, Hedy lifted her glass. "To Friday." And they took a sip of their selected beverages. It was well deserved.

"Not that I just want to jump in and pelt you with questions," began Hedy as Bruce, sitting between the two women, turned to her, "but are we going to be able to get a not guilty by reason of insanity?"

"Patty won't go for it," he said calmly, knowing this might be a long night. He needed to sell Hedy.

"Remember to keep your voices down," said Barbara cautiously. "Just smile, and they'll think you are talking about the menu. Besides, do look at the menu," she said as she handed them forward with a smile plastered on her face.

"What do you mean Patty won't go for it?" said Hedy in surprise. "Patty?"

Bruce laid it out. "She told Dr. Terrell you all treated her like a pet rock, and she wants to take credit for killing Dorothy. That she stepped up."

Hedy paused, staring off into space. She could feel the eyes of the men in the corner boring into her. "Pet rock? She stepped up? Credit for killing Dorothy?"

"Pet rock. She's very talkative. Articulate, even," said Bruce.

"She wants to take credit for killing Dorothy with what? A guilty plea to murder one?" Hedy said in a tone so low Bruce could barely hear it and so filled with disbelief that he could feel it.

"I have talked her out of murder one," began Bruce slowly, giving Hedy the complete picture. "It wasn't easy. That's what she wants." He needed Hedy to understand what he was up against.

"I'm not sure what I can get the prosecutor to agree to, or the judge, but Patty has agreed to nothing less than a guilty plea. She is furious that I pleaded not guilty. Wouldn't talk to me for the longest time. Dr. Terrell had to persuade her. I'm going to try to get the charge reduced because of mitigating circumstances, but both the judge and the Commonwealth Attorney will want a big trial. Roosters, both of them," continued Bruce. Patty was just part of the problem.

"She wants murder one, but that would mean life without parole. I'm trying for manslaughter one. I'll go in with manslaughter two, but that isn't going to fly because of the violence. Everyone will know it's just a starting place," he continued.

"We have everyone's testimony about the child abuse. Plus, the Louisville law firm has an expert who has submitted a strong report about Patty's specific brain injury, the resulting seizures and epilepsy, and how it matches the blow to the head with the golf club." Hedy was trying to grasp what Bruce was saying.

"Tell me again why she wants to take credit?" asked Barbara, a little surprised. "Most defendants want to go for the least amount of jail time, and a guilty plea will mean jail time."

"She feels she has no voice. That while her sisters have taken care of her, she isn't treated as an equal. She also feels that Dorothy took her life, and she wanted to take Dorothy's life. She doesn't care about the consequences," Bruce said.

"Dr. Terrell is very good at painting an accurate picture for her. Bologna sandwiches on white bread, which she apparently hates," said Bruce, while Hedy smiled and thought about Patty's love for Pepperidge Farm rye bread. "And no police scanner. He's trying to get her one, but there are also the bad clothes and mean people."

"And yet she won't cooperate with a not-guilty plea to keep out of jail?" said Hedy as she looked up and saw the staff bringing the setups for dinner. Placemats, napkins with silverware.

"Here's some bread," said a young woman. "Garlic and olive oil." Barbara and Hedy knew the drill and were aware this was just for Bruce's benefit. "Are you ready?" she asked the group.

"I don't think Bruce has had any time to look at the menu," offered Barbara. "Give us just a minute."

"Are we splitting the wedge?" said Hedy to Barbara. Bruce could see the easiness between the two women. He didn't understand being gay, but he also didn't care. He had known Hedy over forty years, and she was just Hedy.

"I'm getting the spaghetti Bolognese," said Hedy, "and I want it all." No entree splitting tonight, as she usually did with Barbara; she hadn't eaten since the buffet breakfast in the Executive Lounge of the Marriott on Michigan Avenue in Chicago. She had just made the Southwest flight out of Midway and the direct ride home. It made Friday travel a little more bearable. She was just beginning to relax a little.

"I like the look of these sliders," said Bruce with an obvious question to his hosts.

"Get two of them. They are great, and they come with fries. Get a salad too," said Barbara. "You look a little thin." Bruce liked being coached by a medical doctor to eat more.

Barbara waved for Shawn and gave him the order and then indicted another beer for Bruce.

"Thanks, but that's it," he replied. "I have to drive back, but it certainly tastes great."

"How has it been?" said Hedy, changing the subject.

"Hard," Bruce replied, closing the menu. "There is no other way to put it. Our daughter, Jess, has just gotten married, so she is settled. Our son, Jay, is an attorney in Louisville."

"Do you eat?" Hedy asked, noticing Bruce's thinness after Barbara mentioned it.

"Not well, and to be honest, I've become obsessed with this case. You never have enough time for research. There is always another case that reflects some aspect of Patty's act of violence, but never a case exactly right. I keep thinking it's out there."

"But would it matter if she isn't willing to work with you fully?" asked Barbara. It was nice having an outside voice who knew how criminal cases worked within the system. Barbara had testified in hundreds. Bruce would love to be able to call her.

"I guess I didn't know how strongly Patty felt about wanting to plead guilty," he said as he looked up and noticed the men had moved to the bar.

"Can we help you with something?" he said directly. "You seem overly interested in our conversation."

"Josh Henderson with the *National Enquirer*," replied the young man as he extended his hand.

Hedy looked up, horrified. "The *National Enquirer*?" she said almost involuntarily. She didn't see the iPhone until it had snapped several photos of the three-person party trying to eat dinner.

The bartender was on it immediately. "Thank you, gentlemen. The beer is on the house, but you'll need to leave," he said as he put a hand under the man's arm.

"What have we done?" griped the camera-phone-toting companion.

"Harassed my customers," said Shawn. "Thanks for coming." He continued shepherding them to the door.

"Maybe this wasn't such a good idea," said Hedy.

"They are gone now," replied Barbara as she looked around at the increased interest among the patrons. People were beginning to recognize them, where before they had seemed like any older adults out for a Friday drink and dinner.

"We've ordered," she continued. "Let's see how everyone reacts after a few minutes. Most people will lose interest, leave us alone. At least the reporters are gone."

"We need to talk," Bruce said as he punched the Caesar salad that had just been delivered. "She had to be convinced to go with manslaughter. Only would take it once I told her that it included the intent to kill."

"You are kidding," said Hedy.

"I know there is no judicial discretion with manslaughter, but the minimum sentence is ten years," Bruce said. "It's ten to twenty, so ten is the best possible scenario."

"So the best we hope for is ten years," said Hedy, pausing her fork in midair.

"There is the possibility of parole, but I'm not sure how long she might have to serve. I'm calling the parole board on Monday, but I think that she has to serve eighty-five percent of her time," said Bruce. "My biggest concern, and the concern of Dr. Terrell, is that she is given the opportunity to serve her sentence at the Kentucky Correctional Psychiatric Center. They have only fifty beds, but he would be there to make sure her medications are monitored. He says if she is sent to the general prison for women in Pewee Valley, the government will quickly decide they are too expensive, and they'll prescribe something else."

"Even if we pay for it?" said Hedy.

"She would be part of the correctional system and unable to receive special treatment," he explained.

"What are our chances for that?" questioned Hedy.

"I really don't know," said Bruce. "I don't know if I can pull all this off anyway. This is best case."

"Best case that my sister serves ten years in prison under psychiatric care," responded Hedy dejectedly.

"She killed your mother in a violent way, wants to admit to the crime, and doesn't care about the ramifications," Bruce said.

"Let's go back to not guilty by reason of insanity," said Barbara. "With a not guilty, she could have day passes in a couple of months, and she would be guaranteed a spot at the psychiatric center, or at least Central State."

"Dr. Terrell won't testify that she is insane, and she won't take a not-guilty plea." Bruce wanted that to be perfectly clear. "My best hope is a reduced charge that she will plead guilty to—manslaughter, because it includes the wording 'intent to kill'—and that I can get her the minimum sentence, and she serves it under a gifted, overworked doctor who has taken a personal interest in her life."

Hedy looked down at her barely touched spaghetti. Maybe she hadn't been all that hungry. "You know Sophie will go crazy," Hedy said to both Barbara and Bruce. She was beginning to realize why Bruce had come to her.

"Sophie, Lily, Eva," said Barbara. "Where do you start?"

"Oh, and she wants a big story in the *Courier-Journal* and *People* magazine," said Bruce as he lifted the small burger to his mouth. "Wow! This is fabulous." Juices dripped onto the plate.

"Has she lost her mind?" said Hedy. "Who has she become?"

"Strong," said Bruce. "She won't be blindsided again. She'll scream out in court guilty to murder one. I have no option but to tell the court what she wants. Dr. Terrell will tell the court she is perfectly sane and able to stand trial. We don't want a trial."

"But big news stories?" Barbara said, returning to the latest twist.

"She wants to tell people what happens when you hit a child," said Bruce. "She thinks Hedy is a big-time advertising person who can get her stories in the *Courier* and *People*. Oh, and I forgot. She also wants Diane Sawyer to do a segment on the case."

"How about the *National Enquirer*? Barbara has been holding off the *Courier-Journal*, and I know plenty of folks at *People*."

"Every news outlet in America has sent fielders," continued Hedy. "No problem there. Barbara and Diane Sawyer are friends. I'm sure she'll happily come back to her hometown of Louisville, Kentucky, and do a special on someone who has killed her mother and insists on pleading guilty. She left *60 Minutes* years ago, but as the anchor of *World News Tonight*, the options are limitless."

Bruce couldn't tell whether Hedy was being sarcastic or actually buying into the plan. He needed her to handle the other family members.

"You know, it's not such a bad idea," said Barbara. "We've hidden it for so long. Aren't we just doing what they did in the fifties? When we see a woman slap her child, do you step in and tell her it's wrong? Probably not. I see dead babies all the time. Give Patty some credit for wanting to tell people the truth."

Hedy just looked at her. Bruce knew to say nothing. This was critical, as he saw the wheels turning in Hedy's head.

"Sophie will go mad. Her whole life has been spent hiding, not talking about things. She would rather die than have our laundry spread over national media." Hedy was adamant.

"You'll have to do some convincing," said Barbara.

Bruce thought he might kiss Barbara right at the bar. "Patty is an adult. Sophie has devoted her life to her, but Patty will tell her story, and the only thing we can do is guide her toward what is the best option for her, without taking away her pride in eliminating Dorothy." Bruce felt as if he had just given a closing argument.

"Do you think we can get manslaughter and ten years at the psych hospital?" said Hedy, realizing what she needed to do.

"I don't know. I just don't know. We have a strong case, but can't you see Kenny Nall wanting a media circus and him sitting ringmaster in the courtroom with a big trial?" Bruce knew Hedy would understand.

"Would you have the trial in Breckinridge County?" asked Barbara.

"If I have to have a trial, I want it in Breckinridge County," said Bruce. "People did know Dorothy. She wasn't just mean to the girls. And they will believe Johnny Flood, who has been practicing medicine there for fifty years. Everyone will believe the truth. I just don't want to put everyone through all that," continued Bruce. "I'm thinking the prosecution may want another venue, but the law says it has to be in an adjacent county most convenient to the parties. That would probably mean Meade County. Not as good as home, but the next best thing."

"So, correct me if I am wrong, but you want me to convince the family that the best thing is a guilty plea to first-degree manslaughter, ten years at the crazy hospital, and publicity all around," said Hedy wearily to Bruce.

"I think I would phrase it a little differently, but basically, yes. You don't want me talking to all of them, spending valuable time, running up your bill. I know you can do a better job convincing everyone. Remember, she is only going to plead guilty to killing Dorothy, and Dr. Terrell will not testify that she is insane. We'll be toast if we try to go in with anything like a not-guilty plea."

# THIRTY THREE

Hedy picked up the phone and called Lily first thing Saturday morning. She knew Lily was an early riser, and she wanted to get her just as the coffee kicked in.

Thanksgiving hadn't been mentioned, and it was coming up on Thursday. Hedy usually did the cooking, but she wasn't up for anything this year. She had maintained a grueling travel schedule and was mentally, physically, and emotionally spent, but she needed to get the conversation rolling. A normal Thanksgiving would have entailed Eva and Don enduring Dorothy all the way to Louisville and back and basically everyone enduring everyone else's company. Tradition. But, if things went according to Hedy's plan, everything would be different this year. At the very least, Eva and Don wouldn't have to transport Dorothy.

The calendar was breathing down Hedy's neck, and she had promised Bruce she'd do the selling. Dr. Terrell would be submitting his report on the Wednesday after Thanksgiving telling the court that Patty was not insane and would be able to assist in her defense. Bruce would be filing all the supporting documents with the court on the thirtieth.

That would mean both the Commonwealth Attorney and the judge would know everything about the case through the filing.

Monday, December 10 had been set for a meeting with Bruce and the Commonwealth Attorney, Stanley Dowell. Bruce was hoping to convince Stanley of what he and hopefully the family thought was best for Patty, yet fair in the eyes of the law. He wasn't asking that an open-and-shut violent murder case be forgiven; he was simply asking for everyone to look at the whole picture. Bruce was even prepared to toss out the desire for publicity. Maybe that would be enough as opposed to a long, protracted trial.

"Is this a good call or a bad call?" said Lily into the phone after reading the caller ID. "The last time you called, it was for cleanup day. That went so well."

Does Lily seem bitter? thought Hedy. Is it all somehow my fault? Lily isn't the only one impacted by this murder. "This is neither good nor bad, but necessary," said Hedy. "We have to talk about how Bruce is going to present Patty's case to the Commonwealth Attorney."

"Can't you just tell me?" said Lily.

"If I tell you, then I'd have to tell Eva, Sophie, Don, Paul, and Howard, over and over. It needs to be a group discussion, and we need to be together. It's not just a matter of me spitting out some of the inevitable."

"Who died and left you in charge?" Lily shot back.

Hedy was so over Lily's bad attitude. Hedy had her own issues.

"What are you proposing?" Lily said, resigned.

"Thanksgiving."

"Oh, please," said Lily. "Haven't we just about had enough of one another? I can't take Sophie wringing her hands and crying much more. I didn't ram the pipe into Dorothy's neck."

"We all rammed the pipe into Dorothy's neck," countered Hedy. "Get over it, Lily."

There was silence, and then, "OK. Thanksgiving. Should we have it at Dorothy's?" Lily said.

"Actually, I was thinking about a restaurant here in Louisville called Captain's Quarters." Hedy didn't like the restaurant at all. Lots of fried food, but she knew she'd get the bill, and the buffet was $21.95 per person, as opposed to the English Grill in the Brown Hotel at $59 per person. Everyone could fill up on fried chicken, turkey, and even green bean casserole. Hedy would have spent more than that on the meat and liquor, not to mention all the cooking, if she actually hosted Thanksgiving.

"They have a private room I can get, so we can talk without people gawking at us and reporters hanging around. Last time Barbara and I went to dinner, the bartender had to escort two reporters out the door." She didn't mention it had been with Bruce.

"That's what you get for having a large-and-in-charge presence in the big city of Louisville," countered Lily.

"Have I done something to you personally, Lily?" Hedy had learned not to take the insults and to call her sisters on their never-ending judgment of her.

"I'm tired," said Lily. "Tired of how everything turned out. It wasn't what I expected or wanted."

Hedy didn't know how to respond. Was she talking about Dorothy's murder? Her personal life? The mess in Washington, DC? The Syrian civil war? Lily never came to the point exactly, but she was always making statements that were vague and unclear with more than just a little snark in them.

"We all have to make adjustments," said Hedy, "and move on. Take what comes your way, and try to make the best of it. Thanksgiving, 1:00 p.m. Captain's Quarters. I'm happy to treat. Will the kids be with you? I have to give them numbers."

"I'm not subjecting my children to a discussion about my sister violently killing their grandmother," said Lily.

Hedy thought about the numerous calls she had made to Drew and how much support he had given her through this wrenching ordeal. "Well, Drew and family obviously won't be coming either. Singapore is too far away, and it's not a holiday there."

Lily made no comment. Anytime Hedy mentioned her son, no one asked about how he was doing. Hedy had sent him to a boarding high school, and everyone thought she had just dumped him, when nothing could have been further from the truth. It had been the best possible situation for him in terms of positive male influences, high academic standards, and a view of the world much larger than the average high school. Today, he was happy, successful, and thriving. Her siblings didn't seem interested.

Eva was her next target because Hedy wanted to put Sophie off until the end. She'd need agreements from everyone else, plus more fortitude than she currently possessed. She hoped the fortitude would build as she put together her plan.

"Thanksgiving," said Hedy after the initial warm greeting with Eva. "Bruce has to file everything with the court next week, and he wants us to know and agree on what he is attempting."

"Why doesn't Bruce explain it to us?" asked Eva in a much nicer tone than Lily's. "Who died and left you in charge?"

"He's going to his daughter's for Thanksgiving," explained Hedy. "She's in North Carolina. He's worked nonstop on this, and the clock is ticking financially." Hedy didn't want to bring up the fiscal aspects too much, but she and Barbara were paying.

"There is this restaurant," began Hedy, and she explained the private room and buffet. No cleanup, no food shopping or cooking. Please, she thought. Eva was normally the most agreeable.

"Don and I will do anything," said Eva, and Hedy gave a sigh of relief. "The kids have other plans, but really, I think it ought to be just us anyway."

"I couldn't agree more," said Hedy, and she proceeded to give out the particulars of the time and place.

When Sophie answered the phone, Hedy could hear the water running. It was always running, and as it was turned off, she could hear Sophie drying her hands. "What's up?" came the reply.

"I've had a discussion with Bruce about the options, and he wants us to be prepared for outcomes. He has to file all the paperwork next week. I thought Thanksgiving dinner would be as good a time as any for all of us to go over things."

"Will Bruce be there?" asked Sophie, wanting to know the lay of the land.

"No. He's going to North Carolina to have Thanksgiving with his daughter," said Hedy. "I'll have to explain the options, but we've gone over them carefully."

"So you have made some kind of agreement, and we are all just supposed to go along," said Sophie.

"No. I didn't have any input at all. Patty is calling the shots primarily" was Hedy's counter.

"Patty." Sophie was not buying it.

"The sister I have taken care of single-handedly most of my life is calling the shots?" Sophie said into the phone. "The sister who doesn't really talk, listens to police radio to calm herself, and rocks to keep the violent seizures at bay. She's calling the shots? Would that be before or after she soils herself in the middle of a cluster attack?" The tone was ugly.

"The medications you have carefully gotten for her are working. I thank you for taking the lead with Patty always. I am personally grateful for everything you have done, and you have done so much it can't be counted," stated Hedy. "But Patty is speaking now, and she has some very clear demands."

"Are we going to get not guilty by reason of insanity?" said Sophie.

"We are not." Hedy didn't want to go into this much detail, but Sophie deserved more. Not telling her would be hurtful and almost like gaming her.

"What do you mean we aren't? Isn't that why we got all the records, made statements, forced Johnny Flood to testify?"

"Initially yes, and it will all be really helpful for Patty in the long run, but she doesn't want not guilty by reason of insanity," said Hedy.

"Doesn't that just show she is insane?" asked Sophie, who had taken a seat and was trying to absorb the information. "They won't let me see her," said Sophie. "I can't advise her. She can't go to jail."

"Bruce is working on all that," said Hedy quietly. "I just thought we could do Thanksgiving in a private room at Captain's Quarters and all have a discussion. A discussion we have to have."

"I'm not sure. Does that mean she'll plead guilty?" Sophie needed answers.

"Yes." Hedy didn't want to go into the details with Sophie alone.

"Jail time?"

"Yes," said Hedy a second time, and she could hear Sophie crying.

"We don't have a choice," began Hedy. "We don't have a choice. Patty took Dorothy's life in a violent manner, and there are laws, regardless of the extenuating circumstances."

"She's better off here," Sophie tried again. "It'll cost the government more to keep her jailed."

"You'll be able to visit her," said Hedy. "Let's put this to rest until Thursday. We'll be able to discuss everything in detail. You'll understand why pleading guilty is the only way."

"No," she sobbed. "There has to be another way."

"There is no other way," said Hedy. "Is Paul there with you?" she asked calmly.

"No, he's working. Somebody called in sick. I'm fine. I'm not going to swallow pills or anything." Hedy could imagine Sophie sitting alone in the house with the dog, crying.

"Will the kids be home?" Hedy tried to bring the discussion around.

"No. They will be in Nashville," Sophie said, almost in a whisper.

"So you have it," said Hedy. "Captain's Quarters at 1:00 p.m. Private room. Thursday."

"I hear you," said Sophie, "but there has to be another way."

"We'll discuss every option," said Hedy. She had read Bruce's rough draft and was convinced that if he could get a reduced charge of manslaughter and a minimum sentence of ten years in the Kentucky Correctional Psychiatric Center, he would have scored a major victory.

When Hedy placed the phone on her desk, she simply stared at it. There wasn't a better way. She felt a complete sickness wash over her. Lily was right—life hadn't turned out the way anyone had originally expected.

Hedy reached for the phone and scrolled through the contacts. She never called Paul at work, but she was worried. He would have to get Sophie to the restaurant, and he would ultimately have to convince her of the overall plan.

"Is something wrong?" Paul said immediately when he saw Hedy's name and number.

"Well, yes and no," said Hedy. Paul was so level headed she could almost feel the gratitude in her body.

"I've just spoken with Sophie. I've had to tell her that Patty is going to plead guilty. I haven't told her everything, and the rest of the details aren't going to be any better. I've had a long discussion with Bruce, and he is going to suggest attempting to get the murder charge reduced to a manslaughter charge. That would mean ten years in jail for Patty at the very least."

"Parole?" said Paul.

"Bruce is going to call the parole board, but since there is violence, he thinks she'll have to serve most of the time. He's going to try to get her into the Psychiatric Center, but they have limited beds." Hedy was rushing though the information.

"Patty will only plead guilty," said Hedy. "Sophie doesn't believe it, but it's the absolute truth. She wants to take credit for killing Dorothy. Says it is the best thing she has ever done."

Paul didn't say anything for a few seconds, and Hedy waited for him to process.

"It probably is the best thing she has ever done," replied Paul with a note of defeat. "What do you want from me?" Paul was no nonsense and without judgment.

"There are a lot more details," said Hedy. "I have proposed we have Thanksgiving dinner together at Captain's Quarters. It's a buffet, and we can have a private room. Nobody wants to do much, but it is a holiday. So everyone is off, and we can discuss all the options. Bruce gave me a rough draft of what he is submitting to the courts. I only got it last night, but I'm not sleeping, so I read it completely. He's done an excellent job."

He stood and followed her without resistance, and they started down the hall, her magnetic card opening locked doors and lights popping on when they detected motion. Hedy just followed.

Barbara wanted to feel Paul's hands to see if they were clammy. She attempted to access him physically. He was moving, but he had a vacant look in his eyes. He moved slowly, but he was responding to her verbal commands. People reacted differently to traumatic events. She need to wear her medical hat.

"I can start making some calls," offered Hedy once they were in the office. She seemed steady and calm. Barbara knew better. "I can call Eva and Lily, but I think the kids should hear it from you," she said to Paul in a slow, calm tone. "We don't have to do anything right this minute."

"She didn't want any more in the newspapers," he said. "It was like Patty betrayed her. She couldn't take any more." He and Sophie had been together so long, had essentially grown up together. He didn't need a note from Sophie to explain her desperation.

"You don't have to explain anything to us," said Hedy. "I just wish we hadn't argued. I wish things had gone better. Maybe I could have explained it better."

"On the way home, she said she had come to realize that Patty really did want to plead guilty. That she remembered that first night how she wanted to take credit for Dorothy's death. She seemed OK with everything, but I guess she wasn't." Paul continued to stare off into space.

The chief deputy knocked at the door, and Barbara went to answer it. She slipped out of the room and held the doorknob behind her so the door couldn't be opened without resistance from her.

"The police beat reporter is here. Wants to know if we have any unusual cases, anything happening. He's just fishing. I don't think he knows anything."

"Have you finished the autopsy?" Barbara asked.

"Haven't even started," came the reply. "She just came in. How fast do you think I can go?"

"I'm sorry," said Barbara, realizing the absurdity of the question. "Well, I guess you don't have anything to report unless there is another case you want to call his attention to."

"Car accident, Twenty-Second and Broadway," he said. "It's been a slow night so far. Probably will pick up once we find a dead body or two after a Thanksgiving gone bad. My family—Thanksgiving dinner is like a WWF SmackDown! Probably a couple more just like mine," he continued, and Barbara tried not to think about the scene at the Captain's Quarters.

"Thanks," said Barbara, making sure she didn't directly tell him to lie to the reporter. She might have to call in another favor from Joe Cross. She reentered the room, and Paul continued to stare.

"You'll need to stay with him," said Hedy, realizing her brother-in-law had grown paralyzed. "I'm going into the office next door and start the calls to Eva and Lily. They can call their children, but I'll caution them that Paul hasn't called his yet. We'll need to do that sooner rather than later," she continued, all business. Barbara worried about when it would all hit Hedy.

Hedy didn't think it was possible that she was back making calls to the sisters. The bad thing was that now, she only had to make two calls.

Howard picked up the phone on the second ring just as Hedy looked down to see that it was about five thirty in the morning. Hedy was grateful they still had a landline, which virtually assured someone would answer in the early morning hours. "Hedy," he said in an urgent tone. "This can't be good." Lily was sleeping in another bedroom.

"It's not," replied Hedy. "Sophie took her life last night. Paul was at work. She hung herself." Hedy didn't know any other way to deliver the news. She was glad she was speaking to Howard.

"Wait," said Howard as if he needed to stop the world from spinning. "Sophie killed herself?"

Lily had walked into the room and heard Howard. "No," she screamed. "No." She took the phone out of Howard's hand. He let go easily and said, "Hedy."

"Hung herself from the back deck. Executed it perfectly. Barbara got the call this morning from her chief deputy. She's with Paul right now. He found her and identified her. He was called into work last night. We are here at the morgue."

There was nothing more to be said. Lily stood looking down at the floor, holding the phone. "I know we argued," she started, "but it wasn't any worse than usual." Lily was trying to make sense of something that made no sense. Didn't everyone argue?

"I don't think it was just last night," said Hedy. "If I thought that, I might have to follow suit because she really only argued with me.

"Paul isn't doing well. Once the body was identified, the chief deputy put it all together, and he called Barbara. Paul just sat in the lobby of the morgue and didn't move."

"Should we come?" said Lily indecisively. "What could we do?"

"I don't know what Paul wants. He needs to call the kids, but he's frozen. He says she was the best he'd seen her in weeks when they were driving home yesterday afternoon. He's just paralyzed."

"What about Patty? Who is going to tell her?" Lily was coming together mentally. "Why would she do this?" Lily almost screamed. "Who knew she was that bad? Why didn't we see it?"

"I feel as guilty as anyone," said Hedy. "I feel I should have explained it better. Maybe cautioned Barbara not to speak. It was hard to know what to do." Hedy felt a heaviness she couldn't shake. She knew she'd have to make most of the calls. "Can you call Eva? I'm going to try to get Bruce. I've got his cell. It'll get to the newspapers. I never know how they put it all together," said Hedy, almost talking to herself. "We'll need to get prepared. They can't get to Patty."

"Patty," said Lily. "What will she do without Sophie?"

"I'm sure Barbara can get me Dr. Terrell's phone number. They have internal phone lists. Maybe Bruce can make a statement. She was just swinging in the wind," Hedy said, closing her eyes and trying to hold back the tears. "We're all unraveling. I don't want to imagine that anything more can happen." Hedy was fighting becoming paralyzed herself.

"We'll drive to Louisville," said Lily, "later this morning. I'll call my kids. No need waking them up with this news when they can't do anything."

Hedy fumbled with the phone. She couldn't seem to make the contact list work. She was confused. Sophie was dead. Her sister. What could she have done differently?

Barbara came to the door and took the phone out of Hedy's hands. She put her arms around her and let Hedy dissolve into tears. Her shoulders shook, and her hands went limp. "What more could I have done? Differently? Better? Why did she think this would be a solution?"

"You don't need to make the calls," said Barbara.

"I do. I always do," said Hedy. "You don't understand."

"I understand," said Barbara, holding Hedy's phone tight. "I know I can call Bruce, and I can call Dr. Terrell. Let Lily call Eva."

Hedy shook her head. No one had ever helped her. No one had ever taken over for her. She was the one who did everything. She made it bearable. Sugar to take away the hunger. Bread and butter in the attic. She looked at Barbara and couldn't imagine someone could take the calls off her plate.

Then she remembered. "You shouldn't have mentioned the Whole Foods thing," Hedy said to Barbara, thinking about Sophie's reaction to the story about the little boy. "Sophie didn't like that." Hedy felt herself slipping back into that little girl. The six-year-old who had to keep the balls in the air. "You don't know how the game is played." Could she trust Barbara? Hedy couldn't feel her fingers.

Barbara pulled Hedy up by her shoulders and looked into her face. "I know how you think the game is played, but the rules are sick, based on Dorothy's mental illness. Me telling the Whole Foods story did not make Sophie commit suicide." Barbara knew she had to get through to Hedy. To the Hedy who had been in therapy for so many years.

"Denial was Sophie's way of coping. Denial. Denial. Denial. It may have worked when she was a child, but the damage it did in adulthood is why she committed suicide. Patty wanted to speak to that mother in Whole Foods, but Patty was pulled along in Sophie's world of denial. Patty is over lying and hiding. She wants to be heard. We needed to put it out there. We need to stop acting like everything was normal."

"Oh, I think we have gone way past that" was Hedy's response. Why was Barbara being so mean? Hedy reached for the phone. "My mother was murdered by my sister, who is in a psychiatric hospital, and my other sister just jumped off the balcony with such precision she let everyone know this was not a cry for help but a loud shout about how much she wanted to die."

"End the pain. End hiding. Stop the playmaking that everything is OK. It's not OK," said Barbara, looking directly into Hedy's face, knowing she was a little too close for comfort.

Hedy got up and walked across the room. She needed to get away from Barbara. She needed to think. "I've got calls to make," said Hedy simply. She would gain control. She was always in control.

Barbara reached over and took Hedy in her arms. "I can do this for you. You don't have to be strong all by yourself anymore. I can do this for you."

Hedy couldn't answer. She didn't know what to do. If she didn't control the situation, something bad would happen. It always did. If she went to sleep, she always woke up with Dorothy standing over her, ready to come down on her with her shoe. She'd be unprepared. She had to stay in control. She thought about the game where little heads popped up and people tried to whack at them and push them back down. She didn't know what to do. She didn't have her phone. She didn't want to be whacked.

Hedy slid down the wall and sat on the floor. Her legs could not hold her. She put her head down on her knees, and she started to cry. A cry she had been holding in for so long she didn't know how she would ever stop. She felt her body go limp as she sobbed.

Barbara knew she needed to let her cry. Cry for years if you have to, thought Barbara. You have earned it.

Barbara had left Paul with her chief deputy. She had written a script for medication that would allow Paul to sleep. Or at least start to cope with what he had found. Sophie was his whole life. Sophie and the children. Sophie, Patty, and the children. Now he had an empty home and a broken life. A pretend life shattered. Denial wasn't good for anyone. She thought about the next generation of Anderson children and the damage that had been inadvertently dealt them. Sophie and the others had tried to give them the perfect childhood the original sisters had been denied but they had failed.

Barbara didn't have enough hands. The mille-feuille of today's challenges kept her from knowing where to start. She was desperately grateful for her staff, who were getting prescriptions, keeping reporters at bay, and making sure the office continued to run. The Friday after Thanksgiving was supposed to be a day off for Barbara.

"I need to call someone," Barbara said to Paul, spelling her chief deputy, who went next door to Hedy. "How about your sister?" Barbara said, referring to Paul's younger sister.

Paul looked up at her as if he were seeing her for the first time. "Sophie really never liked you," he said bluntly.

"I know," said Barbara, "but she sometimes she didn't like herself. I didn't take it personally. I knew what Dorothy had done. Sophie was a victim too."

"I liked you," Paul continued, completely void of the filter he had always operated with, which was actually Sophie's. "I was glad when Hedy found you. I didn't care that you were a woman. I knew you made Hedy happy."

"Thank you," said Barbara slowly, reaching for Paul's phone. "Is her number in here?" She needed to keep him focused and not wander off on a conversation better left for later. She had been around the family long enough to know Paul's sister, Sandy, was her best hope. There wasn't an Anderson who could provide anyone comfort; rather, they would need more comfort than anyone could possibly give. Dorothy was one thing, their sister was another.

When she was finished giving Sandy directions to the morgue, she felt Hedy's phone vibrate. Under usual circumstances, she would never answer the phone. She looked at the caller ID and went into the hall.

"Hedy Miller's phone," said Barbara, wanting to take Mike Dewitt off balance. "It's Barbara Collins," she said, knowing he knew exactly who she was.

"Is Hedy available?" he asked slowly, unsure what was happening. Hedy always answered her own phone.

"No. Her sister committed suicide last night, Mike, and she can't come to the phone." Barbara knew Hedy would be furious.

"The sister who killed the mother?" he asked, as if he were referring to some television show.

"No. The twin sister of the one who killed her mother." Barbara wanted that to sink in. "Doesn't Hedy have sick time or something? Is the agency even open today?" She knew it technically wasn't.

"Sick time?" said Mike, puzzled. Who took sick time? "I guess she does. It's in the benefits manual," he began, realizing he had never taken a sick day. He barely took vacation, and when he did, he managed calls the entire time. He and his wife had had more than one argument about the demands of the agency.

"Suicide? Will this be in the newspapers?" he asked slowly.

"Yes. I'm trying to control the press, but yes, it will be in the papers, right beside the headline about the sister who killed her mother, Mike," she began slowly. "Hedy is hurting right now. Can you cut her a break?"

"I'll try, but you know —"

"I know," said Barbara. "I know as well as anyone. But please, I'll have her call you as soon as she has regained some composure." She hoped he heard the message.

"I'll tell Rachel, but she really won't like this. The mother story was just dying down with the clients. Now this. Will there be a trial?"

"We don't know." Barbara didn't even attempt to be warm. "We are working on a plea bargain, and that will also be in the media." Hedy had learned how to cope with being abused at home, so she didn't even realize when she was being abused at work. How much could Hedy hold, wondered Barbara, before she blew apart? She thought about her crying, sitting on the floor. She didn't want to think about it and knew her chief deputy would come get her if things started to disintegrate.

She took Hedy's phone and scrolled through the contacts until she found Bruce Edwards. It was early, but not as early as it had been when Barbara had first thought about calling him. Paul's sister had arrived, and she was helping. Hedy continued to sit on the floor. Barbara worried about the others. She could only do so much.

"Hedy," said Bruce into the phone.

"No, it's Barbara," she said quickly. "I've got some bad news."

"Something wrong with Hedy?"

"No, it's Sophie. She committed suicide last night." Barbara wanted to give Bruce a moment.

"Sophie?" he said hesitantly. "Sophie. Why?"

"Who knows why? She was abused and living a life of denial. Patty wanting to plead guilty and have news stories was just too much. I don't know," said Barbara. "I do know we need to do something about Patty. The media. It's a lot for me to hold everything down."

"How did she do it?" he said, attempting to process.

Barbara wondered why that was the first question everyone always asked. "She hung herself. Paul found her." She was already tired of explaining.

"I wasn't flying back until Sunday," said Bruce. "I've been working on the case the whole time, but this will change things."

"In a good way or a bad way?" she asked.

"Good, primarily," said Bruce. "Lots of sympathy. The depth of tragedy. The ramifications of abuse."

Barbara wanted to ask Bruce for help, but she could feel that none was coming. She was on her own. He was consumed by the case. She would continue to manage the unthinkable.

"Sophie," he said sadly. "Why didn't she talk to someone?"

There was no answer. Barbara took a breath. "I know this will impact the case," she said, giving into the remoteness of Bruce. She realized slowly that he needed to block everything else out. "Do you need anything from me?" she asked.

"The autopsy report," he said. "I assume she's in the morgue."

"We're all in the morgue," replied Barbara. "Paul is not moving. I've got his sister here. Hedy is beyond buried in grief. The others are coming in. I'm trying to control the media, and I have Patty to think about."

"Patty will have Dr. Terrell," said Bruce, coming around to everything that was happening. "Call Dr. Terrell. He'll know what to do. God. What more can happen?" Bruce said to no one in particular and certainly not to Barbara.

"We had an especially ugly meeting with everyone yesterday," said Barbara, suddenly remembering she needed to let Bruce know they had all discussed what he was proposing.

"Are they onboard?" he immediately asked.

"They know they don't have a choice. Sophie was totally against it. She wasn't able to hear that Patty wanted a voice. That she wanted to plead guilty. It's a moot point now." Barbara couldn't believe she had just said that.

"Call Dr. Terrell. Keep me in the loop. Let me know what to expect from the press," he said. "I assume you have some friends," he said bluntly.

"I do, and I'll call them as soon as I call Dr. Terrell. Call us if you have questions," Barbara said. When she hung up, she wondered what she had expected from him. It was good he was so focused on the case.

Barbara had to go into several files to get the cell number for Dr. Terrell. She knew she was accessing information she probably shouldn't, but she had gone somewhere new. She didn't care anymore. She needed to take care of Hedy and Hedy's family. Apparently no one else had. She thought about Mike Dewitt and got irritated anew.

She used her personal cell phone and waited for him to answer. It was going on eight in the morning. "Yes," came the simple reply. She knew he didn't know who was calling and was a little surprised he answered the phone.

"It's Barbara Collins," she said. "Chief medical examiner," she added for good measure.

"Oh, yes, Barbara ..." She could tell he was confused as the sentence paused in midair.

"I'm sorry, and I know this is probably unprofessional, but I felt I had no choice but to call you. Sophie, Patty Anderson's twin sister, successfully committed suicide by hanging herself last night." She didn't want to answer any more questions about details, so she tried to put it all in one big statement. "It came after a particularly ugly discussion about next steps for Patty. Professionally, I think she felt boxed in by the guilty plea and Patty's need for media."

There was silence. Barbara hoped he didn't feel she should have taken different channels to contact him; it would have just meant hours of delay, and Barbara was efficient if nothing else.

"I'm so glad you called," he said. "I probably wouldn't have checked messages today." He was calm, professional. "The question

336

is that someone will need to tell Patty and manage the ramifications. Of course, the remaining siblings won't be allowed into the facility. Besides, I am sure they are fraught. Her attorney would be able to speak with her and then me." Dr. Terrell was putting everything together.

"I've spoken to Bruce Edwards," said Barbara in an equally professional tone. "He is in North Carolina for the holiday and won't be back until Sunday night. Are you in a position to break the news to Patty?" she said, making it clear they wanted him there when Patty found out about Sophie.

"I think that might be best," he replied, and Barbara felt a sudden rush of relief. "I'm not sure how she will react. I'm surprised by her every day, but I'll watch to see how the information settles in," he said. "I'll go to Patty now. I was just reading the *New York Times*. Nothing like the Old Gray Lady," he said. "You know, Patty is a very interesting case. It's been a bright spot in my professional career. I'll let you know how it goes."

Barbara hadn't expected the last part, but she was infinitely grateful.

Her next call would be the last, and then she would check on Hedy.

"You never cease to amaze me," came the response when Joe Cross picked up the line. "You are definitely on my holiday card list," he said with such exuberance that Barbara was taken aback. She could only assume he knew nothing.

"Another favor," she began, "but this time you'll be glad." Barbara had started to use the word *happy*, but she then realized no one would be happy about this tragic turn of events. He could be glad, though, that she was giving him the inside scoop on the story. The poor beat reporter from last night had left like a lamb and would be kicking himself as soon as he found out Joe had the story. It had taken years to build up the trust, contacts, and luck.

"Patty Anderson's twin sister committed suicide last night by hanging," said Barbara, and she was immediately hit with a wall of silence.

"I'm so sorry, Barbara," Joe said, and Barbara knew he meant it. "How awful. How is Hedy?"

"She's a mess," said Barbara simply, feeling an urgency to get off the phone. "I know it has to be reported, but I hope you can contain it a little," explained Barbara. "I can pretty much guarantee you full-blown access to the whole story once everything is complete." Barbara knew he'd get that anyway, but he didn't have to know it now.

"The police beat reporter didn't pick up on anything," commented Joe easily.

"Sometimes information is slow on a busy holiday weekend," said Barbara, hoping he felt lucky because she could stall things. "I think there was an automobile fatality last night."

"Yeah, I read about that one. Thanks, Barbara. I'll follow up with the chief deputy. Let me know if I can do anything, really." And there was a pause. "I can't imagine how hard this must be for Hedy and the family. I really am sorry." It was genuine.

# Thirty Seven

Dr. Terrell called the correctional facility and let them know he would be coming in and he needed Patty Anderson for a session.

"Really?" came the reply from the nurse on duty. "The Friday after Thanksgiving? She's such a drama queen. Even got you coming in extra hours." He disliked this particular nurse intensely, but he reminded himself he would not stoop to her level. She acted as though nothing was out of bounds. She was homophobic and often left pamphlets from her church that addressed the sin of homosexuality. He routinely picked them up and tossed them in the trash.

"I'll be in for a 10:00 a.m. session," he said, not addressing her other comments. "Just have her in my office, please."

Patty seemed in particularly good spirits when she was delivered to his door.

"Can you tell me why they have given me tennis shoes to wear?" she said without any normal pleasantries.

"Because that is what everyone is given. Khaki clothes and canvas shoes. Have you looked around?"

"I just figured no one else had nice shoes," she said, and Dr. Terrell thought about the drama queen comment. Patty had probably been asking about her police scanner, white gloves, and now, decent shoes.

"You look nice, Patty," he said, "regardless of the shoes."

"Is that inappropriate?" asked Patty. "Sophie always told me not to listen when people started talking about my looks or stuff. That there were bad people out there."

"All correct," he said, "but I'm not a bad person, and I didn't mean it in an inappropriate way. I'll watch it, though. You are absolutely right."

"We had a decent meal yesterday," Patty reported unsolicited. "Turkey and Thanksgiving stuff. It was great. Did you have turkey yesterday?"

"Let's talk about something else, Patty," he said, beginning to set up the conversation. It was inappropriate for him to talk about his meal with a client, even though the meal had been especially delicious. His partner was a gourmet cook.

"Sophie died last night."

"She died? How? Did someone ram a pipe in her throat?" Patty asked calmly.

"No, she hung herself," said Dr. Terrell intently, watching her response.

"Oh," came the answer. "Suicide."

"Yes. Sophie took her own life. She died."

"That is a bad thing to do," Patty said. "A very bad thing. Something Sophie would tell me not to do."

Dr. Terrell remained quiet. He didn't need to say it again.

"Was she angry?" asked Patty as she pulled back her hair, which was growing too long for her to keep easily. Gray roots were becoming pronounced. "I guess she was angry with me."

"Why do you think she would be angry enough with you that she took her own life?" he asked.

"Because I wasn't supposed to ever say anything." Patty looked down and started to cry. "I didn't want to make her mad." She began scratching her arms with her nails, and red whelps began to rise. "I just needed to say what happens when you hit children."

The tears rolled down her face, and Dr. Terrell wanted to reach over and wipe them away, but he instead pulled out tissues from his desk drawer and placed them on the corner of his desk.

"It's good I'll be in jail," she said simply. "I'll have a home and food."

Dr. Terrell slowly began to realize the amount of pressure and dismissive behavior Patty had endured. Sophie probably had no idea. Sophie had tried to do her very best, but she had treated Patty as a pet rock, and Patty's emotions had been squeezed for so long she was dry.

"I love Sophie," she said. "I always have. She took care of me. I know it. I'm sorry if I made her so angry she killed herself."

"I don't think it was you," said Dr. Terrell.

"It was me," she said dejectedly. "I could always make her mad. Sometimes I thought she would hit me like Dorothy, but she never did."

Patty looked around the room, surveying her new reality. "She never came to visit me."

"The judge wouldn't let her visit," Dr. Terrell said. "She wanted to come see you."

"What happens now?" asked Patty.

"Well, I'm sure there will be a funeral, and then you'll have your court date, so you will see the family then. Your attorney will present your case, and then we'll see what the judge says is going to happen next."

"Will I get to go to the funeral?" she asked, already knowing the answer.

"I don't know when it is going to be, but my guess would be no. Are you still going to plead guilty?" he asked.

"Why wouldn't I plead guilty?" she said in astonishment. "What difference would Sophie killing herself make?

"I would like to go to the funeral," she said, "but I guess it wouldn't be good for everyone." She put her hands in the air and said, "Crazy murderer sister attends funeral of twin she drove to suicide." She stopped and looked at the doctor's face but could not read anything. She hadn't had a seizure in over a week, and she wasn't groggy from the medication. "Besides, who would get me dressed? Paul is married to Sophie. I am just baggage."

Dr. Terrell tried to imagine the depth of Patty's wounds. Hurt was an inadequate word. She had been cared for physically but emotionally stabbed over and over and over. He wasn't surprised by her reaction to Sophie's death. There was nothing more that could be taken from this woman.

"I'm tired," she said, looking up at him. "I'm really tired. May I go to my room?"

"Yes," he said, "but I think it would be good if we put you back in the suicide prevention smock."

"Because Sophie killed herself?" she replied without emotion. "Whatever."

# THIRTY EIGHT

The story broke across the country like a crashing wave. Hedy could feel herself tumbling, as if she had lost her balance in the ocean. Things were happening so fast she couldn't keep up, and the waves just kept coming. Other people were pulling the strings. Paul's family had set up visitation times and a mass at the Catholic church that Sophie and Paul had attended for years. The sisters were told when to appear where.

"What should I wear?" she asked Barbara, who, it seemed, had joined Paul's family, making decisions and giving orders. Hedy couldn't remember what day it was or what she was doing. She had stopped making or receiving calls. Dorothy's death had been one thing, but Sophie's had broken her. She wished they hadn't argued.

"That black dress is nice. Eileen Fisher is always in style. It will be a long day, and you'll want to be comfortable."

She heard Barbara, but what did she mean? Hedy reached for the dress.

"It is the visitation," said Barbara, recognizing that Hedy was not functioning. "It's December third. Monday. We'll be at the funeral home from 1:00 p.m. until 8:00 p.m., and then the funeral will be to-morrow, Tuesday, December fourth."

"Yesterday was Dorothy's birthday." It seemed an odd comment to Barbara. "That means we missed Lily's birthday too. Hers is December first," Hedy continued, slipping on the approved black dress. "I guess it would have been inappropriate to celebrate.

"It's not hard to remember everyone's birthday," said Hedy. "Well, except mine."

Barbara didn't answer. She knew every Anderson sister's birth-day was on a first of the month except Hedy's, whose birthday was on the eleventh. January first, December first, and April first for the twins.

"So fat you had to have two ones instead of a single digit," said Hedy to herself, mocking one of Dorothy's favorite sayings.

Barbara had begun watching Hedy carefully, worried about her mental state. Too much had happened, and she had slipped into a world caught between reality and childhood. Everything she spoke of was about Dorothy or Sophie. Past tense. Present tense.

"We don't have to stay the entire time," said Barbara. "We won't know a lot of the people, and that is too much time for one person."

Hedy didn't respond as she applied makeup and attempted to cov-er up her distorted face. So much pain.

People came, and they all smiled. They accepted condolences and tried to put names to faces. There were so many people, the line never abated. Many were sincere, and many more were just curious.

"We haven't seen Patty since the arrest," said Hedy bluntly to some person who attended mass with Sophie's family. "We hear she is doing as well as can be expected."

"Sophie took real good care of Patty. I'd see them at the grocery or the drug store. Always took real good care of Patty," said some woman in a flowered polyester dress.

Where do you buy a dress like that? thought Hedy as she shook the woman's hand and nodded in agreement. "Thank you," she said for the four millionth time.

The funeral was no different. A blur of black cars and people. The priest recalling Sophie's work at the church, the school, sports teams. Her undying devotion to her children, who were in as much of a fog as Hedy and the rest of the family. A note would have answered so many questions for so many.

Barbara seemed to be everywhere. Standing in publicly for the family and making sure Hedy drank from a cold bottle of water.

"No comment," said Bruce as he headed toward his car. He seemed to be in a bad mood. The world was spinning, and the circus music was getting louder. Hedy tried to hold on, but she couldn't grasp anything stable. Things moved all around her. Food was put in front of her, and she ate when Barbara told her to eat. Why are we doing this? she thought, and then she was in front of a gaping hole in the earth. Someone gave her a flower, and holy water was being sprinkled on the coffin. She tossed her flower in with the others, and Barbara was holding her arm. "...return to the earth," she heard. And then the music stopped.

"You seem to have slept well," said Barbara as she sat at the dining room table and folded the newspaper into a neat rectangle.

"What day is it?" asked Hedy.

"Thursday, December sixth. You've been sleeping," Barbara said. "I gave you something."

"I thought you limited your practice to dead people," said Hedy as she reached for a soda and a clean glass. "Am I dead?"

"Not yet," she said. "Not yet, but I do think everyone in Breckinridge County drove to Louisville just for the show. It might have come close to killing you."

"Most of them were really nice," said Hedy as she sat down at the table with Barbara. "But you are right. Some were there to see just how bad we looked. They got a lot for the trip. We all looked really bad."

"Bruce has filed all the paper work," began Barbara, believing Hedy was actually coming back to this current world, and she had no intention of commenting on how anyone looked. "He said he'd call if he heard anything."

"I can't take much more bad news," said Hedy. "Speaking of bad news, did you see that the advertising agency sent flowers?"

"About the biggest one. I guess they don't realize how much bigger you can buy in Kentucky as opposed to New York City," said Barbara.

"I guess you can look at it that way, or they were trying to look as though they cared, which they don't," said Hedy. "They could care less if I jumped off the balcony, as long as I make the numbers in the quarter."

"Aren't you being a little cynical?" Barbara said. "You are a nationally recognized expert. They care about that. They put together an unbelievable package when they persuaded you to leave J. Walter Thompson."

"That was then, this is now. Rachel Weiss hasn't spoken to me in about three years."

"Maybe you should speak to her," said Barbara. "I have to call the governor every once in a while."

"I don't care anymore," said Hedy. "I never thought I'd say that because I've always absolutely loved what I do professionally. But I don't care, and I don't like Rachel Weiss. I don't think she has a soul."

"I've been in touch with Mike Dewitt," said Barbara, knowing she was going onto thin ice.

Hedy's head jerked up, and she asked, "You've what?"

"Did you think he just wasn't calling? For days? Someone had to call him. I let him know you will continue to be on sick leave until at least December fourteenth. The sentencing may be as early as December twelfth, so I thought you needed the time. That would put you back to work on December seventeenth."

"You shouldn't have done that," said Hedy slowly.

"He said he'd call you on December fourteenth, check in, see how you are, how things are with the clients. Nine in the morning."

The roar in Hedy's head almost made her see nothing but black. December fourteenth, she thought. December fourteenth. Almost Christmas.

# Thirty Nine

Bruce waited for a moment before he entered the office of the Commonwealth Attorney. He fully realized the importance of this meeting. Getting Patty the plea bargain would define his career and give her part of her life back. Whatever part was left for Patty. He picked up the files and opened the door of the car.

"Bruce," said Stanley Dowell as Bruce entered the door of a modest office. "May I get you some coffee? Water?"

"I'd love a bottle of water," answered Bruce, not commenting that he hated coffee and had never even had a single cup. Didn't even like the way it smelled.

"You looking forward to the big trial?" said Stanley as he took his place behind a large wooden desk. Bruce took note that Stanley wanted to be in control and comfortable. It would have been normal for the men to meet on more neutral territory, such as a conference table. The gesture was telling.

"Is that what you have in mind?" answered Bruce. Stanley knew what Bruce wanted because it had been filed in his brief.

"I think we should have a change of venue to begin with," said Stanley. "Somewhere in Northern Kentucky. Far, far away from all the people who know the family. You couldn't find twelve unbiased people in Breckinridge County even if you waited a hundred years and everyone alive today had died."

"That's a little dramatic," commented Bruce, thinking how much bigger the media imprint would be if a trial were held within the Cincinnati market. Bruce simply looked at Stanley and cringed at the grandstanding already evident. He should be wearing a cowboy hat and boots and waving a big cigar. "If we have a change in venue, it is supposed to be in an adjacent county to accommodate everyone involved. Meade County would be the most likely," said Bruce, letting the idea of the change of venue play out.

"No. No," said Stanley. "Dorothy's brother practiced law in Meade County. Everyone knows the family there too," he continued.

"At this point, everyone in the United States pretty much knows the family. I don't even turn on the television anymore," said Bruce. "I used to listen to *The Today Show* while shaving, but I don't want to hear about the murder in Kentucky anymore."

"Yes. Murder," said Stanley, making a point.

"Do you really think murder in the first degree is the appropriate charge?" asked Bruce, happy to move away from the image of a big public trial. "The next thing you'll be telling me is that it needs to be a death-penalty case."

"She rammed a rusty pipe into her mother's neck, crushed everything possible—jugular, carotid artery, you name it. Violent. Premeditated. She had purchased a hunting knife at Walmart. Did you read where she told the doctor, up there in Louisville, she wanted her mother to know she was the one who did it? Are you going to tell me that's not murder one and it could be the death penalty?"

"What I'm going to tell you is there are mitigating circumstances," said Bruce. "To start with, she's fifty-six years old, and she was abused as a child and marginalized as an adult. Marginalized because her mother took a nine iron to her head and caused such damage she dropped forty points of IQ and developed seizures that will define her for the rest of her life."

"The doctor says she is above average in intelligence, especially on good days," said Stanley. "Says she absolutely isn't insane."

"Yes," said Bruce carefully. "And that makes it even worse. She knows she's been reduced. She's aware she'll never get better and will most likely get worse."

"It's a terrible thing," said Stanley in understatement.

"Terrible all the way around. Think about her sister, Sophie," said Bruce, carefully bringing up one of his ace cards.

"Why did she do that?" asked Stanley, scrunching up his face. "I mean, was she unstable?"

"Not until her twin sister went off the rails and stabbed her mother. Before that, she was a regular mother, wife, registered nurse, caregiver of a sister who required pretty much around-the-clock guidance."

Bruce didn't have the stomach to listen to Stanley Dowell anymore. "Look, Stanley, the mother beat and emotionally abused the children routinely for eighteen years before they got out, went to college, and became tax-paying citizens. They have reared children, and they've continued to help their mother by cleaning up the yard and overpaying people because no one wanted to work for her, she was so mean. They never got help from anyone. I assume you read where Johnny Flood, the teachers, and anyone else who knew them even slightly said it was the worst case of child abuse they'd ever seen."

"Please," interrupted Stanley. "Kids are beaten all the time. My parents certainly whopped me. I read about children dying in the papers all the time. The girls didn't die. How bad could it have been?"

"Bad," said Bruce. "So bad that Patty Anderson doesn't care what you charge her with. She's going to plead guilty. Is that what you want? To put a needle in her arm? She doesn't care."

"Doesn't care?" said Stanley.

"Does. Not. Care. The family wants manslaughter because they want to save a little part of her, but you don't have to argue with me anymore about this. Stop playing games. I'm over it. The family is over it. You tell me what you plan on doing because Patty Anderson is going to stand before Kenny Nall and say she did it and that she's happy about it. Whatever the charge."

Bruce was just winding up. "Charge her with the max. There isn't going to be a big trial—not in Breckinridge County or Meade County or Northern Kentucky. Erase that out of your mind. Not going to happen. She doesn't care. She will plead guilty to anything you want to charge her with.

"You know what she's grateful for now?" asked Bruce, his face becoming more animated. "She's grateful she's in jail because she now has a home. She blames herself for her sister committing suicide, and she feels like she has nowhere to return.

"She claims nothing in jail could be worse than her childhood, so she's prepared for anything. She's endured it all. Charge her, Stanley. Be the big man and charge her good."

Stanley hadn't counted on this reaction, and he did not speak.

"They can work out a deal in New York where a man with epilepsy stabs his mother repeatedly and kills her. He loves his mother. She never beat him or belittled him, and she never hit him in the head, giving him epilepsy. Those professionals just agreed to send him to a private psychiatric hospital so his seizures could be controlled. But here in Kentucky, we want to charge a woman who, just once in her life, took control and said, 'Look at me, hear me, see what happens when you hit a child.' Charge her, Stanley. Charge her big.

"Oh, and one last thing, Stanley. Patty wants media coverage. She wants a story in the *Courier-Journal*, *People* magazine, and an interview with Diane Sawyer. All that will be easily arranged. I can't wait to hear how they paint you," Bruce said, ending his tirade. He placed his hand on his briefcase, as if he were ready to leave. "Tell me what it's going to be, Stanley, and I'll have the family there and prepared."

"How can you get media coverage like that?" Stanley said, questioning.

"With a couple of phone calls. There isn't a major media outlet that hasn't already called, but because the family knows Diane personally and because they want some control, Patty has been persuaded to say it a few times and then fade into obscurity. She really doesn't care that you want to put her away for life. At least she has a home, a bed where she can sleep and food on a regular basis."

"A family from Breckinridge County knows Diane Sawyer personally?" Stanley was stuck on the news coverage.

"People in Breckinridge County do get out and meet people," said Bruce, resenting the fact Stanley was dismissive of his home. "Maybe you have forgotten that part of the family is the chief medical examiner of Kentucky."

"She's not part of the family," responded Stanley with a toss of his hand. "What is Hedy thinking?"

"She's part of the family, and Hedy is one of the most rational people I know."

There was a slight pause from Stanley Dowell as he mulled things over. "What are you proposing?" he asked, knowing the power had shifted in the room. He reached for the papers Bruce had filed with the court. He knew what Bruce was proposing.

"Man one, minimum sentence of ten years, credit for time served, and stories in three major media outlets," Bruce answered.

"I can go with that," said Stanley. "There were mitigating circumstances. How soon will the media be covering the case?"

Bruce looked at the man before him. He had never realized just how paper thin he was. He felt disgusted that he could be bought so easily with some television time, but he, Bruce, had gotten what he wanted. He had gotten Patty the best possible plea agreement.

# FORTY

The sun was bright as Hedy and Barbara left their home at 1400 Willow. Hedy knew it would be shocking to see Patty again. She didn't know exactly how she felt about anything because so much had happened. It had been forty-six long days since that fateful afternoon when Patty had decided she'd had enough. Hedy felt overwhelmed, but Barbara kept a steady presence at her side.

"I guess we should be glad Bruce got the plea bargain," said Hedy as Barbara turned the car toward I-64. They would be taking the Indiana route to Breckinridge County. Court wasn't scheduled until 2:00 p.m. central time—three o'clock Louisville time and just perfect for all the news shows.

"I don't know what to think anymore," said Barbara. "I'm surprised the Commonwealth Attorney agreed to the plea, but then, who knows his motivation? I heard he has a sister with Down's," she continued. "Maybe he sympathized with Patty. I think manslaughter is the right charge personally, but then, I'm totally biased."

Barbara had no idea Stanley Dowell was swayed by media coverage and how he might be portrayed in an hour news special or how he felt about her relationship with Hedy. It was better she didn't.

"I called Paul to see if he wanted to ride with us, but he said he wanted to make the drive himself," said Hedy. "I can't imagine how he is feeling. He used to have two wives, and now he has none."

"You think Patty will live with him when she is released?" asked Barbara. "That's pretty much the only home she has ever known."

"I can't imagine that Paul won't have moved on by then," said Hedy. "He's an attractive professional man. Ten years is a long time. Eight and a half is a long time. I hope he does, because he deserves a full life." Hedy paused, thinking. "That would be asking a lot of some woman—having the dead first wife's mentally challenged sister living with you. A wife who committed suicide because the sister killed their mother. Jesus."

"I don't want to think about it," said Barbara. "I want to get this over. I've got to get back to being a full-time employee of the Commonwealth of Kentucky. The last six weeks have aged me."

"I know. Thanks for standing by me," said Hedy. "I couldn't have asked for more support." Hedy felt bad, but Barbara simply smiled.

Hedy didn't mention that she was beyond worried about her own job. She hadn't been very productive the last forty-six days. End-of-year billing and just about everything else had slipped by without her input. Normally she would have been consumed with the numbers and keeping the investors happy. Rachel Weiss was nothing other than obsessed with posting bigger and bigger profits. She didn't care where the money came from, the state of the economy, or what it cost anyone personally. It didn't matter whether it was good or bad for the client. They were all expected to hit their inflated targets. Hedy didn't know how much longer she could endure the environment.

"Have you heard back from Diane?" asked Hedy. "As in Sawyer?"

"I did," said Barbara. "She called right back, herself. She couldn't believe her good luck at getting the interview. She wants to do it pretty quickly because it's hot news. I told her the *Courier* and *People* were also in the mix. She says they'll do it very differently."

"I'm not sure what that means," said Hedy. "More in depth?"

"She says it will be a full hour special, television, and that *People* won't do more than a couple of pages. I also let Joe at the *Courier* know what was coming his way."

"Isn't it ironic that they feel lucky, and Patty feels lucky she gets to tell her story?" said Hedy. "I guess it's a win-win."

"Things tend to work out the way they are supposed to for odd reasons. I'm supposed to call Diane after the hearing today. They already have a team assigned and are doing research. I FedExed her a copy of Bruce's final document."

"I'm not sure how to respond," said Hedy, looking out the window as they started across the Ohio River. "I guess they will be looking for input from all of us. As much as I don't want to do it, we owe that to Patty. It's all so ugly. Can't wait."

"Look how muddy the water is today. I guess from yesterday's rain," commented Barbara.

Hedy nodded and felt good talking about anything other than death, court dates, reliving old wounds, and loss. Her job popped back into her head. A call Friday morning at nine wasn't a good sign.

The media was everywhere when they pulled into Hardinsburg. It didn't even bother them anymore. They both looked with disdain and dismissal at the microphones being shoved into their faces. They were headed to Bruce's office across from the courthouse, and they didn't especially hurry. The media would get out of the way, or they would simply step over them.

"I had no idea we'd be the last to arrive," said Hedy as she sized up the group in the office. She'd seen more of her sisters in the last forty-six days than she had in the last forty-three years. "Ten till," she said. "I had no idea we were cutting it that close," Hedy said, looking at her watch. "I'm sorry."

"We do need to get over there," said Bruce, all business. "The judge is a stickler for time. Honoring him and his court."

As they made their way in, everything hit Hedy as déjà vu. Bobby Clinton was holding the front seats for them. They smiled and thanked him and felt the eyes of the room on their backs. Hedy felt she might throw up, remembering the last time they had been in these same seats.

When they brought Patty in, she was wearing prison orange, handcuffs, and leg chains. Nothing shocked the family anymore. Her hair had grown out, and a wide swath of gray roots split down the top of her head. Sophie had always maintained her hair with frequent colorings, and the realization of that not existing anymore tore at the hearts of the remaining sisters. They all moved from one foot to the other.

"All rise."

They rose. They now knew what to do, and Kenny Nall entered the courtroom waving his black robe with his outstretched arms. Hedy wondered if he thought this was the US Supreme Court or something. She put herself into endure mode and sat down.

Things seemed to go quickly with papers being exchanged, Bruce and Stanley nodding to each other. They approached the bench and then moved around, waiting for something or someone. Hedy heard the words *manslaughter one* and then Patty speaking in a clear voice.

"Guilty, sir," she said. She seemed stronger than usual. She had smiled at everyone when she was escorted in, but beyond that, she did not look back at them for any kind of support.

"Are you aware that you will be sent to prison and that you have admitted that you killed your mother, Dorothy Jackson Anderson?" asked the judge.

"I am aware that I am pleading guilty to manslaughter. I am aware I killed my mother. I am aware that Bruce has told me he has worked out an agreement that I don't have to plead guilty to murder, but I want to plead guilty to murder," Patty said in a voice that did not waver.

"Mr. Edwards, are you aware of your client's wishes?" said the judge.

"I heard them for the first time just now," said Bruce in astonishment. "We have a plea agreement. I worked it out personally with the Commonwealth Attorney."

"It doesn't appear you worked it out with your client," said the judge, who seemed pleased at the surprising turn of events.

The family sat up and stared at Patty, their backs all ramrod straight.

"I was told..." began Stanley Dowell.

"I know. I know," said Judge Nall.

"The state is willing to give you a chance to rehabilitate yourself and be readmitted into society," the judge said to Patty.

"I'm never going to be rehabilitated," she said quietly. "I'm never going to get better. I'm as good as I will ever be."

"If you plead guilty to murder, you will never get out of jail," said the judge. "It's mandatory."

"They have a library where I have been staying, and on some days I can read," began Patty. "If I plead guilty to murder, you have to give me at least life in prison," she explained. "No judicial discretion. Or you could kill me. That would be OK too." No one in the courtroom uttered a sound.

"Did you know my sister Sophie committed suicide?" she asked the judge.

"I object, Your Honor," said Bruce, grasping for straws, time, anything.

"You object to your own client speaking?" Judge Nall laughed. "You've lost this one, son." Bruce hated it when he called him son. The judge was about two years older but a pompous ass.

"I can fire you." Patty turned to Bruce and then whirled around to Hedy. "Sorry, Hedy. I know you are paying."

"You don't want to fire me," said Bruce as calmly as the situation allowed.

"Yes. I do. You are fired." Patty was collected. Bruce sat down.

"Now that Sophie is gone, I have no home to go back to, so I think I want to stay in prison the rest of my life. There are people who talk to me. There are meals. I don't like the food, but maybe I can have some money and buy candy bars in the canteen. They have Snickers. If I'm in prison, I'm not bothering anybody."

Paul put his head down, and tears rolled across his cheeks. How could she feel this way? he thought. "Patty," he called out in desperation. He had cared for her willingly.

"She's gone, Paul. She's gone," whispered Patty. The judge did not even attempt to stop this unorthodox hearing.

"The only thing I want is to be able to tell people what happens when you hit a child. When you make them feel so unloved they hate themselves. If you call them millstones around your neck, you break them. You kill their spirit. She killed every one of us, and no one stopped her. I wanted to stop her, and I did," said Patty.

"I want to plead guilty to murder. I murdered her. I took the pipe, and I put it into her neck. I wanted to. I planned it, and I did it. That should give me the right to have a home in prison." She paused. "For the rest of my life. Not for eight and a half years, but for life. I want to know where I'll be and that I'm not a millstone around anyone's neck anymore."

"But you may regret this later," said the judge. "If you plead guilty as charged, without taking the plea agreement, then I have no choice. And there won't be any going back."

"I've never been so sure of anything in my life," said Patty, and then she paused. "Except for the fact I wanted to kill Dorothy Jackson Anderson."

There was nothing more to say. The family could not speak. Tears streamed down their faces as they attempted to figure out what had happened. Patty would rather be in jail than be with them. Pet rock.

Millstone. They had thought they were taking care of her when they were just picking up where Dorothy had left off. She certainly had found her voice.

Eva got up and walked out of the courtroom, Don trailing behind her. "I just have to breathe," she said, sliding into the empty sheriff's office. "I have to breathe."

Hedy and Lily looked at each other and did not speak. What would they have said?

"I am very reluctant to accept your guilty plea to murder one, but I feel I have no choice," said the judge. "You came in here charged with murder, and now, without representation, you are pleading guilty to the original charge of murder. That carries a mandatory life sentence without the opportunity of parole. Is there anything else you have to say before sentencing?" he said to Patty.

"Do I get to grant interviews with the media so I can tell my story? So I can maybe save one child from being hit in the head? I want to do three stories," she said.

"Three stories?" asked the judge, with his head tilting to the side.

"*People*, the *Courier-Journal*, and Diane Sawyer." One thing you could say about Patty was that she never wavered once she made up her mind.

"If they want to interview you, I don't think there should be any reason to stop that," continued the judge.

"Thanks," said Patty, and then she turned around. "I know we don't ever say we love one another, but I love you all. Thank you for your support, but don't plan on visiting me in jail. I don't want you there. I have a new family in the prison, and they are just as crazy as you are." She smiled, pleased at her joke.

"I won't put you on the visitors list. They won't let you in. Go on with your life, but I will appreciate anything you can do to help me with my three stories. I want to tell our story."

Patty turned her back on her family of origin and took a deep breath. She felt free. She felt Dorothy run off her. When she was a child, Dorothy had never touched one of the girls unless it was a blow physically. Patty didn't have to feel the blows ever again, and she didn't have to be reminded of them. She knew they all loved her, but she wanted to be free.

"Patricia Anne Anderson," began the judge. "You are hereby sentenced to life imprisonment for the premeditated murder of Dorothy Jackson Anderson." Aware of one thing he could help Patty with, the judge added, "Where you will spend the rest of your life will be determined by the staff at the Kentucky Correctional Psychiatric Center in LaGrange. Court adjourned."

As if just remembering, she turned to the family and smiled as broadly as they had ever seen. "I snuck one other thing out that day I killed her, and you'll want to get it. We'll need it for the stories."

Mouths did not open, but faces begged for more. "The shoe. The one with the wooden heel that she used on us all the time. It's under the bed. Way back and in the middle. Make sure the shoe is part of the stories."

# FORTY ONE

No one spoke. The family did not move. "I'm sorry," said Bruce. "I'm sorry." He had waited until Patty had shuffled out the door.

"We're all sorry," said Hedy finally. "You did everything you could. We should have listened to her that first night. She knew what she wanted, and she got it."

"Do you think she'll never speak to us again, really?" said Lily. "Forever?"

"I don't know what to think," said Hedy. "Don't visit her in prison. She won't put us on the visitors list?"

"She'll need us for the Diane Sawyer special and probably for the two print stories," said Barbara, and everyone turned to look at her. "More than just producing the shoe. I'm to call Diane after the court hearing. This turn of events will just make it all the more interesting. We have to do this for Patty. She certainly isn't asking for anything else."

"She got the damn shoe," said Eva. "The one with the back broken down. How old could it be?"

"Never aged in my mind," said Hedy.

People weren't leaving the courtroom and they were listening to the family, so Bruce suggested they go to his office. "There's no reason for me," said Hedy. "I'm spent. If Barbara weren't driving, I'd have to just curl up right here on the floor. I need some time. I can't take anything more."

"Me too," said Lily slowly. "It's morbid how people want to eat off you, eavesdropping, never getting tired of someone else's misery." She said it just loud enough and people started moving in their seats and gathering plastic purses and old sweaters. "When do they decide the sideshow is over? Circus gone to the next town."

Hedy remembered walking to the car and pushing the cameras out of her face, but she didn't remember the car ride to Louisville. She and Barbara were quiet, in their individual worlds. There was nothing to say.

Barbara guided Hedy into the bedroom and helped her put on her sleep suit. She shook a small burned-orange-colored pill into her hand and then shook out a second. She handed Hedy a glass of water and did not speak. Hedy did not question Barbara and took the medication. Sleep enveloped her, and she was grateful when she felt the blackness come. Tomorrow was another day.

The call from Mike Dewitt was scheduled at 9:00 a.m. on December 14, which allowed Hedy a day to gather her notes. She had seen it coming and was prepared, but when she heard the words, the roar in her head was overwhelming.

Mike wanted to get this over with. He wanted to catch an early flight out of New York.

"Not performance related."

"Effective immediately."

"Position eliminated."

"Health insurance will expire at the end of the month."

"We'll not fight you on the severance agreement."

"Not performance related."

It didn't matter. None of the offered statements mattered. Hedy was sixty-one years old and as of December 14, cut adrift professionally. It had taken nineteen minutes to go from being the senior vice president of a New York advertising agency overseeing North America for health care clients, which accounted for 35 percent of the agency's business, to nothing. The week previous, Hedy had flown first class, and uniformed men carrying cards bearing her name met her at the baggage carousel, pulled her luggage, and walked her to waiting black cars. Clients assembled in conference rooms to hear what she had to say, and her speeches were booked a year in advance. Life was fast, exhausting, and exciting. People waited for her. People wanted her. Today she had no one to call.

She had been eliminated. No justification required. Not completely, of course, but it was just a matter of time. People would call and act surprised when they really were just grateful it wasn't them. Invitations to speak at less important conferences would come in for a few months, and then what? Hedy looked down at her computer and wondered what her next steps might be.

She tried not to think about the cruelty of the timing. If it had been one day later, she would have had another month of health insurance.

Eleven days before Christmas. Two days after the she lost yet another sister. This one to the locked doors of a lifetime in prison.

She looked out the window and saw the first little snowflakes beginning to fall. Dorothy had once told her the only reason she had a job was because she could lie. It had driven Hedy to be extra careful about what came out of her mouth. She considered how she wanted to handle the message of her leaving professionally. They had given her that option.

She thought about Rachel Weiss and could not even muster anger. Hedy sort of laughed and then said out loud, "You'll never have to speak to me again, and I'll certainly never have to speak to you."

Chernobyl, she thought. I won't have to stand next to Chernobyl. Rachel Weiss was a miserable human being. Hedy felt almost good.

She calmly picked up her phone and started typing. As Barbara was leaving for work, Hedy had told her she'd probably be axed with the 9:00 a.m. call. And now it had become a reality.

"We'll be fine if that happens," Barbara had said as she went out the door, "but they would be fools."

The text came back simply. "Turn on the news."

Hedy started to get up but then sat back down. Did she really want to hear one more commentary about Patty, her mother, child abuse, murder one as opposed to manslaughter, rusty pipes, and epilepsy?

"You have problems?" Barbara typed a few minutes later, and Hedy went to the bedroom and turned on the television.

The scene of parents crying and running toward their hysterical children jumped off the screen at Hedy. At almost the exact time

Mike Dewitt had been destroying her career, a deranged young man had fired his way into a grade school in Connecticut and shot twenty children. First graders whose little faces promised magnificent things were now lifeless bodies. Parents wept in each other's arms, and other babies huddled in broom closets hoping to stay alive. Six adult staff members were killed along with the shooter. The irony that the man responsible for the tragedy had also killed his mother was not lost on Hedy. Matricide, she thought. Doesn't happen that often.

The fact that other people were dealing with events much worse than those she had processed in the last six weeks did not necessarily make Hedy feel any better. It just made her sick to her stomach. She thought about Drew, Anaya, and little Amy in Singapore and silently gave thanks for the rigidity of that society. The United States pretty much had the corner on mass school shootings. The television just kept sucking her in, and she finally got up and punched the button to turn off the disturbing images.

Hedy pulled out her long coat and put her arms though the sleeves. She headed out the door and into the elevator. Patty may not want to hear from her, but she was going to make sure she had enough money in her account at the prison to buy candy bars at the canteen. Walking quickly, she made it up a small hill and went into her bank.

"Hello, Ms. Miller," sailed a pleasant reply.

"Hi, Nick." Hedy was always greeted warmly by the head teller. She thought he was gay and hence the special service.

"I want a $200 certified check," said Hedy to Nick. "I guess the Kentucky Department of Corrections," she said when asked about the payee.

"Is this for your sister?" he asked, as if sending money to jail was something Hedy did every day.

"Yes," she replied.

"The prisons don't take certified checks," began Nick. "My cousin is in for drugs. The Department of Corrections used to take money orders, but now you have to send it by JPay." He was writing it down on a small piece of paper. "Wish I could help you," said Nick. "You'd get a money order or a certified check for free because you're a gold-account member, but you'll have to pay like eight dollars to JPay."

"But the website?" started Hedy.

"Just not updated. JPay is relatively new. Saves salaries and time. The state gets some kind of kick back."

"That's really unfair," said Hedy. "Eight dollars is a lot of money for some families sending cash to inmates."

"Tell me about it," he said, pushing the paper toward Hedy. "Takes more money to be poor."

"Where do I do this?" Hedy asked.

"I'd say go online. You can send money, music, e-mail. All kinds of stuff. I'm thinking you'd stand out at any of the local offices. Besides, there aren't any here in the Highlands."

"You are kidding," replied Hedy, completely amazed.

"That there aren't any JPay locations in the Highlands?" asked Nick. "Or that you can send money and music to inmates by way of the Internet?"

"Both, I guess. Well, not so much the Highlands. I'd assume we don't have a lot of inmate family and friends."

"More than you think," said Nick. "You'll need her prison ID number," he continued helpfully, cracking his knuckles. "The drug charges ruined my cousin's family. I can't imagine about you. I know it sounds morbid, but we read everything we could about your case. I'm really sorry."

"It's fine, Nick," said Hedy. "I'd read everything too, if it were about you. How often do you actually know the people caught in these hideous circumstances?" Hedy paused and then realized how much Patty wanted people to know the story. "Part of my sister's wish was that Diane Sawyer would do a story about her and child abuse," said Hedy boldly. "They are sending in a crew from New York to do the story, so there will be more you can read and see."

Hedy couldn't believe she was talking so openly. She felt emboldened and free. She didn't care what Rachel Weiss thought or whether they were going to make their numbers. She wanted to help Patty tell the truth about child abuse.

"I won't tell you to have a great day, but I will tell you it will get better," said Nick.

Hedy smiled at Nick, acknowledging the gay handshake. "It will get better," she replied.

The wind was blowing harder, and the walk home seemed longer than usual. She pulled her black cashmere coat around her and wondered if she and Barbara had enough money. She liked nice things. Bruce's bill had come by way of e-mail that morning, and even though she had written him a $10,000. 00 check, he had billed her an additional $64,444.10. The Louisville law firm had yet to submit their bill, but she knew the unused legal advice would run more than $100,000.00. It could have been much worse.

Patty was in jail for life. Sophie had killed herself rather than accept the fact that everything wasn't just dandy in her life, and now Hedy was unemployed. She wondered about Lily's marriage and guessed Eva and Don might be the happiest.

And then, she said, "I'm happy," to no one and seemed almost surprised at the thought. She waved at the guard, and he buzzed her into the building. "Hi, Ms. Miller," said the building manager as she entered the lobby. "We are all real sorry," he continued. "If there is anything we can do…" He let the sentence trail.

"If I knew what was needed, I'd ask," said Hedy, embracing her new freedom. "I have no idea." She smiled and walked to the elevators.

Hedy spent the next hour perusing the JPay.com website, sending money and music to Patty. She had no idea what kind of music Patty liked. She had never asked. Then she made a list of clients she wanted to reach out to personally, letting them know about her "retirement."

The e-mails came fast and furious. She took the high road and said nothing. Job offers followed. Did she want to be senior vice president over Human Resources at a California hospital, or managing partner at a competing advertising agency? Do freelance writing for requests for proposals at yet another competing agency? She didn't. She knew that much, but she was grateful for the offers.

When Barbara came home, she was carrying colorful brochures. "I booked us on a Christmas cruise," she said quickly. "This guy at the office cruises all the time, and he had all these books," she continued, waving fat catalogues with smiling couples looking off into the sunset, champagne glasses in hand.

"I know I sound like a bitch," began Hedy, "but I don't want to pack sun block and think about squeezing into a bathing suit."

"Good, because we are going on a river cruise. Much calmer clientele than the Bud Lite Beer–drinking kind you have always thought were the only people who cruised over the holidays in the Caribbean. You have no idea. We start in Amsterdam and end up in Budapest. Well, Buda and Pest," said Barbara, smiling. "I love that they are two separate cities. I think St. Paul and Minneapolis should have been so clever. Pauleapolis. Minnepaul."

"I've been eliminated professionally, the legal bills will be over $100,000.00 and you want to take a holiday cruise," said Hedy to a smiling Barbara, grateful for her perfect teeth and wide supporting smile.

"I upgraded us to a veranda suite," she continued. "Christmas markets, and get this: we make a stop in Wurzburg. We can skip the tour of the baroque Residenz Palace and just see my sister." Barbara had one sister in Germany and another in Brussels. Instead of killing themselves and their mother, Barbara's family had just moved as far from one another as possible.

"We've seen the Residenz," said Hedy. "It won't be a big skip. What about your work?" Hedy grew serious. "Lots of dead bodies over the holidays."

"You are right, and I don't want to see them. I want to see you. I want to be with you. We need to heal. My shoulders are killing me. When they say dead weight, they really mean dead weight. I've been pushing and pulling bodies for too many years, and it's taken its toll," she continued, attempting to rotate her right arm.

"We need to enjoy what we have," continued Barbara. "I called Tom at the bank, and we are fine. Your salary was great, and we have saved. We. Are. Fine," Barbara emphasized. "Besides, I'm still pulling in some cash."

"I'm happy," said Hedy again, surprising herself. "I'm grateful they ended it. I couldn't have gone on much longer balancing the clients' needs with Rachel's need to post higher and higher profits."

"All good. We'll need to fly out on Sunday."

"It's Friday," said Hedy, as if it were an impossibility when she knew now it was not. No clients to worry about and a sister in prison who didn't want to see her.

"Cruise starts on the eighteenth, and we get to Budapest on December thirty-first, just in time to celebrate the new year. It's is going to be a great year, 2013."

# FORTY TWO

What Barbara left unsaid was that 2013 would start with a bang. Diane Sawyer was scheduled to come to Louisville just after the new year to start filming, and her team was already working behind the scenes getting releases, developing scripts, working out shooting schedules, and doing background filming. It was amazing how much filming went into an hour show.

*People* magazine needed to postpone the jailhouse interview for two weeks because of the Newtown, Connecticut, school shootings, and Joe Cross was poring over the court documents Barbara had supplied him. There were already enough quotes and information for a huge story, but he wanted to interview Patty before he finished his piece.

Barbara and Hedy would have a little over two weeks to collect themselves. Barbara was being overly cautious about who had access to Hedy. Another day would be a better time to brief Hedy about what would be needed from her for the television special and the print stories.

Somehow, Barbara had become the spokesperson for the family in terms of the media. Lily had done exactly what Lily always did, and that was to check out. She had quit answering phone calls from anyone in the family or anyone even remotely associated with the family. She had gone back to work acting as if nothing had happened. She spent long hours at the office and returned home to a dark house. Howard was always home, but Lily chose not to notice.

Eva and Don were more than agreeable, but they had little experience in dealing with the media, and they deferred to Hedy or Barbara. Hedy's departure from her position with the advertising agency had left her almost numb, so Barbara had seamlessly taken over. It was better that way. As the chief medical examiner, she had been in the news more than a few times and knew, better than most, how to manage the aggressiveness of those seeking a story. There would be three stories, period.

Hedy cashed in frequent-flyer miles and upgraded the duo to first class. Delta doesn't need to know I won't be making Diamond Status next year, she thought as she hit the upgrade button, which gave them flat-bed compartments on the international legs from Atlanta to Amsterdam, and then, coming back, from Budapest to Charles de Gaulle Airport in Paris, and from Paris to Atlanta and Louisville. She had plenty of miles, a small perk for half a life spent on the road.

After they reached Atlanta, it was over an eight-hour flight to Amsterdam. They were scheduled to leave Atlanta at 10:40 p.m., after a four-hour layover that gave them plenty of time to go to what Hedy considered a private haven—a restaurant called One Flew South in the E Terminal of the sprawling airport complex.

Hedy knew the Atlanta airport better than most of the people who worked there, and she guided Barbara to the restaurant, which offered good wine and even better fresh food, something rarely found in any airport. They had plenty of time not to worry about missing connections and delayed flights.

People hustled outside the oasis, which was partially secluded by cleverly placed wooden slats, while Hedy and Barbara had sushi and white wine. They were scheduled to get into Amsterdam at 12:55 p.m. the next day and didn't need to check into the river cruise until their second day in Amsterdam. The world seemed to slow down just a little, and Hedy focused on everything for which she was grateful.

"Do you think Patty will have any kind of holiday?" she asked Barbara as her chopsticks went in for another bite of broiled eel, cucumber, and rice.

"I have heard that people—churches and the like—donate gifts for the inmates' children, and a little more money is allotted for the food so the inmates have a better-than-usual meal, but I think that's about it," she said. "Did you send something to her?"

"I put the $200 in her prison account," said Hedy. "You know how she mentioned she wanted to buy candy bars. I called and asked about getting her a new police scanner, but I think the comment was, 'A police scanner is never going to happen,' so I essentially gave up. I feel bad, but I have a partner who came home and gave me a few hours to get ready for an international trip," said Hedy, smiling. "Besides, wouldn't the $100,000.00 in legal fees cover us for at least a few holidays?"

"It's prison," said Barbara bleakly. "They don't get too many rights. She chose that, and she chose to keep everyone off the visitors list. It's time you take a little care of yourself. It's OK. Christmas was never a really big deal anyway, especially with everyone living in Singapore."

"I did get Amy some cute things. Shipping cost more than the gifts," said Hedy with a laugh, referring to her little granddaughter. "I'll be glad when she's old enough to come and visit for the summer, or at least meet us in Paris or something. She's such a little hellcat baby. I just love her."

The time in Atlanta went by amazingly fast, and the women felt relatively at ease when they flashed their first-class tickets, passports, and tagged carry-on bags. "Have a nice flight, Ms. Miller," said the blonde checking in passengers. "Thank you for your loyalty." Soon the notifications of being one of Delta's best customers would be gone. Soon she would be like every other Joe who bought a ticket. Hedy knew she would miss that, but she also knew she had paid a very high price for those small pleasantries.

The flight was long but certainly tolerable in the front of the plane. As much as Hedy loved a good glass of wine, she never drank on airplanes because it simply dehydrated her. Barbara was another story, and Hedy noticed more than one Pinot Noir being poured.

"Take an Ambien," said Barbara with an outstretched hand holding two pills. "Ten milligrams will put you out, and you'll wake up in Amsterdam. I want to do a little sightseeing before we get on the boat. These will slow down that racing brain. Trust me on this one."

Hedy would trust Barbara on anything, especially medications. She was generally very conservative, but of course her patients didn't need many pills since they were normally dead. Nonetheless, the increase in deaths by overdose kept Barbara constantly studying interactions and outcomes of all medications. She'd had a colleague who worked with live patients write the script.

Emerging from Amsterdam Schiphol Airport, both Hedy and Barbara were surprised by the grayness of the weather. Rain threatened, and it seemed odd they had arrived for a cruise. Hedy thought perhaps they should have considered a lodge with a roaring fireplace.

The taxi Hedy had arranged through their hotel was waiting, and they effortlessly slipped into the back. Taxis in Amsterdam were historically known for overcharging, so Hedy had prepaid the fifty euros to ensure easy transportation even though she could have secured something less expensive with a little effort at the airport. She was too exhausted, and the euros didn't seem that outrageous.

Hedy had spent more than 1,500 nights in various types of Marriott Hotels over her professional years and had reached lifetime Platinum Status with the chain. It provided her with a variety of amenities that were more luxurious at international hotels than domestic ones. She felt at home knowing she was headed to a Marriott, but a feeling of extreme exhaustion started engulfing her. Was it emotional or physical or both? She felt tears cloud her eyes as she looked out the taxi window, taking in the distinctive architecture and the networks of canals. She didn't know why she was crying.

"What's wrong?" said Barbara.

"I don't know," Hedy responded. "I have no idea. I feel like two people. I am strangely comfortable in the back of an international taxi, and then I am reminded I will always have a foot in Breckinridge County."

"You haven't been in Breckinridge County for forty years," said Barbara.

"Really?" was Hedy's response. "I never left. I mean, I wanted to leave and did. New York, Los Angeles, the world, but I can't forget the horrible times there or the unbelievable kindnesses shown to us over and over by the people there."

"It's been a lot," said Barbara in support, but not understanding totally. She had grown up in the exclusive enclave of Santa Barbara. Her family might have been one of the poorest in town, but the region was beautiful and full of successful professionals. She had learned Russian in high school and taken rides in her friends' family jets. She had been exposed to what the world offered, and going to medical school wasn't a big dream, it was something that was expected. Hard as she tried, she could not understand the emotional trappings that came with growing up in a small, poor, rural community.

The red awnings of the Marriott came into view, and Hedy pulled herself back into her real life. She gathered her backpack and slung it over her shoulder, exactly the way she had done hundreds of times in front of hundreds of Marriotts.

"Nice," said Hedy as she walked back to Barbara, who was sitting in the lobby waiting for Hedy to take care of the details. Hedy extended the room key cards and said, "We've been upgraded to a corner room overlooking the Leidseplein. We are on the eleventh floor, so the view should be good, and the Executive Lounge opens at 5:30 p.m. Full breakfast in the morning starting at six."

"I think we should push through and not think about the time difference," Barbara said after they had gotten settled.

"I'm the one who taught you that," said Hedy, smiling. "No fight from me. You will want to see the Ann Frank House," Hedy continued. "I was here with Drew years ago. I think maybe he was ten; that, and the Van Gogh Museum."

"Actually," began Barbara, "the Van Gogh Museum is under renovation. A group of his most famous works is being shown now at the Hermitage Amsterdam Museum. They told me when I booked the cruise."

"I didn't know there was a Hermitage in Amsterdam!" said Hedy. "Got to work that Russian in somewhere," she joked, referring to the fact that Barbara loved most things Russian and spoke the language as often as possible, which was not much in Louisville, Kentucky. "The Hermitage has an Amsterdam location," she continued, almost laughing.

The Hermitage was the most impressive museum Hedy had ever experienced. It was located in Saint Petersburg, Russia, and she had been stunned when she had walked from room to room with priceless pieces stacked almost on top of one another. Sculptures by Rodin were butted against Rubens and Rembrandts. Monet and Degas works lived by those of Gauguin, Matisse, and Monet. *The Three Graces* sat almost forgotten in a corner.

"The Russians are opening satellite museums so more people can see their impressive collection," explained Barbara.

"Have they thought about selling some of it and providing a little infrastructure for their citizens?" asked Hedy. "Have you looked at the electrical work and the pipes?"

"I've looked," said Barbara. "You know how the police scanner is never going to happen? Well, the Russian people are never going to be treated fairly in our lifetime."

Hedy always felt good when she could carry on a conversation about things that had been left out of her education. She knew she had giant holes and had worked for years at studying and filling those holes, but oftentimes, it seemed there was never enough patch.

The Ann Frank House was located a little over a mile from the Marriott, and both Hedy and Barbara embraced the ability to pull their coats tight and take in the scenery while walking. Amsterdam was an amazing concoction of colors and row houses along a network of canals. As they walked, they looked up and saw big pulleys that were still part of the structures, a throwback to when goods and furnishings were pulled from boats along the canal up and into the buildings.

"Wait till you see how small their hiding place was," said Hedy to Barbara. "You cannot imagine how they survived for over two years in such a small space."

By virtue of profession, Barbara had not traveled as much as Hedy. When one was anchored to a specific government job, especially a job in the morgue, there wasn't a lot of opportunity to travel. Hedy loved showing her areas she had previously visited. Hedy was a master at organization and travel planning, and over the past fifteen years, she had engineered great trips, from beaches to cities on most of the continents. Barbara loved Europe the best, and while a river cruise was not something Hedy would have planned at the end of December, she loved Barbara for knowing how much Hedy needed a break. Her life, as she had known it, had been crushed in a short six weeks. Hedy was the walking wounded, and they both knew it.

When they emerged from the small museum and had walked through the tiny space where a young woman had written and lived the nightmare of persecution, they did not speak. There was too much to say and only inadequate words. The experience was just layered onto an already weary soul.

"Maybe we shouldn't have come," said Barbara as she saw the grayness of Hedy.

"Of course we should have come," said Hedy. "You don't come to Amsterdam and not go to the Ann Frank House. I'm fine. Stop worrying so much. A lot of shitty things have happened, and I just have to process." Hedy reached over and took Barbara's hand, something she would never have done in the States. But Amsterdam was different, and she didn't have to worry about clients and judgment.

It was nearing 6:00 p.m., and the night was fully on them. "I have a great restaurant picked out for us," began Hedy.

"No wonder you didn't have time to think about packing. You were too busy planning Amsterdam," said Barbara, knowing Hedy would have every minute on a schedule.

"It's what I do," smiled Hedy as she raised her hand to flag down a cab. "It's not always easy to get a cab," she said, explaining her quick response to one sitting outside the museum. "And the restaurant is in the Red Light District."

"Have you lost your mind?" said Barbara. "Why would we want to go to the Red Light District?"

"Because that is where the restaurant is located, and it's actually very safe. It's Amsterdam! Come on, don't be silly! You can look at the prostitutes in the windows or maybe stop by a coffee house and pick up a quick 'space cake' or have a puff of weed."

Barbara was at a loss for words, but she got into the cab. She thought about what a space cake might be and what impact it could have on an individual who did not normally use marijuana.

"Blauw aan de Wal," said Hedy. Barbara knew she had worked on the pronunciation because sometimes even English posed a challenge for Hedy. Any foreign language sent her into a spin. Back to those gaping holes in her early education.

When the cab dropped them off outside a graffiti-adorned tunnel, Barbara once again turned to Hedy and gave her a look.

"Right through here," said Hedy, never pausing, and soon they were walking toward a tranquil courtyard garden. Hedy opened the door, and Barbara walked into a rugged space that had exposed brick walls and the ambience of a bar. The building itself dated back to the Middle Ages and had previously served as an old spice warehouse, but the French-Mediterranean restaurant was very contemporary.

Bert, the current owner, greeted the two woman and asked them politely it they had gotten a chance to inform the restaurant about their presence in advance. Hedy nodded and handed the man a card from the Marriott indicating the concierge had made reservations.

The prix fixe menu gave them limited choices, but the veal rolled with sushi-grade tuna was stunning for Hedy. Barbara was a little less adventuresome and decided on the pea soup with pancetta.

"We fly the peas in when we can," said the waiter in perfect English. "Just like the fish. Our airport is a gateway to Europe, so when peas are fresh in Australia, we have this great pea soup."

The waiter guided them on wine pairings and the lamb in an herb crust for the main course. Flan with candied fruit and chocolate mousse was a perfect end, considering the restaurant served appropriate proportions as opposed to the oversized ones regularly placed in front of diners in the United States.

They had been seated upstairs, where the white tablecloths and thin wine glasses were much more sophisticated than the exposed brick and raucous attitude of the downstairs.

"I'm not sure when I've had a meal this good and this different," said Barbara as she leaned back and held her wine glass midair. "I'm feeling the effects of jet lag, however."

"It's a far way from the KFC in Hardinsburg or the Kentucky Correctional Psychiatric Center," said Hedy quietly. "This was a good idea, Barbara, getting away. Thanks."

"What are you going to do now that you don't have to get on a plane four days a week?" said Barbara, without a hint of pending judgment or advice. "You know we are fine financially, even with that $100,000.00 hit."

"I think we should get rid of some of the property. We don't need two places, and we don't live in two places. The tax benefits were good when we were both working, but seriously, we are property rich. I'd like to be a little lighter," continued Hedy as she savored the last of her wine.

"I love my house," said Barbara. "And the Willow. The monthly maintenance fee is almost $1,100.00. It's so outrageous. It was perfect when you were all over the place working, but now we don't need someone who manages your dry cleaning or takes the groceries you've had delivered and puts them in the refrigerator. That was only necessary because you were so often coming home from a business trip past midnight."

"Your house has four floors," said Hedy. "If I am trying to get ready and realize the only pair of jeans that fit are down in the laundry, I'm running down two flights and up two flights. Do you think that makes sense? Especially in the long run."

"I honestly don't know," said Barbara. "I'm not wedded to the house, but it's paid for, and I've poured my heart and soul into it." One of Barbara's favorite places was Home Depot because she loved puttering, and the house was a perfect palette for repair and loving touches.

"I can hardly think about putting one foot in front of the other, much less what I want to do for the rest of my life," said Hedy as she motioned discretely for the check. "Let's walk. I want to see the Red Light District as it is just coming alive for the evening."

Women sat perched on tall stools with their legs crossed in wide picture windows. Garters and dark sheer hose were the preferred choice of clothing, along with black lace bras and long, red, tapered fingernails. Open-toed shoes swung seductively and only slightly from the bar on the near bottom of the seat. Other women stood leaning, with one leg tucked behind them, both shoulder and leg pressed against the wall.

Come-hither looks were obvious but not pronounced. These women knew what they were doing and had men standing outside staring with hands in their pockets. Every once in a while, someone would enter the door, and the curtains would be pulled, indicating the woman was occupied. People walked hand in hand along old buried railroad tracks, and Barbara and Hedy took each other's arms.

It was cold, in the thirties, but as they looked inside the coffee houses, where people of all ages smoked marijuana and talked easily, they felt a rush of freedom. "How many people get to do this?" said Hedy.

"We made choices. Studied hard and worked harder. Not everyone had the options, but I'm grateful every day" was the reply. "Travel isn't appealing to everyone."

"I'm glad it's appealing to you," said Hedy. "I absolutely could travel the rest of my days."

Hedy wondered how it could be that someone would not want to travel the world and be exposed to different cultures and ways of thinking. She did not speak but just continued the walk toward her home away from home. She cringed a little, thinking how they always stayed at a Marriott, a Western hotel, as opposed to some of the small boutique hotels that screamed of culture and unique locations.

"I'm going to sleep well tonight," said Barbara. "I'm exhausted."

"Who are you kidding?" said Hedy as the red awnings of the hotel appeared in the distance. "We'll be up in the middle of the night because it's six hours ahead here. We'll be there when they open the Executive Lounge for breakfast."

"I know. It's just that I'm so tired right now. I feel like I could sleep for days. This whole ordeal has taken its toll on everyone," replied Barbara.

"I know you've carried so much when I just couldn't," said Hedy. "I'm so grateful. You have no idea. To be able to share this and not be responsible singularly—you cannot imagine."

# FORTY THREE

Patty enjoyed the ride back to LaGrange, where her little white room awaited. She didn't care that it was so small and that the bars interfered with the view out the window or even that she was locked inside. She wondered, now that she was a permanent resident, whether or not she might get her police radio scanner. She'd given up on the gloves, but she really missed knowing what was going on in Chicago.

The weather was gray but not too cold. The wind cut through her orange jail clothes as she emerged from the police van with her hands chained. It was Friday, and there was more than the usual activity around the facility because it was Visitors' Day for the inmates who were on good behavior. I won't have to worry about that, she thought, knowing she could never gain the privilege. Besides, she wasn't going to put anyone on the visitors list. She didn't have anyone she wanted to visit with.

Patty thought about Sophie a lot. She was sorry she had killed herself, but it didn't make sense. It was like Sophie waiting and waiting in that playpen until the older sisters came home and let her out and changed her diaper. Why would you just give up a husband who loved you and two children, a professional job, and freedom with Patty out of the way? Why give up now? Who cared what people thought? Sophie never made total sense to Patty.

Patty was looking forward to Monday, when she had an appointment with Dr. Terrell. She was anxious to tell him what had happened in court. How she had fired Bruce and cut the family free. She breathed deeply and saw that a tray of food had been left in her little room. They had to make sure you ate on travel days. Transport for her was at 5:00 a.m., so she'd had breakfast at 3:00 a.m. She was hungry.

Bologna sandwich, Doritos, and red Kool-Aid. Patty smiled as she looked at the bologna. They'd never had Doritos when they were growing up, but bologna was fifty cents a pound, and Hedy had tried to make sure there was bread to go along with the bologna.

Patty picked up the sandwich, released it from its little bag, and took a bite. The bread was stale but not too bad. She would have liked a little mayonnaise or mustard, but you didn't get any of that in prison. Just like in the attic when Hedy fed them before they went to bed.

Patty knew Hedy was probably sending her money, so she thought about what she would buy first. Snickers and the squeeze cheese. She hadn't seen any vegetables or fruit. Sophie wouldn't like that. Well, Sophie was dead. Stupid move, Sophie, thought Patty as she took a sip of the Kool-Aid. For once, you should have waited, and everything wouldn't have seemed so bad.

Dr. Terrell was waiting for Patty when the attendant walked her to his door. "Hello, Patty," he said immediately. "How are you feeling?"

"Pretty good," she said, smiling. "Hedy loaded up my account, and I got to eat a Snickers bar. They didn't have any police scanners to buy, so I thought it would be all right to dip into my funds. She gave me $200. How much do you think the police scanner will cost?"

"There's not going to be any police scanners, Patty, seriously. No way. I tried. I told you that."

"I'm not going to accept that," she said simply. "They can't just take away my police scanner."

"Yes, they can. This is prison," the doctor reminded her. "You are not here to be entertained."

"Oh, that's right, you are supposed to rehabilitate me. How's that going to work? What's first on the rehabilitation list for me?"

"Do you want to tell me about court last Wednesday?" asked Dr. Terrell.

"I fired Bruce. I'm here for good. No one has to worry about keeping me tucked away in some room upstairs. This is my home. What about Pepperidge Farm rye bread in the commissary?" she said, all in a hurry.

"No police scanner and no rye bread," said the doctor, looking at her with sad eyes. "Patty, why didn't you take the plea?"

"Because I killed her, and I wanted to take credit for doing something no one else had the nerve to do," she said, a little sad that he seemed disappointed. She wanted Dr. Terrell to like her. She loved that Dr. Terrell talked to her.

"But if you had taken the plea, you would have been out in eight and a half years. Now you are in prison for a lifetime."

"I've been in a prison all my life," said Patty. "First the playpen, and then the seizures, and then Sophie's bedroom. What's the difference?"

# FORTY SEVEN

P atty sat in her room and rocked. She hadn't expected Dr. Terrell to dump her. She had expected to stay right here. Forever. Nothing ever turned out the way she wanted. Every time she planned something, it changed on her. The Kentucky Correctional Institute for Women, she thought. What would that be like?

"Are you ready for your pills, Patty?" asked the woman Patty liked. She was standing at the door of the cell.

"Sure," said Patty. "Got to keep the seizures at bay. What do you know about the Kentucky Correctional Institute for Women?"

"Are they sending you to Pewee Valley?" came the response.

"I guess so," said Patty with a deep sadness. "I thought I'd get to stay here."

"I knew they'd send you there eventually. You ain't crazy enough for here."

"I'm pretty crazy," said Patty. "How crazy do you have to be?"

The thin African American girl holding out the pills nodded her head toward the woman in the next cell. "Now there's some crazy."

"I can yell all night if that would keep me here," offered Patty.

"They know when you are fake yelling. Fake crazy. That's what they specialize in here. Are you really crazy enough to do something terrible, or are you just mean?" said the woman, not much more than a girl.

"I guess I'm just mean, then," said Patty.

"You ain't mean," the woman said quickly. "You like those women who kill their husbands just 'cause they so tired of being hit. I did think you were a little crazy when I heard you didn't take that plea deal."

"I know it sounds stupid, but I have my reasons," said Patty.

"They must be some pretty good reasons," came the reply. "Now take these pills, and I'll be making a mental list of what you'll need to do to fit in at Pewee Valley."

Patty got the message she was to have a session with Dr. Terrell, but she said she didn't feel well. "It's my stomach," she said to the guard assigned to take her to his office. "Maybe I haven't been pooping enough. There's not a lot of roughage in this place."

Roughage, thought the guard. She had no idea what Patty meant, but she turned around and shrugged. Most of the inmates loved it if they got the kind of time with Dr. Terrell that Patty had been getting.

Four days passed with Patty rocking and looking out the window. She didn't bother to get up early to get the best food at breakfast, so she just didn't eat. She had been told Eva had called to be put on the visitors list, but she had shaken her head no. She didn't speak. She missed her police radio scanner. She did have Snickers, and she watched her "loaded up" card shrink as she bought chips and ramen noodles for the woman who screamed for her baby. She didn't care if she used up all her money. There wasn't going to be a police scanner for her to buy. She stopped taking a shower at night, and she didn't change her clothes. She needed a plan.

Her pill-passing friend said she'd need to be tough at the prison in Pewee Valley. "Them women is tough," said the girl as she brought Patty her meds. "You'll probably be put with another murderer. They pair you up like that." Patty didn't mind. She could cope with whatever they handed out. She was used to it. She wondered when the transfer would happen. She wanted it to be soon. She wanted to get on with the next phase of her life.

"Are you sick?" Dr. Terrell was standing at the cell door. "Why have you stopped coming to sessions?"

"What's the point?" said Patty. "When are you going to transfer me?"

"Soon, because if you don't get treatment here, there is no reason for you to take up one of these very valuable beds."

"No problem. You want me to get my things together now?" asked Patty in a defiant voice. To hell with him, she thought. She wasn't going to be a bother to anyone anymore, especially some shrink.

"Do you want me to put in the paper work?" he asked calmly.

"It's whatever you want, isn't it?" she responded.

"Patty, I don't want to have to stand here. Come with me to the office so we can talk," he said, coaxing her to stop rocking and come to the office for a session. He needed it more than she did.

Patty looked up at him and stared. "Nobody is going to hurt me ever again. I can take care of myself. I know what it's going to be like in regular prison with the other women. I know my cellie will be another murderer. I'm fine with everything." Patty felt herself shut down. She knew how to stop herself from crying. She had learned that early. If your own mother wanted to toss you into the FFA camp lake with a brick around your neck, where you ended up spending your days really didn't matter. "I'm just fine."

"I don't think you are fine," said Dr. Terrell. "I think it is important you understand why the transfer needs to take place, what it will be like, and what you can expect. You need to be prepared."

"I'm always prepared," said Patty. "Always ready for the next blow. I never rest. I'm always aware. Those women better be afraid of me because I got nothing, nothing to lose."

"I'm going to ask you one more time to please come with me for a session."

"No thanks, Dr. Terrell. You have your other patients to tend to. She's looking for her baby," said Patty, motioning to the next room. "Did you put in a prescription for my police scanner? That would be nice before you send me out the door." Patty spit out the words.

"I can't get you a police scanner," said Dr. Terrell. "They have said absolutely no at every level."

"Then you're not so powerful after all. I don't even know who you are." She continued the assault. "Maybe you're not a doctor at all. What real doctor would work here? I bet you couldn't get another job." She was just getting started.

"You couldn't find me crazy enough to stay in this precious hospital. You can't get me my police scanner, and you can't even muster the guts to take me on as a patient. Have fun with your life, whatever kind of life you have. Dull, I suspect."

Patty felt herself channeling Dorothy. She hated when she sounded even a little like her mother. Mean and bruising. The aura surprised Patty because she felt so in control. She had no idea what was happening to her life.

She felt her body tense and get stiff. She bowed and fell out of the chair. Her body reacted violently to the spasms. Her head hit the floor hard time and time again. Her hands fell loose and began shaking like leaves in a strong wind.

"Nurse, nurse," shouted Dr. Terrell as he stood helpless on the other side of the bars. "Open this up, now."

Keys rang out, and Patty continued to convulse, her head pounding the hard floor in a rhythmic beat. Staff ran to the cell and pulled a key from a large group of identical keys attached to a leather belt. "It's open," said the guard, and the doctor ran in. He held Patty's head against his upper thigh and let her convulsions continue and then lessen. She finally stopped and immediately began pulling herself out of the attack.

She clutched the arm of the chair and felt her head roll back in an unnatural position. She wanted to be away from him. She didn't have total control, and she kept letting saliva run down her chin. She hated it when she was coming out of an attack because she was aware she had no control. She pulled herself up and toward the chair, and by sheer will, she sat down and let her head roll against the back. She tried to focus her eyes. She felt the grogginess descend, and she reached for the tissue in her pocket. She hated when people saw her slobber.

Dr. Terrell reached down and picked her up from the chair. He was not a big man, but he was strong enough to lift a woman not much more than five feet two inches and 117 pounds. He placed her in her bed and pulled up the sheet. "You'll need to rest after this," he said. "It'll take you some time to come back around. I'll check on you. They'll be bringing you some medication."

Dr. Terrell nodded to the nurse, who had come to witness the event, and she turned to check the standing medical orders for when Patty had an especially difficult seizure.

"I can take care of myself," mumbled Patty. "I don't want to bother anyone. I want my police scanner, and I want to tell what happens when you hit a child." She was barely awake.

The nurse came in with a hypodermic needle. She slowly injected it into Patty's arm, and they watched Patty succumb to the medication. Dr. Terrell thanked the nurse and turned to walk to his office.

He pulled out his computer and wrote a letter asking for a professional transfer from his current position at the Kentucky Correctional Psychiatric Center. There was a similar position open at the Kentucky Correctional Institute for Women. He carefully worded the request to reflect his need for a professional change, his fatigue of doing daily evaluations.

The state was currently paying for an outside company to provide the psycho-social assessments and psychotherapy counseling at three times what Dr. Terrell would cost them as a regular employee. He knew it would take time. The wheels of government turned slowly, and the higher-ups would be completely surprised. They would probably have to pay the same company to cover what Dr. Terrell was doing now at KCPC.

The wheels weren't turning as slowly when it came to Patty. The pressure was on for him to transfer her to the women's prison in Pewee Valley. When the news teams for the *Courier-Journal*, *People* magazine, and Diane Sawyer descended, they wanted her in a regular prison setting, not a psychiatric facility. Life in prison should be for someone who committed a heinous crime, not someone who did not appear mentally incapacitated. It was a fine line of understanding how the public reacted to violent crimes.

Kenny Nall, the presiding judge, had received a surprising amount of bad press for taking Patty's plea of guilty to murder one. Editorials asked about the child abuse and the need for consideration. The heartlessness of his actions. The judge was not happy, but he'd ruled, and he had to live with the ruling. He waited for the media opportunities to at least tell his side of the story.

Everyone in the system wanted Patty to appear in an appropriate setting. After all, New York had worked out an agreement for a young adult who had stabbed his mother to death so that he was getting help controlling his epilepsy. Patty needed to be seen behind bars for violently killing her elderly mother when there had been no seizure. Cold blooded and well executed.

Jack Terrell hit send and listened to the familiar sound of an e-mail dashing to its intended receiver. He could almost feel the shock waves. He needed to be cool and unassuming. He certainly didn't want it connected that this transfer had anything to do with Patty. Not everyone would react like Garrison and know there was nothing but a professional connection.

His phone started to vibrate against his thigh, and he thought momentarily the call might be in response to his request for transfer. It was not.

"The warden wants to know when she is going to be released out of your care," came the blunt response from the only female deputy warden, Nora Evans. She had earlier been the officer for the assessment programs, so she was a logical choice to extend the still-pleasant inquiry. If Dr. Terrell didn't move quickly enough, the warden would step in, but not yet.

"She just had a really violent seizure," said Dr. Terrell. "We've had to medicate her, and it'll take days for her to be completely out of the effects."

"I thought you said she was controlled," said Evans.

"She was until today."

"Was there a cause?" Evans wasn't going to cut him any slack.

"She is angry about the police scanner," he replied, telling part of the story, "so she has been postponing sessions. Claims she isn't feeling well."

"So she's refusing treatment?"

"I spoke with her at length today," he said, indicating there had been a session when, in fact, there had not. "She claims she is ready to go to KCIW. But then she had the seizure, and it was a very bad one."

"We have to get her transferred by the end of the year," said Evans. "The news media is scheduled. We absolutely don't want her here. Do what you have to do, Jack," she said, trying to be collegial. "Is there some medication that will stabilize her and the attacks?"

Jack knew he could dope her up so that she would hardly know where she was, and that might control the seizures, but he didn't want to do that. "The options are not good," he said. "If we had a way to really control them, you wouldn't have that kid in New York in a private psychiatric hospital." He knew he was playing with fire.

"The New York case is not the same," the deputy warden said, keeping the official message on point. "The Anderson woman was not coming out of a seizure. She killed her mother in a premeditated, violent manner. Let's remember what we're dealing with. Let's get her transferred. I'll call in a few days to get the date." A presumptive close.

Jack slid the phone back into his pocket. He didn't have much time, and he wanted to prepare her for what was coming, but he couldn't force her. If she didn't agree to sessions, then he'd just have to write the orders to have her released from his care. Healed. Ready to go back into mainstream prison society. He closed his eyes and tried to envision what might happen if she had a seizure before she had been able to build a network. At least she had money for bribes, he considered. Items from the commissary would go a far way in smoothing her path if she handled things appropriately. Otherwise, she'd just be threatened every day for her "loaded-up card." He needed to warn her. He needed her to come to sessions.

"Are you ready?" asked the guard as he stood outside Jack's office. "I've got one for eval. Two o'clock?"

"Yes," said Dr. Terrell as he looked up at a man covered in tattoos and sporting a bald head and a few brown teeth. He was handcuffed and extremely thin. He was hunched, overaccommodating for the handcuffs. His prison clothes hung on his frame, and he walked with a slight limp.

"The Swastika tat on your neck is nice," said Dr. Terrell as he opened the prisoner's file. He knew he had crossed some invisible line. He didn't care anymore. They really needed to grant that transfer.

# FORTY EIGHT

"Well that was reasonably awful," said Hedy as they walked out of the dining room and down the stairs that would take them to their corner veranda suite. "Do you want a nightcap before we turn in?"

"A Bailey's would be great," said Barbara, and they turned to enter the bar, which was filling with people who had just enjoyed dinner. The boat had pulled away from the dock and was headed overnight to Cologne. Barbara put in the order, knowing Hedy would stick with her Cloudy Bay.

"I'm so sorry to bother you, dear," said a woman with white hair and a thick British accent. "But aren't you the one who lost your mother? My son lives in the States, and I keep up with the news. My husband, Edmund, said it couldn't be, but I never forget a face. You're the one, aren't you?"

Hedy looked up at her and did not speak. Barbara turned from the bar holding the two drinks. "I'm sorry," she said to the woman. "We were just going to the room."

Hedy got up silently, took the glass of wine from Barbara's hand, and turned in the direction of the cabin. She left the woman with her mouth open.

"I'm so sorry, dearie. We just wondered," they heard as they walked down the hall.

"And you thought it would be the Connecticut Yankees," said Hedy as she inserted the key card into the lock and pushed down the handle. "At least they had the good manners to hold their tongues. They didn't speak all dinner, but they didn't ask."

"I'm so sorry," said Barbara. "Do you want to abandon ship?" She sat down and took off her pumps and tried to smile, her attempt to lighten the mood.

"Maybe I should just make an announcement. Yes, I'm the one. Tune in for a sixty-minute special. Don't ask me questions. Leave me alone." Hedy was despondent thinking about her options. "I sure as hell didn't see the British coming. It will be all over the boat by tomorrow. If you think there were some stares tonight, just wait for breakfast."

"Room service," said Barbara, picking up a little door hanger that let passengers order breakfast and the time it would be delivered. "Do you want the full American breakfast or the lox plate with bagel?"

"You can't make it go away," said Hedy, "and we can't just sit in the room and hide. What the hell were you talking about earlier? Going naked tomorrow? You know I'm not going to do that."

"Don't count that out," said Barbara. "The guy from the office, who apparently works to cruise, said it was the best thing!"

"Sure. That's so me," said Hedy. "Did you just meet me today? I'm going in and getting ready for bed."

"Well, if you don't mind, I'm going out," said Barbara as she reinserted her feet into the shoes.

"Out?"

"Let me take care of this. I want to make arrangements for a table for two from now on. We don't need to put people in a bad place. The poor Connecticut couple didn't enjoy their dinner any more than we did. I'm going to talk to the captain or whoever is in charge. We don't have to be victims," said Barbara.

Hedy knew this was a good thing, and she was so grateful to Barbara. "You know it really is just too much for me. I hate for you to have to deal with this," she said.

"I do it well," said Barbara. "Try telling grieving parents their daughter was a prostitute and died from a combination of heroin overdose and her pimp beating her when they were under the impression she was on track to graduate college. That Brit will be crushed if she opens her mouth again." Barbara pulled down the ends of her sweater so that she was completely put together, her black slacks breaking perfectly over her shoes, her colorful scarf tied just right. She took a quick look in the mirror and went out the door.

Barbara did not expect to find a woman in charge. She was blond and thoroughly German. She was a little overweight but neat in her uniform and maybe in her early forties. She smiled as the woman from the front desk eased Barbara into a small office. The two employees from the ship had conversed in German over the phone about the American asking to speak with the most senior official, and while Barbara could pick up a little, she wasn't exactly sure

428

what had transpired. What she felt, however, was that this was very unusual.

"How may I help you?" said the blond as she rose and extended her hand. Her English was so perfect she must have spent time in the States.

"Your English is beautiful," said Barbara.

"Thank you. My parents sent me to Colorado to study each summer of my high school years. They thought it was important."

Barbara smiled in approval, wondering slightly about how one would pick Colorado. "I'm here to ask for some special treatment," she said, wanting the woman to know she realized this was highly unusual. The Germans expected people to follow the rules. "My partner, with whom I am here with on the cruise, is Hedy Miller. Her sister is the woman who murdered her mother. Another sister committed suicide."

The woman was not shocked. "Yes, several of the passengers have asked. I looked it up on the Internet. I'm so sorry."

"I am not just asking for Hedy, but for the other passengers. Tonight we were told we would have to sit at a communal table. It made people uncomfortable because, while they figured it out, they didn't want to ask, and it certainly made Hedy and me uncomfortable."

"Yes, yes. I understand, but if I set up a table for two, wouldn't that also make things uncomfortable? You would be the only ones. We can't reconfigure the whole dining room for one sailing. We only have big round tables, plus some long rectangular ones. What about room service?"

"Do you think we should only have the option of eating in our room?" replied Barbara, a little irritated that her request had not been automatically granted.

"No. I don't think that should be your only option, but it is a delicate situation. We welcome you and your partner and are happy that you have selected our ship to celebrate the season. I imagine you also wanted to get away, have some privacy outside the States. There must be a lot of coverage."

"Yes," said Barbara, "but tonight we had a British woman ask Hedy directly if she was the one whose sister murdered her mother."

"We can't be held accountable for the ill manners of the British," said the woman pleasantly.

Barbara almost laughed, but the fact was, she needed some answers, not little jabs at stereotypes. "It's not just the British, but the Germans, people from the States. Soon it will be everyone. What can you do?"

"What would you do if you were at home?" asked the officer pleasantly.

Barbara stopped to think. "Well, we'd stay in a lot, probably, and when we went out, we would go to places that would respect our privacy."

"For the most part, wouldn't you guess?"

"Yes, I suppose there would be some people who would approach Hedy if we were eating out at home." It was the first time Barbara had given the situation adequate thought.

"Let me suggest that I can instruct the maître d' to always seat you with a couple from Australia who are traveling with their two daughters. They are also unhappy with the dining arrangements. They don't want to talk with anyone but their daughters and themselves. We will reserve the inside window seats, across the table, for you and your partner, we will explain the situation to them, and no one will have to speak to the other. Sort of a table for two hidden in plain sight."

Barbara smiled. "That would be very nice." She knew everyone would be too busy eating and drinking to take much notice if they were there but not at some chatty table.

"How would you like to handle the occasional inquiry about whether your partner is the one currently in the news?" asked the woman cautiously. "I could write a letter to all the guests and explain the situation and ask that they apply decent manners. Slip it under the doors tonight."

Barbara sat back. "No. I think that might just draw attention."

The woman smiled noncommittally. She wasn't going to make this decision; she would do whatever Barbara and Hedy wanted.

"Let's see how it goes," said Barbara. "Maybe as a last resort."

"I noticed you selected one of our veranda suites for your cruise," said the woman. "I hope you are finding everything acceptable."

"Yes, yes. Very nice," said Barbara, already distracted with how she was going to break this to Hedy.

" Since you're one of our best customers, I would like to offer you a private tour for our stops, as opposed to going on the group buses."

Barbara turned and wondered who had trained this woman and how she could thank her enough. "We're skipping tomorrow. I was trying to talk Hedy into the Cologne Baths."

"Yes, yes, a must-see. It wouldn't be something we could put on our itinerary." She laughed. "Not for everyone. I'll have a car waiting for, say, 1:00 p.m. A leisurely breakfast after the group has left for the Cathedral Tour. It leaves at 10:00 a.m., and I'll make sure the wait staff knows you will be coming by after that for a big brunch. You'll need it with all the swimming. We sail at 6:00 p.m., so I can have the car at the baths at 4:00 p.m. Yes?"

Barbara smiled. She liked this woman a lot.

"I would suggest that you talk with your partner and let me know what you would like to see, and I can make arrangements. Nuremberg, Melk, Vienna, and then, of course, Budapest would be my suggestion. Private tours with our compliments.

"I can't school everyone on the definition of impudence, but I can try to eliminate as many opportunities for it to be exhibited as possible. You and Hedy will no doubt need to manage a few rogue passengers," she continued. "Please, from all of us, know that we are sorry for her situation. If we can do anything more," said the young woman as she rose.

Barbara had no doubt that each staff member would be reminded of the definition of good manners and exactly how they should be played on this particular cruise with this individual situation.

When Barbara returned to the room, she found Hedy sleeping. She silently congratulated herself on being able to earn Hedy's trust in handling the situation. Hedy didn't trust many people, and she certainly wasn't used to relinquishing ugly situations. She had juggled them all her life, for everyone.

The next morning, they stood together and looked out their big windows as the other passengers disembarked and walked toward waiting coaches. Hedy had slept late, but they were ready for their brunch and were anxious for the buses to pull away.

"There she is," said Hedy about the Brit and her husband, Edmund. "Who names their child Edmund?"

"People all over Great Britain—especially back in the day. What are they? In their eighties?"

"Let's not venture into age. Eighty is looking younger and younger." Hedy laughed as she turned from the window, tiring of watching the milling of passengers. "I guess we would have to handle some rudeness even in Louisville," said Hedy, enforcing the woman's observation.

"Especially in Louisville," replied Barbara. "I don't know what I expected last night, but man, she did everything right. Brunch, table for two in plain sight, complimentary tours."

"I'm still not getting naked," said Hedy. She had laid out her bathing suit and a little dress designed for the beach, not Germany at Christmas. She'd go in plain clothes and then change at the baths.

"They are gone. Zoom. Zoom. Out, out buses," said Barbara with a toss of her hand. "Let's eat."

"Good morning, Ms. Miller, Dr. Collins," said the headwaiter. "We have a perfect table for you right there in the middle, by the window," he said, pointing. "That way, you can look out at the beautiful city of Cologne." He headed them into the dining room, lifting white starched napkins and moving water glasses. "We can fix anything, so I gathered up all the special breakfast and lunch menus on offer this cruise, plus the menu that is always available. Maybe somewhere in here, you can find something to your liking. If not, just instruct us!" He smiled and went to get water.

"Quite the assortment," said Hedy, leafing through the menus. "I don't want to be any more of a bother than we already are." She continued looking at the more standard fare. "I'm going with the eggs benedict."

"Spanish omelet with Romesco sauce," replied Barbara. "English muffin in honor of our rogue rude passenger," she said with a smile.

At 1:00 p.m., a black car with a uniformed driver waited at the end of the little bridge connecting the boat with the land of Germany. Barbara and Hedy had picked up an extra towel along with their little packs carrying everything from iPhones and hair products to their bathing suits.

"Why did you bother?" Hedy asked Barbara, picking at the bathing suit sticking out of the bag. "Thought it was just naked all the way."

"It is, but when you are in the front pool, there are children, and most people wear suits. There is also the fact people have lunch overlooking the big pool. I'd hate for anyone to choke on their sausages."

Hedy never understood Barbara's complete disregard for exposing her body. The fact she had such a nice body certainly helped, but naked? Hedy paused in the women's locker room at the gym.

The pool was warm, even on the outside, where there was a slight sprinkle of rain. One section of the main pool had a built-in current which helped people float in a circular pattern. As Hedy let go and went with the motion, she, felt the tension pull away from her muscles. She had been holding everything in for so long, she hadn't realized just how tired she really was.

"I made a massage appointment for you," said Barbara as she returned to Hedy's side. "You need it."

"What about you?" asked Hedy, getting excited about the possibility but not wanting to be selfish.

"They only had one cancelation, and besides, I want to get hit with the branches and stretch out in the wet sauna. I want my pores opened up."

"And is that the clothing-optional portion?" asked Hedy.

"Exactly," answered Barbara. "Come find me among the naked pools when you are finished. I'll be a wet noodle."

Hedy felt extremely guilty with all this pampering. She removed her suit and climbed between the Egyptian cotton sheets to wait for the masseuse. It was hard to even bring her sisters into focus. What might they be doing? She thought of Patty and squeezed her eyes shut. She just couldn't think of her now. She didn't want to cry.

"Is there anything you'd like me to work on?" said the light-brown man as he entered the room, rubbing his hands and showing off his body, which was beautiful and worthy of display. His accent was hard to place.

"Every possible place on my body," said Hedy. "It's been a rough couple of months."

"That makes me happy. It means I can make a difference," he replied. "Let me know if it is too hard. I usually do a deep massage," he said, oiling his hands and placing them on her back. Hedy was face down, and she felt the warmth begin to penetrate her muscles.

"The harder the better," she said quietly as she let go. Do I deserve this? she thought as she felt his fingers run down her spine and then out along the back.

"What is this?" he said as he hit the top middle part of her back.

"Oh, please don't take offense, but my mother hit me as a child, and I would roll into a ball, exposing my back. It took the brunt. Somewhere around T-1 and T-2. The muscles don't fit right. I've gone to a lot of doctors, but there isn't much they can do. If you can just help them loosen," she said. For the first time, she didn't try to lie about why her back was a mess. Eighteen years of beatings had taken a toll.

"Guess she was a treat," he replied.

"You have no idea," she said, "but look where I am now. How nice is this?"

"I will make it as nice as possible." His hands began a rhythm that allowed Hedy to go into another world, where she was treated kindly and with respect. Hands that did not hurt her. The music was low, and candles burned in the room, filling it with pleasant smells.

When she finished, she did not bother to put on her swimsuit, but rather wrapped a bath towel around herself and went to find Barbara. She looked in various bathhouses where people were being slapped and folded back into shape. Finally, she spied the back of Barbara's head. She was laid back in the winter rain in a mineral pool completely naked and next to any number of men and women.

Hedy had always been uptight about her body. It was never good enough, tall enough, thin enough, firm enough. She held the towel tight. The first to emerge from the pool was an overweight man with his stomach folding over itself. He smiled as he exited and walked toward one of the small houses, completely at ease with his body. The next man had a penis so small Hedy looked quickly and then looked away. Was it a penis? It was so small.

Once, Hedy had done research for the Mayo Clinic and learned that one in every 1,750 births in the United States resulted in babies with ambiguous genitalia. *Intrasex* was the politically correct name. Hedy had been stunned at how common it was and that in earlier years, almost all of the babies had been quickly surgically corrected to be female. Just easier to dig a hole than build a pole, but oftentimes completely wrong in how the children would later identify.

The next to exit was a woman who must have been a body builder. Muscles on top of muscles. Barbara looked up and smiled.

In one quick movement, Hedy pulled off the towel and laid it on a bench. She then walked toward Barbara and got in.

"You are just beautiful," she said, and Hedy knew she was lying.

"Get into the mineral water; it's warm," said Barbara. "How was the massage?"

"Fabulous. Some man originally from Turkey. At the end, I thought about asking for a cigarette, and I've never smoked in my life," she said, laughing.

The car was outside promptly at 4:00, and it whisked them back to the boat. Most of the other passengers had returned and were milling about looking in the gift shop or reading in chairs that were strategically placed about the boat. Hedy looked up and saw her coming. She reached out and indicated to Barbara to step back. She was prepared.

"I've looked for you everywhere," said Edmund's wife. "You weren't at breakfast, and you didn't take the tour."

Edmund himself then stepped toward the two women. "You have upset my wife terribly," he said directly to Hedy.

"And why would that be?" she said in a low voice, not wanting to attract attention, but people were beginning to take notice of the confrontation. Edmund was not as quiet.

"You just walked off. You were rude. You didn't answer her question. She didn't mean any harm."

"It would be impossible for me to compete with your wife on rudeness," began Hedy. "Yes, my sister killed my mother with a rusty pipe rammed into her neck so violently that she bled out in about fifteen minutes. My other sister committed suicide as a result. She hung herself. My family has been through the mill, and I am trying to regain my composure with a trip uninterrupted by people like your wife. Do you want details? My mother was a borderline schizophrenic. She beat all her children our entire lives. She deserved everything she got. More details? My sister pleaded guilty to murder one when she could have taken a plea agreement. The plea agreement would have resulted in her being imprisoned for eight and a half years as opposed to the rest of her life. She did that because she wanted to take credit and tell the world what happens when you hit a child. There will be a Diane Sawyer special in January. Tune in. You'll get everything answered. Every last detail," said Hedy, using her hands to indicate smallness.

"Now leave me alone. Do not come near me. Do not ask me any more questions. If I have upset your wife, I am sorry, but there is a limit to what I have to take from the likes of her."

A small crowd had gathered, and people dropped their heads when Hedy ended. She reached out and took Barbara's arm and strode toward her corner suite. She did not speak until they were inside the room, and then she laughed. "Do you think I was rude?" asked Hedy.

"I thought you were fabulous," said Barbara, taking her in her arms. "Absolutely fabulous."

"Get off my back, Dorothy. You are dead. I don't need your ugliness any longer. I'm happy. I'm really happy," said Hedy. "What were you thinking about wearing to dinner tonight?" she asked Barbara.

# FORTY NINE

Jack couldn't put it off any longer. The year was coming to an end, and Patty refused to see him. He could not help her if she wouldn't talk to him. The staff had told him she had packed her meager belongings and placed them in a paper bag. She was ready to go.

He had taken a call from the warden shortly after Christmas and had assured him she would be in Pewee Valley before the first of the year. Next week, a small picture of Patty was scheduled to appear on the cover of *People* magazine along with a fairly in-depth story. Jack had been interviewed. He knew it would show old photos of the five girls, Dorothy in her younger years, and Patty smiling in a prom dress in front of a green-painted fireplace. The details would be briefer than what was scheduled for the other two stories, but it was just the first in what would soon be a media onslaught. He didn't think it would end with Diane Sawyer and the *Courier-Journal*. The warden wanted it to be clear that in Kentucky, there was no special treatment for a murderer, especially a white woman from means.

Jack printed out the forms and paused before he put his pen to the paper. He so wished he could have spoken with her. He had never seen anyone with such a steel will. He signed his name and got up from the desk.

"Here are the release papers," he said as he walked into the deputy warden's office. "She's as well as I am going to get her here," he said.

"I heard you asked for a transfer to KCIW, Dr. Terrell," she said, looking at him with renewed interest. "Something going on with you and Patty Anderson? Just a coincidence?"

Jack looked at her and then said, "You know I am a gay man. I have a partner I have been with for thirty years. A lawyer," he added just in case she wanted to worry about his possible future legal bills if someone erroneously questioned his desire for a transfer.

"There is nothing going on with Patty Anderson other than she is a very interesting case whom I think I could help under the right circumstances. I've been here twenty years, and I'm tired of doing evaluations of sex offenders and other people so broken they can never really be helped. I need a change. That's it. Here are the papers."

"I hear it's gone through," said the deputy warden. "That you'll be transferred right after the first of the year."

"That would be very nice," said Dr. Terrell as he walked away.

It didn't take long for Patty to be moved. Everyone knew she was coming, and everyone was ready. She was aroused at 3:00 a.m. Breakfast and then transfer at 5:00 a.m. It was standard. She had been issued the orange suit prisoners wore only when traveling. She picked up her brown paper bag filled with state-issued underwear and walked off. She waved at the woman who cried for her baby.

Patty was now used to being processed. She smiled for her picture, rolled her fingers in the black ink, and stripped in front of the guards. They checked her cavities, and she saw just how hardened they had become. "Find anything?" she asked as the female guard pulled her gloved hand from her vagina.

"Never know what you'll find," she said. "Last week I got a whole bag of weed. I'm not finished."

Patty had always been good at disassociating, and she put her mind somewhere else. She stood with her legs spread as the woman dug a little deeper.

"She's clean," said the guard as she turned Patty toward the shower. "You'll need to wash up. I had to use some jelly. Nobody been down there in a while."

Patty did not let any of this bother her. She needed to know where she was going to be for the rest of her life. She needed to make her way. If she could endure Dorothy as a child, this was going to be easy.

She was issued numbers and clothes. She recognized the outfit and the canvas shoes. Why hadn't they just let her keep her shoes from KCPC? Waste. She would have rather they had left her with old clothes and given her an apple.

"So you the new cellie," said a large black woman twice Patty's size. Her hands were on her hips. "You killed your mother?"

"Yes. Yes, I did," said Patty, not batting an eye. "In the neck with a rusty pipe."

"Gurrll, you got to be kidding," said the woman.

"No. I had it all planned, and it went off without a hitch," said Patty.

"Everything but you getting caught," said the woman, whose hair was as wild as her eyes. "I killed my man."

"Really?" said Patty. She knew not to ask questions. This place was so different from KCPC. Everyone appeared normal. Sort of. Patty was scrambling mentally to eyeball the place.

"I shot him. Tired of him beating on me," said the woman. "Drugs too. I'm in for life."

Patty looked at the woman discreetly and wondered just how big the man must have been to get away with beating her.

"Me too. Life," said Patty. The young girl had told her not to ask how long people were in for because it was rude and would piss them off. Only if they offered, and both Patty and Tasha had offered.

"I guess I get the top," said Patty.

"Un hun. That's right," said Tasha. She crossed her arms. "You want me to make your bed?"

"No, thanks," said Patty.

"But what if you don't get it right?" asked the bigger woman. "You need to get it right."

Patty said nothing as Tasha took the sheets out of her hands and went to make the bed. "We all get judged, and I don't want you dragging me down. You understand?"

"No," said Patty. She made sure it was in an earnest voice.

"I want to go to breakfast first, and if your bed isn't made up right, we'll get the leftover shit."

"I'll try not to drag you down," said Patty. "I appreciate your help."

"You the one that's going to be on TV, right? The idiot that turned down a plea bargain. You nuts or what?"

"I'm not nuts enough, apparently," said Patty. "I wanted to stay over at KCPC, but I'm not nuts enough."

"You sound nuts to me," said Tasha as she executed a perfect hospital corner.

"I really didn't have anyplace to go, so I might as well just stay in jail," said Patty.

"You sound like Martha," said Tasha. "She been here so long she won't even sign up for the parole board. They going to send her out, though. She just about done her time."

"Maybe she can do something else and get sent back. You know— not hurt anyone, but something bad enough," offered Patty.

"I like the way you think," said Tasha. "Maybe we ought to put that in Martha's head."

Patty sat down on the toilet. "No chairs?" she asked.

"Not a damn one. They want us to sit on the bed, but then you just mess up those nice hospital corners."

Patty wondered if she was taking the good seat and slowly slipped onto the floor. She saw a small stack of books on a shelf along with some letters. "Do you read a lot?" asked Patty.

"If I couldn't read, I'd lose my mind. The library cart comes around. Do-gooders donate used magazines. Two thousand six is a young one."

"What about the food?" asked Patty.

"What do you think? They feed us for something like fifty-two cents a day. I never know what it is most of the time. Everything is stale. When my daughter comes to visit, she'll maybe bring me some money. I like the beef jerky from the commissary."

A buzzer sounded, and Tasha went over to the bars. Patty followed her. "Noon roll call. They come by and count us, like we are going somewhere."

Patty stood rock still when the guard came by counting. "You the new one?"

Patty nodded her head, and the guard moved on.

"I guess I missed lunch," said Patty to Tasha. "Transport day, and I got breakfast before five o'clock this morning. I'm not a big eater anyway," she said.

Tasha answered, "I am," and then she started yelling for the guard.

"This woman ain't had no lunch today. Transport day. You better bring her lunch. It's in the rules," said Tasha.

Patty smiled at the guard.

She watched as Tasha ate the stale bologna sandwich, Doritos, and red Kool-Aid. She guessed the same people who cooked at KCPC did the cooking at the women's prison. She really wasn't hungry.

"So, we can get mail?" said Patty to Tasha carefully, noting the stack of letters on her bookshelf. Patty didn't want any mail, but she did want to know how things worked at her new home.

"You can get mail," said Tasha. "They read everything, but I like getting letters, and I save them. You want mail?"

Patty saw that Tasha was careful not to ask about who she had on the outside. You didn't ask questions. "Nobody really." Patty knew Tasha knew everything about her because she had been in the news and they had access to television.

"My sister killed herself," said Patty. "I don't want to hear from the others. They need to get on with their lives."

"That's a bad thing about your sister," Tasha noted a little off-handedly. "I've got kids and grandkids. I like hearing from them. Four kids. Two boys. Two girls. Their grandkids are growing up without me. The kids too," she continued with a note of sadness.

"It's good they write you," said Patty. Then she took a breath. "I have epilepsy, and that means I have seizures—fits." She hated that last word, but she knew it was the best way for her to describe it to Tasha. "It's pretty scary and ugly." She knew she needed to get it out.

Patty continued while Tasha looked uninterested. "I'm sorry about it, but I can't help it," Patty said. "If I have a seizure, you don't have to do anything. Well, if you roll me over on my side, it would keep me from choking if I vomit. I usually don't vomit."

446

"That's some bad shit, girl." Tasha looked up from finishing off the Doritos. "How many times you do that?"

"It depends," said Patty. "You could just call for the guard, but by the time they get here, it might be too late."

"Maybe they ought to just put you in the infirmary," Tasha offered, knowing she did not want to have a roommate who went into some kind of fits.

"It doesn't happen all the time," she said. "I work really hard with my meds."

"We'll see," said Tasha, standing up and towering over Patty. "I don't want to have to be standing around watching you have a fit."

Patty didn't answer. She wondered what Tasha had dealt with in her life. She couldn't be immune to bad luck, or she wouldn't be in KCIW for life. Four children and an abusive husband. Drugs. Didn't sound like an easy life. Patty turned and looked directly out of the cell, trying to figure how she could survive.

Patty thought she heard a dog, but that couldn't be right. They didn't lock up dogs; they just put them to sleep if they did something like pull a child's face off or kill an abusive owner. She thought about how it would have been if they had just put her to sleep. She could feel the coolness of not having to worry about surviving. She closed her eyes and wished for that coolness. She took a deep breath and then exhaled. It was a trick her former therapist, Dr. Levy, had taught her. She hooked her arms around her legs and closed her fingers into one another. She could do this. She just had to stay calm and figure things out.

The guard appeared at the door. "You ready?" she said to Tasha.

"I'm so ready," she replied. "What are you thinking putting me in here with a nut case that has fits?" she said, pointing to Patty. A wave of betrayal washed over Patty. She had thought things were going so well.

"Did she have a fit?" asked the guard.

"Not yet, but I don't want to be around."

"Well, for the next hour, you get to be in your NA meeting, so enjoy." The guard unlocked the door and ushered Tasha out.

Narcotics Anonymous, thought Patty. That meant there would be AA and other programs. What could she join? She wanted to get out for an hour. She didn't drink or overeat, and she certainly didn't do drugs. Well, recreational drugs. She did plenty of other drugs.

Time crawled for Patty, even after Tasha had gone and come back from her meeting. She didn't ask Tasha anything more, and Tasha kept looking at her. Finally, she said, "How can I tell if you are going to have a fit?"

"They are normally called seizures," began Patty, but she knew it wouldn't make any difference. "They come on without warning. I sometimes get a feeling, an aura, but it's just seconds. My body becomes rigid, and I'll hit my head on the floor. Thirty seconds. No more than a minute, almost always. If I have more than one in an hour, they'll probably take me away. I'm sorry."

"You ought to be sorry. Visiting that kind of shit on people," said Tasha in a dismissive voice. "I don't need any of that shit."

"Me either," said Patty, "but I don't have a choice."

"You have a choice to keep to yourself," said Tasha. "Don't be following me to dinner."

Patty nodded and moved closer to the back wall. She wondered when dinner might be. She was pretty hungry. When it came time for the dinner bell, Tasha was up quickly from reading a young children's book. Patty had taken note that all the books were written for children about eight or nine years old. The guard came and let them both out at the same time, but Patty walked slowly. She didn't want to be accused of following Tasha. She wasn't sure where to go, so she followed the crowd. They apparently went in shifts. She hung back, observing.

Hot dogs and beans, thought Patty as her stomach growled. She hadn't had a chance to get to the commissary, so she was without her safety food, Snickers and squeeze cheese. She'd had to leave her stash at KCPC. The staff had taken everything. She slowly edged in line. Patty looked down at the hot dog that was placed on her tray and could see it wasn't an ordinary hot dog. She looked at the corn bread and wished for a little butter. Water would be so much better than this diluted Kool-Aid. She sat at an almost-empty table with an attached bench for seating and then kept moving toward the middle as other inmates came to sit down.

"You the new one?" asked a woman with hair shaved like a man. L-O-V-E was tattooed across the tops of her left fingers. She wore glasses and pushed them back as she took a seat across from Patty.

"Yes," said Patty. "My name is Patty."

"We all know what your name is. Killed your mother. You going to eat that corn bread?" asked the woman as she took it off of Patty's tray. Patty watched as the bread left her plate. That was the only thing she had planned on eating.

"Why did you just take my food?" said Patty, remembering how Tasha had eaten her lunch.

"Take your damn corn bread," responded the woman, and she threw it back to Patty. It bounced off the tray and onto the floor. Patty looked down but didn't pick it up.

"You too good to pick it up, now that you've taken it away from me?" said the woman as she stood up.

"You took it from me," said Patty. "Now it's on the floor."

"Well la de da," said the woman. "On the floor! Oh my."

The young Hispanic on Patty's right reached out and placed her hand on Patty's arm. "Pick it up, honey. We don't waste corn bread."

Patty turned and retrieved her bread from the floor.

"Leave her alone, Jane," said the woman, who couldn't have been more than thirty years old. "Why do you always have to start in on the new ones?"

"Got to break them in," said Jane. "This one especially. Killed her mother and then didn't take the plea. Some kind of nut job."

"She's not a nut job. Well, we don't know if she is or not," agreed the young woman, and she turned to Patty. "You some kind of nut job?"

"Yes," said Patty, "but not nuts enough to keep me out of here."

Patty wanted to fit in, but she knew she couldn't be taken for granted. These women needed to know she was not afraid of them. That they had better step back from her. She absolutely didn't care.

"I'm Ana," said the young woman, and she smiled. "How about the franks and beans? It's one of the best dinners," she said, laying into a big forkful.

"The franks look funny," said Patty to Ana, and she took a bite to show she wasn't too good to eat them.

"They are called turkey franks," said Jane. "Not up to your country-club standards?"

Patty worked hard not to react to Jane's anger. "I've never belonged to a country club in my life, but I am thinking we all probably ate a little better when we were on the outside. I'm just trying to figure things out." Patty wanted to turn things down a notch. She took another bite. They were disgusting.

"When my parents had us working the fields," began Ana, "we would eat so many of the tomatoes we'd be sick. They were so good, right off the vines. I'd never tasted tomatoes so good until we got to Kentucky."

"I've always thought we had the best too," said Patty. "It's nice to hear from someone who has eaten tomatoes in other states say it too." Patty like Ana.

"Florida, Georgia, Tennessee. They were all good, but Kentucky was the best." She smiled at the thought. "I should have kept picking the food, but, you know…a boyfriend, and then carrying the drugs. Now I'm here, and my mother has my baby. I got ten years, with barely three served."

Patty oddly felt at home with these women. She had spoken more just today than she had in weeks with Sophie and Paul. Every woman had a story, and Patty being hit in the head with a nine iron didn't seem so bad. It wasn't that Sophie and everyone didn't love her, it was just that she was such a reminder. She smiled at Ana. "Maybe it'll go fast, and you'll be out for your baby's teenage years."

Patty was exhausted. Some of the women had the right to sit in a communal room and watch television. She didn't have any rights and was headed right back to her cell. She assumed Tasha had a meeting or was watching television because she wasn't in the cell when Patty returned after dinner. Patty climbed the steps and stretched out on the bed. Her back hurt, and she was hungry. The sheets felt good, and she quickly dropped off to sleep.

Just like days of old, Patty was ripped awake with a jerk. This time it was Tasha and not Dorothy, but the effect was the same. "What are you doing?" said Tasha, pulling the sheets off Patty. One hand on her hip and the other on Patty's bedclothes.

"If you want me to have a fit, then keep doing stuff like this," said Patty. "Why are you on me?"

"Oh, honey, I'm so not on you. You not my type. So not my type. I'm trying to tell you the facts of life, and life don't include you curling up like this is some damn hotel." She pulled her head, indicating for Patty to get up.

Rising slowly, Patty wondered what would be an appropriate re-action. She descended the bunk bed and stood by the cold bars. She crossed her arms for effect.

"I made this bed perfect for it to stay perfect," Tasha began. "Now look. Sleep on top of the damn thing. Not under. How else we going to get to breakfast early?"

Patty didn't exactly understand, but she was willing to go along. She didn't move.

"You be the only one in here sleeping snug like under the covers. Sleep on top so when the guards come, they will see a perfect bed, and then we'll get there before the pancakes run out."

It began making sense to Patty, as she watched Tasha remake the bed. "Do you want me to help?" asked Patty.

"If I'd wanted your help, I'd a asked," said Tasha.

"Fine. But you don't have to be so bitchy about it," said Patty, knowing she couldn't take this from Tasha on a regular basis.

"Don't you be calling me out of my name," came a swift response. "You mind your street and I'll mind mine. We don't have to be best friends. Just don't drag me down."

"I'm not dragging you down," said Patty. "I'm just trying to find my way. I appreciate your help."

Morning came quickly, and Patty jumped up to smooth out her bed. The sheets were tight and beautiful when the guard passed by. The pancakes were still being handed out. She saw Ana and went over and took a seat. She didn't want to assume anything. "May I sit here?" she asked, holding her tray in midair.

"I guess," said Ana offhandedly, nowhere near as friendly as yesterday.

Patty looked up and saw the most beautiful thing she had ever seen. She could not pull her eyes away. "There are dogs here?" she asked Ana so breathlessly that the whole table turned in her direction.

"Puppy Prison Program," said a woman Patty had never laid eyes on before. "They train them here during the week, and then the dogs go out to the mall and to the grocery store with people on the outside during the weekend. For people with disabilities."

"You mean the inmates train them?"

"For about fifteen months or so," said the woman. "Don't worry, honey, you won't be getting no dog."

"Why not?" asked Patty. "I could train a dog."

"You probably have your GED," said Ana, "but it takes more than just being educated to be selected. You have to be in the Honors Program, and anyone with a violent charge, liking killing their mother, wouldn't qualify."

"Honors Program?" said Patty, slowly putting down her fork.

"If you have a nonviolent charge, you get seven days' credit a month for good behavior. After a while, you get in the Honors Program." The old Ana had returned.

Patty couldn't stop looking at the yellow Lab as he walked alongside his human inmate. She had always wanted a dog, but Sophie said they were too much trouble. That dog was beautiful.

"There are only about seven or eight women who get to be in the program," Ana added, "but it's nice to have the dogs around. We all enjoy them."

Patty thought about Dr. Terrell. If he were there, maybe he could do something to help her get into the Honors Program. She had been so mean saying he had a dull life and everything. So what if he hadn't gotten her the police scanner? If she could just have a dog, she could put up with anything, even Tasha. Even life in prison.

# FIFTY

Barbara and Hedy barely left the room on the fourth day of the cruise. The boat stopped briefly for the group to tour the ancient medieval Marksburg Castle, and then it made a quick stop in the city of Koblenz. They didn't care about either and didn't want to take advantage by asking for a private car. The day was really designed for the guests to enjoy looking out at the hilltop castles nestled along the Middle Rhine River as the boat slowly made its way to Miltenberg.

They had made the discovery of DVDs in the library and had picked up the first two seasons of *Glee*, a show they had heard a great deal about but had never watched. One episode after the other sucked them further into the ridiculous, over-the-top musical numbers that would never have been created on a weekly basis in a public high school in Ohio. The talent on display was more than entertaining, and Jane Lynch as Sue Sylvester made them laugh out loud. They had a friend who had gone to high school with Jane, and apparently, in real life, she was a lot like Sue.

"I've had about enough *Glee*," said Hedy, getting up from the bed. The cleaning attendant had made the bed, but Hedy had chosen to stay on top of it as opposed to getting between the sheets. Old habit. She had a blanket sporting the cruise logo on top of her. "Not that it hasn't been wonderful," she said, referring to the show, "but it's almost six o'clock. Even the castles have gone in for the night."

Barbara punched the button on the control to turn off the television. She got up and went to look out the window. "Actually, the castles have lights, lots of lights. Look up." She and Hedy stood transfixed as the boat slowed to accommodate the view.

"Are we going to dinner in the dining room tonight?" Barbara asked, giving Hedy all the room she needed. They had avoided both lunch and breakfast.

"I think we should," said Hedy. "I mean, we paid for the cruise, and if they want to look, let them look. I'll answer their insidious questions, if they have any. Hell, when we get back, I'll have to stand in front of television cameras and answer questions."

Barbara didn't comment but felt somewhat responsible.

"Am I still the only one?" asked Hedy.

"Lily refuses flatly," began Barbara. "She told the producers they should be glad she was getting the still photos together. Eva says she just can't. Whatever that means."

Hedy knew what it meant. Eva wasn't built like the others. She hadn't gotten the mean, steel-will gene. Too nice. If pushed too far, she would respond, but it took a lot. She didn't deserve being pushed.

"Whatever. I'll tell our pitiful tale," said Hedy. "I guess we want high ratings."

"Oh, the ratings are going to be just fine," said Barbara. "Lots and lots of hype."

"Maybe we can just move into this little room permanently, floating up and down the Rhine. Once, Drew sent me an article about how older people were just staying on cruise ships because they were cheaper than nursing homes. Three meals a day, a doctor onboard. Sounded good."

"We'd have to move to a smaller room, down several levels," said Barbara as she combed through her hair, which required little effort. "I'm not dressing up," she said, surveying her jeans and polo shirt. Barbara always looked good. Thin went a long way.

"Let's get a drink before dinner. We'll be late, but who cares? The bar will be empty." Hedy was ready to walk out the door. She stood straight and headed down the hall.

"Cloudy Bay," said Barbara, knowing Hedy never veered. "What kind of beer do you have?" They were in Germany, after all.

The bartender was different, and he appeared to be struggling. "My English is poor," he said, smiling. "So sorry."

Barbara looked at the young man and his smooth, beautiful complexion. He wasn't German. Asian of some sort?

"Sprechen Sie Deutsch?" Barbara spoke a smattering of German and thought she could maneuver through a drink order.

"No," he said, smiling with big white teeth.

"How is he working on this boat," asked Hedy, "if he can't speak English or German?"

Barbara tried one last thing.

"Вы говорите по-русски?" No Russian either.

He shook his head in such a pleasant manner that Barbara and Hedy both smiled. Hedy rose from her seat and went behind the bar. She pulled open the little refrigerator and pulled out an open bottle of the sauvignon blanc. She motioned for him to hand her a white-wine glass, and she poured herself a drink. Then she reached in and pulled out a frosty mug. "What's your pleasure?"

"That Pilsner looks interesting," said Barbara, and Hedy slid the cold mug under the tap. "My father taught me how to pour a beer so the head would be just right," said Hedy, remembering her years as a small girl pouring beer every night for her father. A case a night, without exception.

They were just heading for a seat in the deserted bar when the blonde officer who had been so accommodating came into the bar. "I'm so sorry, ladies," she began.

"No problem, obviously," said Hedy, and she held up her glass as if in a toast.

"It's the holidays, and we are so short staffed. Benz doesn't normally tend bar, but with everyone upstairs, we had to take a chance. He wants to tend bar desperately, but his English isn't good enough. He normally cleans rooms. I'm sorry."

"Please," said Barbara, "you have done so much for us. He was wonderful. How will Benz learn enough English?"

"I don't know, but I'm not even sure he can even stay cleaning. People leave notes in English, and he can't read them. The others try to cover for him, but many of them don't speak Thai. He is such a good worker, and his family depends on his wages.

"It's hard to get really good workers," she continued. "The Germans want to start at the top, and they don't like being away for eighteen months on a ship. It's the Asian applicants who will do anything. They look at these jobs as something very special. They make a good wage and have good living conditions compared to the ones who work in the textile factories making T-shirts for Gap. Then there is the sex trade. Families selling little girls to old men. The children are their only valuable possessions."

Hedy and Barbara listened carefully, occasionally looking over at Benz, who continued to smile and polish the wine glasses. The bar was perfect, and he looked perfect with his gold-and-black-patterned vest, starched white shirt, and black tie. He just couldn't communicate and take orders for the bar. He was nothing more than a guard for the glasses.

"I'd best run. We're having wiener zwiebelrostbraten as the special tonight, and there will be a lot of questions. I'll say sirloin steak and sour cream forty times tonight." She laughed. "Have it. It's quite good. Potatoes, too." And off she went.

Barbara turned to look at Hedy, and she knew something had happened. "What?" she said in a small panic. "What?"

"That's it," said Hedy. "It's so perfect I can't believe I didn't think of it before."

"Think of what before?" Barbara looked at her beer and then at Hedy's wine. They had barely taken a sip. She should be lucid.

"Teaching English as a second language in Asia," said Hedy. "We could teach English as a second language in some Asian country.

Cambodia, Thailand, Vietnam. We'd be close to the baby, and we could make a difference in the world. English for Emerging Cultures," said Hedy, as if she had just seen the words written out on a school sign, ever the marketeer.

"English for Emerging Cultures?" said Barbara. "No. How about English for Hospitality Employees? Think practical."

"Perfect. English for Hospitality Employees," Hedy said. "You are right. Makes a lot more sense."

"You're the one not making sense. I have a job in Louisville, Kentucky," said Barbara.

"And you enjoy it how much?" said Hedy.

Barbara looked down and thought about how she felt about going back to the morgue. It used to be great fun, but the hierarchy had changed, and the rules were now draconian and soul crushing. She could no longer protect her team, and they were becoming as despondent as she had already become. Her shoulders ached from pulling dead bodies out of the zippered bags and onto the steel tables for their last examination. She simply put in the hours until she could go home to Hedy and her real life.

"I'm a physician," said Barbara. "Shouldn't I do something like Doctors Without Borders?"

"How do you feel about actually practicing medicine on live people?" asked Hedy. "How long has it been?"

Barbara knew Hedy had a point, but she didn't want to admit it. She also didn't want to admit just how tired she was of suiting up and going in every day. Writing reports. Testifying and answering insulting